Fallen Colonies

Fallen Colonies

Ashley Ashforth

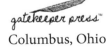

gatekeeper press™
Columbus, Ohio

Fallen Colonies

Published by Gatekeeper Press
2167 Stringtown Rd, Suite 109
Columbus, OH 43123-2989
www.GatekeeperPress.com

The editorial work for this book is entirely the product of the author. Gatekeeper Press did not participate in and is not responsible for any aspect of these elements.

Library of Congress Control Number: 2021947942

ISBN (hardcover): 9781662920486
ISBN (paperback): 9781662920295
eISBN: 9781662920301

Contents

CHAPTER

1

The large windowless room is lit only by a dim blue glow from the rusted old capsule embedded in the wall. A flash of sparks and smoke spew out of the shattered screen of the electrocardiogram. The screen flits on for only a few seconds, showing her vitals. The machine ticks with her heartbeat and sets off an alarming sound when it no longer can. The glass door is fogged with the condensation of her breath. The drips form vein-like streams, mimicking the prominent black veins spread across her face and body. Her pale skin causes the veins to stand out like cracks in a porcelain doll. Long wavy auburn hair sticks to her beading skin, matted.

Her breaths become irregular. Occasionally her muscles twitch as if an electric pulse has run through her. The blue gel mat forms around the impression of her body. Convulsing, all of her muscles tightening before her eyes shoot open, she inhales sharply as if she had been underwater for too long. Her chest rises and falls heavily. The taste of copper is overwhelming. Warm liquid dribbles out of her mouth as her tongue swells from being bitten during her seizure. Her eyes glaze over. The smell of a musty basement permeates the air. *Where am I? What is this? I cannot move, why can't I move?* Her heart races as more sparks light the room for a second. Feeling panicked, she closes her eyes, breathing deeply to calm herself. Not knowing she has drifted into sleep, her eyelids twitch as she begins to dream.

Running. Running so fast the forest of trees are a streaking blur of green and brown. Something or someone is chasing her, but she doesn't dare look behind. The trees dissipate, opening up to the Dark Sea. The sand sneaks into the heels of her shoes as she kicks it up with each step. The black water crashes upon the peach-colored sand. She continues to run to an old decaying dock. The wood creaks under her weight. There is a young boy standing there, facing the ocean at the edge. A wave of relief rushes over her, but she runs straight through him when she tries to embrace him, hitting a wall of cold water.

Her eyes open wide with a gasp of breath. The glass door has opened, exposing her naked body to the biting air. A strange sensation vibrates against her neck. Her eyes roll with the pounding pressure in her skull. Pins and needles prick her skin as her muscles come back to life. *Where am I?* Gaining control of her limbs, her fingers wiggle and she finally bends her wrists and elbows. As she grows more aware, she notices her right hand is gripping something. Unable to move her head much, she struggles to bring her hand up into view.

A small black device with a screen is strapped to her hand. Green letters flash, and she blinks away the fog in her eyes as she focuses on the words:

Eject and Reformat: ___Execute___

The word "execute" blinks silently but strikes fear in her heart. With her free hand she reaches up to her shoulder and feels up to her neck. Her hair rises, prickling her skin. A warm metal tube is clamped into the nape of her neck. The strange vibration is the machine embedded in her body. She turns green with terror.

Breaths come quickly, realizing she is attached to the Anamnesis Manipulator. Her hands tremble at the thought of the inevitable pain she will feel soon after entering that command. No one is meant to be awake during removal. She tries to call for help, but the little voice she has falls short in the darkness. She takes deep breaths through her nose, trying to prepare and calm herself.

The command is entered. The machine whirrs with its new objective to release its patient. Her body becomes hot as the hair-like strings attached to each organ and muscle in her begins to retract. A broken screech pierces her ears. Only when she feels the tearing of her own throat does she notice that the ungodly sound is coming from her. As her eyes roll back, she loses consciousness.

This time it is peaceful. No running, no fear, just sorrow. Watching the tide come and go, she sits at the edge of the woods digging her toes into the peach-colored sand. The dock is older and worn out. A plank is clanking against one of the barnacle-layered pillars. The stars shine bright in the dark sky even though it is day. To the west, the sun is setting with streaks of pink, lavender and orange. The sun hides behind the storm clouds that forever linger over the broken city across the water. Lightning consistently strikes the high-rise buildings. It's so distant you never hear the thunder that follows. Beside her there is a cooing. She lays back, snuggling up to an infant no older than three months. An image flashes of her rubbing her swollen belly.

Once more she comes to, but finds herself draped across the floor in front of the open capsule. Her body shivers from the cold cement, making known all the new aches in her body from the fall. Her cheekbone throbs and warm liquid drips down it. She struggles to sit up as her arms wobble like jelly. She leans up against the stainless-steel table in the middle of the room. The change in altitude sends her head into a spiral. Heaving, blood and bile fills her mouth and spills onto the floor. Feeling herself being lulled back into a slumber, she pulls herself away from the table.

Shivering once again, she looks down at her naked body. Seeing her abdomen flat and thin, her eyes blur and she chokes on her tears. "My baby," she rasps. *What happened to me? Where is my baby? Who took him from me?*

With a deep breath she turns her despair into anger. She rips the tape from her hand, tossing the remote. With a new determination, she drags herself past the table to the cupboards lining the walls. Her hands crush something below and a sharp pain shoots up her arms. Broken glass cuts into her hands. The floor is littered with debris. It is as if someone destroyed the lab. Smearing blood across the cabinets and drawers, one by one they open. Tools, glass, metal, finally fabric. Grunting and straining, she manages to wrap herself in what looks like a hospital gown. It sticks to her body where blood has fallen down her back and chest. She reaches up and somehow finds the strength to stand on her tottering legs. Across the room there is a light flashing red and green. Slowly she makes her way, only to step on more shards of glass. Her legs crumple beneath her. She pulls out the larger pieces but eventually gives up on the little ones and continues walking, digging them deeper into her flesh.

She reaches the exit and hits the green button. The wall she leans against swiftly opens, almost dropping her to the floor. Stabilizing herself against another wall, she is able to catch her breath. The door leads her to a hallway that shows no signs of light. Looking back at the chamber, the room has become more visible, an abandoned laboratory that somehow looks vaguely familiar to her. No one has been here in a very long time. The gel bed she was once resting upon is dripping with blood. Shivering, she touches the back of her neck. It stings when her finger brushes past the hole.

Left or right? Both paths promise an abyss of darkness. Choosing a path at random, she blindly leads herself down the hallway, turning corners for what seems to be hours. The sound of her breathing is her only company. The longer she wanders, the heavier her breath comes. Her hands and feet are swelling. Just as she is losing strength and hope, her hand swipes a screen and it lights up. She gasps at the sudden shock of light. Hope is renewed. The blue square shimmers as a bar scans up and down the screen. She wipes the less damaged hand on her robe and presses it to the glass.

It takes its own sweet time but successfully unlocks the door. With a sigh of relief, a very thick heavy wall slowly slides open. The dim lights of the hallway are bright enough to make her eyes cringe. She shades her eyes as she takes a step forward into an adjacent hallway, and as her feet are cushioned by dingy brown carpet she is ready to cry. There is a staircase leading up. Climbing those stairs seems like an ominous task. The wall begins sliding back closed, leaving her with no way to open it again, completely sealed.

There is chatter at the top of the stairs, and the smell of chemicals and something sweet laces the air. Looking down at herself, she knows she is what nightmares are made of. The swelling in her cheek is beginning to affect her sight in her left eye. She tries pulling out any visible glass from her hands and feet before making the trek. Her hands still dripping with blood, she tries to rip her robe for bindings but can't gather the strength. Making her way up the stairs on her knees and arms, it opens up to a living room. Smoke blanketing the ceiling, she gets to her feet. Young men and women lounge on the couches and chairs, draping themselves across each other, kissing and laughing. The coffee table at the center has glasses filled with a green liquid that looks to be absinthe. The decanter stands empty but dripping onto the table.

She recognizes some of the people in the room but can't recall their names. By their body language she can tell they are too far gone to be of any help. When people notice her standing in all her glorified horror, there is a shrill scream. The sound is like a hammer to her skull. As she brings her bloody hands to her ears, silence strikes the room.

"She's dead," one of the men whispers with his face twisted in disgust. One of the girls begins to whimper. The couple she recognized have tears in their eyes, but don't dare take their eyes from her. "Back from the dead," another says aloud.

"Please help me," she cries as she holds her hands out to the couple she recognizes. "I'm bleeding... Please." As they ignore her and cling to each other, crying, she makes her way across the room. The others cringe away, making random comments about ghosts and nightmares. Giving up, she crosses the room again and opens the front door. The sun is high and all but blinds her. For a moment it is a struggle to open her tear-filled eyes.

Holding her hand up to shade herself, she is finally able to adjust enough to see the porch steps. She stumbles down them onto the dirt road. Sand and dirt sting her feet as the tiny rocks embed themselves into the cuts. Turning around in circles, she tries to decide which direction would bring her to something she might recognize. Either side of the path leads into a forest of trees. Seeing the seagulls circle in the distance, she decides to follow their lead.

It is midday and sweat mixed with blood is dripping down her spine. The ground is dancing from the heat. Finding someone quickly, before she loses any more blood, is imperative. Keeping her clenched fists above her chest leaves blood dripping down her elbows. Darkness is closing in on her. She is losing the battle. Dropping to her knees, she starts to drift away. Falling forward, she just misses a fallen log, and her head is padded by a bed of clover. The air is warm and the smell of trees and dirt calms her. In the distance she hears music, a classical tune she would listen to often as a child, "Clair de Lune," though she can't be sure if it is coming from her head. She feels cold even though the sun warms her skin. Her eyes are blinking slowly. She fights to stay awake.

"My stars," a woman with very thick curly hair gasps. She clamors down off her porch, seeing the girl fallen down in the road, smeared with black slime. The curly haired woman is fit for being as old as she is. She rushes to the girl's side, lifts her head onto her lap, then wipes away the hair stuck to her face. "Violet!" she shouts, recognizing her as the girl who had been banished. Violet's eyes opened slightly but hadn't the strength to respond in any way.

"Oh Violet..." She touches Violet's swollen cheek. "Wake up my dear, you cannot fall asleep!" she yells. If the woman could only hear Violet's complaints. *Violet, yes. I am Violet. So loud. I can hear you, stop yelling.* "Open your eyes, sweetie," she says as she lifts her into her arms. Violet's head lulls back and her eyes open slightly. "Come on Violet, stay with me." *I am with you,* she wants to say. The woman is running out of breath as she adjusts Violet's weight in her arms. Her shoes clank on the hardwood floor and the door squeaks back and forth as she pushes through it. Bells jingle. The trees and sky disappear as a ceiling with intricate gold trim and painted roses now comes into view.

"Stay with me, darling." She breathes. The woman drapes Violet across a floral tufted chaise. The scent of fresh roses permeates the air. She leaves Violet to rummage in her medicine cabinet. Coming back with a silver tray, it is overflowing with gauze, ointments and tools. Quickly, she prepares a syringe with a yellow liquid. The needle is small and sinks into Violet's neck. The pinch from the needle is nothing compared to the pain in the rest of her body. "This will help you get your strength back."

The woman cracks open some smelling salts and holds it under Violet's nose. With one breath she gasps from the sharp scent. Her eyes flutter open. "There you are, poor thing. What have they done to you?" she asks more to herself than to her. Violet looks around the room. The room is decorated in such a cheerful manner. She has never seen a room look so feminine.

The woman rushes off and comes back with a bowl of steaming water. She sets everything on the side table. Sitting down in the wood carved chair next to Violet, she is smiling apologetically. She sets the bowl upon her lap. Gently lifting Violet's hand, she dips it into the bowl. The water bites at her open flesh. She winces and watches the woman rinse her hand, then pick out the bits of glass that had become lodged in her skin using cold tweezers. The woman has strange black muck on her white blouse, but it doesn't seem to bother her as she carefully cleans Violet up. Silently, she works as Violet studies her face. She has a long nose, pink cheeks and soft blue eyes. She has to be in her sixties.

Lightly spraying her hands with a mist, the stinging begins to subside. She moves on to Violet's feet, glancing at her with empathy. "It'll be alright, my darling. I'm here to help you now." She wipes at Violet's cheeks with a damp cloth, and her tears blacken it. As she realizes she is crying, she becomes concerned about the ink-stained tears that have begun to seep from her eyes. It reminds her of the Dark sea she jumped into in the dream. The woman strokes her cheek and continues to rinse the dirt, rocks and blood off from her feet. After binding her wounds, and stitching the hole in her neck, the woman shines a light into Violets' eyes.

"You need to stay awake for a little while. You have a slight concussion," she says, propping her up with pillows. She brings over some tea and biscuits on a tray. For Violet, eating will take effort with her ever-swelling tongue. "My name is Clara. Do you remember me?" She smiles sweetly.

Violet shakes her head and instantly regrets it as the room begins to spin. "No," Violet rasps.

"I'm a friend of Jack's." Violet looks at her curiously. *Am I supposed to know who that is?* She sips at her lemon honey tea but can barely taste it. Clara stays at her side keeping her awake.

Eventually Clara allows her to sleep, though checking on her every half hour. Once she has nodded out for the first time, Clara makes a call, whispering into the mouthpiece so to not wake Violet. "She's here, Jack. She's in bad shape but she's here. She could've died if I hadn't found her... Well, you shouldn't overwhelm her. Let her rest and I'll bring her to you. Alright, I love you too. Bye."

* * *

After a dreamless sleep, Violet wakes up with Clara asleep in the chair beside her, holding her gauze-wrapped hand. Her kinky hair is pulled into a loose bun atop her head. She has changed into a fresh blouse of white lace. It looks uncomfortable, with a collar tight around her neck. Violet gently takes her hand back and sits up in the chaise, jolting Clara awake. "Oh shoot!" she says, startled. "Are you alright? What do you need? I'm sorry I fell asleep."

"Don't apologize, you need rest too." Her voice still rasps and her tongue, still swollen, gives her a lisp.

"I'll make breakfast. You sit tight."

"I bit my tongue. It hurts to eat." Violet cringes at the idea of having to chew salty foods.

"I'll make something simple. It'll help."

Violet shakes her head vigorously, making the room spin. She catches her head with the palm of her hand. There is no arguing with Clara, and she eventually comes back with berries and cream, as well as a little medicine mixed in. Violet is able to eat with mild discomfort, and afterwards she is able to stand with assistance. Clara walks her to the bathroom, having already started a bath. The steam spirals up into the air. Peeling the laboratory robe from her body, Violet notices more of the ink stains. Her brows wrinkle

9

in concern. Clara washes her hair and face gently with a soft cloth. Parts of her scalp are tender from clumps of hair being torn out as she fell out of the chamber. The water quickly turns murky with dirt and suds. The opening at the nape has already been sewn shut, but still stings as the suds drip down. She studies her hands, which have already closed up and began to scab over. "Are you a doctor?" she asks.

Clara giggled. "Heavens, no. Though living outside of the colony for so many years forces you to acquire certain skills."

"How long?"

"Too long." She sighs, scrubbing at Violet's back with a sponge.

"Your medicine is magical."

"Oh?" she laughs. Clara looks down at the healing hands. "My medicines don't work that well. You're healing very quickly. Perhaps it's you that is magical."

Violet becomes quiet as she studies the skin on her arms. She rubs at the veins incessantly, until Clara gently places her hand over hers, saying quietly, "You'll rub your skin raw." Clara wipes her hands on her floral apron and grabs a hand mirror, holding it in front of Violet. Her ivory skin is webbed with dark veins spreading across her face. Not only her face, but she notices it has spread down her neck, shoulders and chest. Purple bruising surrounds the cut on her cheekbone. The veins on her arms are more faded than the rest. Haunted by the creature reflected in the mirror, she becomes silent.

After draining the tub, Clara rinses Violet once more with clean water before drying her off. Clara re-dresses her hands and feet, binding them snuggly. Dressed in a lace nightgown, Violet looks even more ghostly than before, with her veil of auburn hair that runs past her waist. Clara helps Violet brush her thick hair and braid it, then turns down the bed in her guest room, complete with a plate of cheese and bread on the side table. She checks Violet's eyes once more and lets her rest. For a while Violet stares at the ceiling, occasionally nibbling at some bread, listening to Clara bustling around. Racking her brain of any memories of what happened to her and why, at long last she falls asleep.

* * *

A man stands in front of Violet, looking fierce. His hair is slicked back, letting his large blue eyes shine viciously. She is no longer in Clara's home but on a small path in the middle of the woods. "Listen to me!" *he shouts.* "You have to forget about him, he was never good enough for you. This is proof! He's dangerous, Violet!"

She stands silent, bewildered. Her knuckles turn white as her fists shake. "He was protecting me, Charlie. He would never hurt me or anyone else who isn't threatening my LIFE," *she spits.*

Charlie scoffs. "Henry is DEAD. Your own father! How can you say he wouldn't hurt anyone else? How can you be so stupid?" *He grips her shoulders tightly, shaking her.*

"I can't believe you'd be so ignorant," *she responds, tears stream down her cheeks.* "You knew... You knew everything since we were kids, yet you ignore the idea of him being innocent! Why? Jealousy? You have no idea what you've done. That man you call my father was strangling me. He was trying to kill me!" *She pulls at her collar, revealing the red marks around her throat.* "If he hadn't hit him, would you blame him for doing nothing? HE's the reason I'm here." *Violet pushes him away.*

As she starts back up the path, Charlie grabs her arm harshly, spinning her around. "I'm sorry," *he whispers before crushing his lips against hers. The palm of Violet's hand collides with his ear. Breaking free of him once more, she screams in frustration. He falls to the ground, howling in pain.*

"What is wrong with you!?" *She wipes her mouth.* "You're disgusting." *Running into the woods, the air seems to carry a song and she can't escape it:*

I watch you turn away and
You walk on out the door
I'm holding my chest tight
As I crumble to the floor

Charlie chases after her. She runs as fast as she can until she finds the withered old dock and jumps into the Dark Sea. The cold water hitting her body shakes her awake. The song continues:

Now here I am waiting for your return
But it's been so long, I beg, remember me
When the sun's shining
When the rain falls and soaks in
Remember me
When you lie awake
When it aches, when your heart aches so

Clara wipes Violet's forehead with a cold wet cloth. Once again she is surrounded by the scent of roses, but the song continues. Violet sits up abruptly, knocking the cloth from Clara's hand. Blood rushes to her head and the room spins. "Turn it off!"

Clara jumps to her feet and quickly removes the needle from her vinyl record. The gramophone above her piano goes silent. "Are you alright?" she asks, coming back to Violet's side.

"I'm fine." She rubs her eyes and temples. "I just had a bad dream. My head felt like it was going to explode."

"I can help you find him, you know."

"Who?"

"Charlie. I know where he is."

"I... I don't know. I'm so confused. I think Charlie did something terrible. Ah, my head is killing me."

Clara gets up and goes to her medicine cabinet. She comes back with a purple root. "Here, chew on this, it will help with your tension." It smells of artichokes and has the flavor of cloves. "I fear you may have hit your head harder than I thought. Do you remember who you are?"

"Yes. Violet..." She thinks for a moment, rubbing her temple. "Violet O'daire."

"And where are you from?

"Safe Haven."

"Do you remember your family?"

"They're all dead."

"You have Jack."

"Jack..." The name is familiar, but his face she cannot recall.

"I think you need to see Jack. Do you remember him?"

"Jack Wiseman?" Violet recalls the name but the face is still missing.

"Yes." Clara smiles warmly.

"Yes, I do need to see him. Did he kill my father?"

"No." Clara was shocked. "Jack wouldn't hurt a soul."

"Someone saved me from my father. Do you know who?"

"I'm sorry, I don't," she says curtly. "You need to see Jack."

"I can't remember much. I have bits and pieces of memories, like a dream, but nothing makes sense. I can't tell if they're real or not." Violet chokes. She bumps her fist on her forehead, trying to remember.

Clara takes her fist and pets her hand until she loosens her fingers. "Everything will be alright," she says. "We'll sort you out soon enough." Clara reaches for a cup of broth on the table, then brings it up to Violet's lips. "Here, drink this. We'll get you clothed and fed, then we can go see Jack."

Nodding, Violet falls back into the pillow. "Thank you for finding me, Clara."

Clara brushes her cheek and smiles warmly. "Eat up, then come out to the front room."

CHAPTER

2

Violet finishes the cheese and bread before following Clara to the front room. When Violet had initially been carried in, somehow she missed Clara's parlor. The room is stocked with fashions of all sorts. It's such a large room and so cramped with racks and shelves filled with clothing, it looks as if you're stepping into a history book. Clara has articles from many different eras and for every occasion. At the center of the room is a display from the 1700s. Behind it is a table with jewelry and other accessories. This is no ordinary clothing shop, Violet quickly realizes. Most shops have three styles that change only when the stock is gone. Here, though, there are many strange uniforms and pieces that seem very impractical for Safe Haven, but the detail and time spent on each piece is inspiring.

Clara notices Violet taking in her surroundings, and says, "Before the Great War, I was a collector. I loved dressing differently from others. Some of them I recreated from old books. I really adore this one." She touches the gold trim of a very elegant navy blue Renaissance dress.

"It's very pretty," Violet says, admiring the color.

"Thank you. Now, take your pick. You can't be running around naked, or in my nightgown."

"Um... I'm a bit overwhelmed. I don't even know where to start. I've never had so many options." Violet sighs while turning through the hangers.

"Poor thing." Clara disappears around a tall rack. She comes back with a pair of lace-up boots. "Here are some good boots to start. You have very small feet, but these should fit." She begins to pull things off the racks and hold them up to Violet's neck. "You're so small," she says under her breath. Violet looks down at her arms self-consciously. They're so thin that she looks sickly.

"Oh, I have the perfect thing!" Clara announces. She comes back with several pieces of clothing hanging from her arms. She hands her a brown jumpsuit and nudges her into a closet with red velvet curtains. "Go ahead and try it on. Let me know if you need help." She pulls a gold rope and the curtain closes behind Violet. On the stool in the corner are some undergarments already prepared. Everything slips on easily. The beige blouse fits perfectly, light and comfortable. The jumpsuit fits snug around the waist with a double-breasted flap on the front. It fits loose in the legs so she can move easily.

Violet comes out to make sure it's on correctly. Clara smiles, giddily remarking, "Very fitting." Violet nods, complimenting herself. She wraps a holster around her waist that buckles in the front and around her thigh, then attaches a brass compact with a long chain to the jumpsuit and into the belt.

Clara sits Violet on the stool and helps her with her socks and the lacing up of her boots. Bells sound at the front entrance, alerting her of new guests. Standing up, she holds her hand out, indicating that Violet should stay where she is. Two men stand in the doorway with mechanical armor that covers them from head to toe. On their arms are badge numbers illuminated in red.

"Good morning officers!" she says brightly. "Let me finish up with this customer and I'll be right with you."

Ducking back down, she quickly grabs a messenger bag from under one of the shelves and stuffs clothing into it. Rushing, she wraps a grey cloak with black leather cuffs around Violet and pulls up the dramatic hood, whispering, "They cannot know you are here; you were banished two years ago. This is a compass." She taps the brass compact. "I'll delay them. When you leave, head for the forest and keep heading south. Stay off of the roads. Put on those gloves." Violet quickly does as she is told and Clara slides the messenger bag over her shoulder. She pulls Violet to her feet and quickly walks her past the men, saying, "There we are. Those boots suit you so well. Thank you for your patronage and have a wonderful day."

Violet nods, eyes wide, as she moves towards the exit. The men stop them and say, "Have either of you seen a strange woman wearing a robe with a black substance, no shoes, with dark hair, roaming around?"

"Oh my, no! Has something happened?"

"It's nothing to worry about. We believe someone was playing a practical joke, but we did see some irregularities in some of our samples. Someone or something may have gotten past the barriers." He holds out a card for Violet, who keeps her head low. "We appreciate your cooperation. Please contact us if you see anything strange."

"Of course, thank you." Her heart is pounding so hard against her chest she is worried he might hear it. She slips the card into her pocket.

Clara clears her throat. "Actually, now that you mention it, I noticed some of my vegetables missing from my garden this morning. Would you mind taking a look?"

"It may have been wildlife, ma'am."

"Even so, I'd feel more safe, if you would kindly."

With that, Violet takes her leave, the bells chiming behind her. Briskly stepping off the porch, she leaves the dirt road and heads deep into the woods. The adrenaline pumping through her veins numbs her feet. When the house is no longer visible, she opens the compass and waits while the arrow finds north. Heading the opposite direction, she begins to relax, with the sound of trees swaying and birds singing occupying the silence. The heavy brush crunches under her steel-toed boots. The trees are covered in such thick moss that it hangs from the limbs. Looking up at the leaves, the sun highlights them almost as if they radiate light. With each breath she recognizes the scent of salt in the air. Home.

* * *

She has been walking south for at least an hour. Her feet are surprisingly comfortable. Clara must have slipped pain relief into her broth earlier. Suddenly, Violet's insides snarl in anger for the lack of food. She would have gone longer without noticing if it weren't for the smell of fried chicken wafting through the air. Unknowingly she has followed the smell into town, and now finds herself in an overgrown garden with peppers, tomatoes and strawberries hanging from arches. She plucks some strawberries and a large tomato and quickly devours them. Her tongue, though tender, surprisingly doesn't sting from the acidity. She plucks a few more and stuffs them into her bag. Walking around to the side of the house, the scent of meat is too luring to resist. She peeks around the side of the house to find the roads clear from any people.

When she comes around to the front she recognizes the red door and blue siding, and says to herself with surprise, *This is my house.* For the first time in her life, she is happy to see her front door. Memories begin to flow. This house had once only brought bad memories, the loss of her mother and abusive father; but now, consoling memories of Charlie overwhelm her. Charlie's warm embrace, Charlie's laughter and love. Now she is happy, knowing the man inside this home loves her and would do anything for her. *Charlie will help me.* Without delay she opens the door, ignoring the sign hanging from the porch reading 'Jenna's Tavern.'

She steps into what once was her living room. Now, the back wall has been knocked out and replaced with a long wet bar. A jukebox in the corner of the room is playing music. There are several tables about the room and most of them are empty. Behind the bar, a woman with black hair pulled into a bun is standing, preparing some drinks. She sees Violet and freezes, turning pale. The bottle in her hand crashes to the floor. Violet knows her as Jenna, a friend who clung to Charlie most of their childhood. Though she had always been nice to Jenna, the kindness was never returned. Charlie's disinterest in her only caused trouble between her and Jenna. When they were kids, Jenna was not the most attractive little girl; but looking at her now, she's gorgeous. Pangs of rage and jealousy smother her.

The entire room stares silently at Violet. She didn't notice that in her haste, her hood had fallen back. Violet turns to bolt towards the door, only to find Charlie standing in the doorway. His sandy red hair is styled with a wave and brushed back, making him look very sharp and clean shaven. He was always keen on keeping a clean appearance. A little boy is impatiently holding Charlie's hand. When the boy sees Violet, he pulls at Charlie's grip. Charlie appears stunned.

When she sees the boy's face, Violet instantly recognizes him. "Nathan!" she exclaims, her voice still hoarse. Dropping to her knees, memories of her child flood her mind. Nathan breaks free of Charlie's grasp and runs straight into her arms, hugging her tightly. No longer the infant she cradled at the beach, he is still that same beautiful boy with chocolate brown hair and eyes, and sun-kissed skin from playing outside. For a long moment she holds Nathan tightly to her and kisses his cheek and forehead. Then she stands, keeping Nathan's hand tight in her grip. Closing the distance between her and Charlie, Violet gently presses her lips to his, wrapping her free arm around his chest. Charlie is stiff at first, but quickly recovers from his shock, wrapping his arms around her tightly. He laughs and presses his lips into the crook of her neck as he embraces her. Memories of Charlie swarm her mind and she begins to feel uneasy. Some of those memories do not match up to reality. Something is off. Even though these warm emotions are overwhelming her, she feels the urge to run away from him.

Jenna drops a glass intentionally, letting it shatter on the floor. The sound shakes Charlie and Violet and they separate. Violet smiles. "You couldn't wait for me, Charlie? Strange for you," she teases. Speechless, Charlie looks at Jenna and back at Violet with a look of shame and frustration.

Jenna crosses the room, livid, and grabs Nathan by the wrist. Nathan holds tighter to Violet. "You told me she was *dead*." Jenna is disgusted as she looks Violet up and down.

Violet hits her hands away, lifting Nathan into her arms. "Don't touch my son," she says as she pushes past them. Charlie follows after them out the door.

"You can't take him!" Jenna protests.

"You've been gone for almost three years!" Charlie says.

"You knew I was alive. I was hidden away in your drug addict friend's basement." Violet continues walking. "You had to have known."

"Charlie, do something!" Jenna screams from the doorway. Both Violet and Charlie ignore her.

"I didn't know if you would ever wake up. You were barely alive when I found you, Violet."

She turns to look at him, stopping in her tracks. Jenna stands at the top of the stairs of the porch, her father's porch, yelling at Charlie furiously. "I'm glad you found someone to love you, honestly. From what I remember, I couldn't love you like you wanted me to. Keep the house. It's not my home anymore." Violet walks towards the woods, Nathan in hand.

"You can't let her take him, Charlie," Jenna yells. Can't you see *that* isn't Violet? That's… a monster!"

She starts after Violet but Charlie catches her by the arm. "Shut up, Jenna! I knew I shouldn't have listened to you." He twists her arm, pulling her back to the porch. Jenna cries out in pain as she protests.

Hearing their conversation and the severe change in Charlie's voice keeps Violet moving quickly, pulling up her hood back into place. "Do you know how to get to Jack Wiseman's house?" Violet asks Nathan. He nods. She sets him down and he pulls her along in the right direction. "You've gotten so big. How old are you?" Nathan holds up five fingers. Violet thinks back, trying to find her most recent memory of him. She recalls seeing him take his first steps, but not much more. She had been gone for almost three years, Charlie told her. Yet, Nathan recognized her immediately, unfazed by her terrible transformation. He holds her gloved hand, skipping along.

* * *

It's close to noon and the cloak is becoming too much, though she can't risk someone walking by and seeing her without it. Drips of sweat slide down her body, making her clothing stick to her in an uncomfortable way. "Have you been living with Charlie all of this time?" Nathan nods. "Has he been treating you well?" Nathan shrugs. "Has he done anything to hurt you?" He thinks for a moment and shakes his head. His delayed response sparks concern. Her chest tightens with the thought of him having the same experience she had had when she was a child. She stops in her tracks and squats down to his level, turning him to face her. "I am so sorry I wasn't here for you. Can you ever forgive me?"

Nathan looks into her eyes. Seeing her sincerity, his eyes fill with tears. "I'll make it up to you," she says, wiping the tears that had spilled onto his cheeks as tears begin to leak from her own eyes. He nods in agreement and wraps his arms around her neck, squeezing tightly. Though the pain of his embrace is unbearable, she refuses to let it show, gritting her teeth. For a long moment they hug each other in silence.

Eventually they begin walking again, staying off the main road. Violet has so many questions, but she's noticed that no matter what questions she asks, he won't answer back. "Why haven't you said a word to me?" Nathan looks ashamed. He keeps his eyes low. Violet sighs but doesn't push him further. She combs her fingers through his hair and he leans into her hand.

Violet is starting to recognize the path. Though it has become a little overgrown, she notices an old shack covered in moss and ivy. "Hold on! What's that over there?" Nathan pulls at her arm, knowing she is going the wrong way. "I just want to look," she says. He sighs and follows along. Making their way through the overgrown brush, they reach the old shed. Nathan tries peeking through the windows, but the glass is blackened. Pulling at the overgrowth, she finds the door. It isn't locked but jammed. She shoves her shoulder into the door. Pain shoots through her arm and into her chest as they squeeze through the opening. The roof is caved in and everything is scorched. The shed looks like a small bedroom, with a burnt-up cot in the corner. The desk on the other side isn't in too bad of shape. Nathan kicks at the rubble, revealing an old yellowed tin box.

Violet takes the box into her hands and the pressure in her head pulses. She stashes it in her bag. "We should go, I'm getting lightheaded." No more time is wasted in the old ruins. Before long, the trees open up to a valley where an old brick house comes into view. Behind it is the Dark Sea. Cutting into the water is a dock built specifically for Jack's airship, one which has not been moved in ages. The waves wash upon the shore, memories coming along with it. Memories of playing tag with Charlie and Jenna in the yard, while Jack reads a book and laughs at them when they fall. Memories of pulling weeds in the garden and catching two-headed lizards. The sunlight dances upon the water. The view is breathtaking and comforting.

Nathan and Violet walk up to the front of the ranch-style house. The front garden is layered with more flowers than she can name. Upon the porch sits Jack's old wood carved rocking chair and a worn-out pillow. The flower pattern on the cushion has faded. Nathan runs ahead and, without knocking, bursts through the door, letting it swing wide open. He disappears into the house. The aroma of stew makes her mouth water, and her stomach growls angrily. She removes her wool cloak and hangs it on the hook near the door. The oversized leather couch sits in the middle of the room, facing the fireplace. Terrariums hang from the ceiling in the corners on either side. The terracotta walls are decorated with the old blueprints of his projects, and his collection of taxidermy insects.

One of the blueprints catches her eye. The tag in the bottom corner titles it "Bio-scout." It is a machine with spider-like limbs. Its body is fitted with a large lens that can scan for human life and assist with alerting authorities if anyone needed assistance, or if that human turned out to be a fugitive. Though it was a machine built to assist humanity, Violet shivers as her hair rises on end. Something about it is too familiar and puts her on edge.

To the right of the living room is a hallway leading to the bedrooms and Jack's office. To the left is the dining room, painted a rustic blue. Bay windows on either side of the room let in so much light. You can see the view of the ocean. In front of the windows are waist-high cabinets with model ships displayed on top. In the center of the room is an exceptionally large farm table with benches on each side. Violet sets her bag down behind the couch. Coming to stand in front of the window to see the ocean, she spots a dock, although this is not the one from her dream. This one is in good condition, and a sleek silver ship accompanies it, sparkling as water does when the sun hits it. A model of this ship sits at the center of the cabinet in front of her. Though the docked ship looks somewhat small, the model reveals its true size. From this view you can only see the open upper deck and the bridge, and just below it the five portholes, including the hatch. Hidden under the water are two large jet engines on either side that steer the ship. The bow has a sharp curve like a crescent moon, and at the stern the largest engine, giving it speed.

Roaring laughter bellows through the house. An old man with wispy white hair and full beard comes through the white door leading to the kitchen. He is intimidating at first glance, with his broad shoulders and wild eyebrows that seem stuck in a permanent frown, even with the grin reaching ear to ear. He spots Violet and sets down a bowl of stew on the old farmhouse table. Nathan follows behind him with a large grin. The man sets his hands on her shoulders and kisses her on the cheek before hugging her so tight she cannot breathe. Instant relief floods her, as if all the weight of the world has been lifted from her. This is the man she has known most of her life. He helped her through the worst of it. Gave her a safe place to reside when her father was on a rampage. He clothed, fed and loved her unconditionally, as he did with any other child lost in this world. Tears fill Violet's eyes and spill onto her cheeks as she clings to Jack.

"How is this possible?!" Jack asks in a slight Scottish accent. The smile on his face turns to fear as he pulls her away from him, worrying over her black tears. "Nathan, why don't you help the girls in the kitchen," he asks gently. Nathan does as he is asked and disappears behind the swinging white door.

"What's wrong with me?" She wipes her blackened tears from her cheeks with the back of her arm.

"Maven's blood," he replies grimly. "It was never filtered out. You still have it inside of you. You shouldn't be alive."

"Maven? What do you mean?"

"I need to take some blood samples, run some tests. For now, make sure you wash your hands thoroughly. You might... spread it or make someone sick." Jack leads her to the bathroom and turns on the hot water. Violet removes the gloves and gauze, and is astonished to find fresh pink skin where her cuts had been. The wounds have healed abnormally fast. While she washes her hands thoroughly, looking in the mirror, she studies the wound on her cheek. The only trace of a scar is the yellow and green bruising.

Jack runs into the hallway and comes back with his leather medical bag. Rubber gloves snap at his wrists. He takes the gauze and puts it in a tin can. "Open up," he says, swabbing the inside of her mouth and enclosing the swab in a vial.

"I had cuts all over my hands and feet. Clara cleaned me up."

"Did she wear gloves?"

"I honestly don't remember."

Jack ties a strip of rubber snugly around her arm above the elbow. "I'll check on her. For now, make sure that if you get any cuts, you take care not to let anyone come in direct contact until we know more about your condition. Keep all bodily fluids...to yourself."

Jack leads her back to the table. She sits at the bench and he hands her a spoon. "Eat, I made your favorite." He pats her on the back and pulls out a sterile needle. Not needing to be told twice, Violet uses her free hand to dip her spoon into the bowl, finding large chunks of carrot, onion, potatoes and the juiciest beef that melts away in your mouth. Before the first bite hits her tongue, she is salivating. Not noticing the pinch of the needle Jack draws her blood, careful not to spill any. Jack chuckles as he watches her lick the bowl clean. He hands her his handkerchief. "Would you like some more?"

"Yes please."

Jack leaves for a moment and returns with another steaming bowl of heaven and a large glass of water. He brings the vial of blood, as well as the tin can, back to his office, but returns quickly, knowing Violet will have questions. Sitting across from her, he is content for now with just watching her stuff her face with food. "I hope this doesn't hurt your stomach. It's been so long since you've needed to digest anything so hearty."

"I've eaten cheese, bread and fruit since waking up. I haven't had any problems."

"Let's hope it doesn't come back up to say hello."

She is so hungry she could eat a third bowl, but decides to wait and see how she feels. More laughter comes from the kitchen. "Who's in there?" Violet asks.

"I took in a couple of strays who wandered into our town. Jolene is seventeen, Ember nine, and Lilly five. Nathan has a way with the youngest. Quite the charmer," he chuckled.

After some time in silence, Violet finally says, "Alright, Wiseman, spill it."

"Spill what?" he asks playfully.

"You know what I mean. You know everything that goes on in this town. You have eyes everywhere. Tell me why I was attached to the Anamnesis Manipulator. Why are my memories a jumbled mess? I can't tell dreams from reality."

"Why were you attached to my machine? Because you made several huge mistakes. You were brought to me on your deathbed. The manipulator was the only thing that gave you a fighting chance. With a few tweaks it was able to keep you alive as long as it did. And here you are," Jack says proudly.

"What did I do? Why was I dying?"

Jack frowns. "Because you were stupid enough to leave the boundaries of this colony. You left the protection of our shields to explore uninhabited cities surrounding us. You would leave in the

26

middle of the night while Nathan and Charlie slept. No one knows what you were looking for. One night Charlie followed you, and thank the heavens he did. There was an explosion in an abandoned building. You, a maven and one of my bio-scouts were in the rubble."

Mavens are humanoid creatures, typically seven to nine feet tall. They do not have skin but a white bulletproof exoskeleton. One hand has three appendages, while the other is shaped like the barrel of a gun, and can shoot shards made from its own bone. Though if it is close enough, it will save the shards and stab you with the two spikes of bone sticking out on either side of its built-in weapon. Its entire blood mixture acts as white blood cells, destroying any foreign entities. No one knows where these creatures came from, but they're one of the reasons humans are in hiding. Jack believes their only purpose is extermination. When he retired from his government job, back when there *was* a government, they were dabbling in genetic engineering for their cause.

"The bio-scout was underneath you. Three of its limbs had run you through. The concrete from the explosion crushed the maven, and its tar-like blood had seeped into you. Charlie rushed you home and we immediately started dialysis. It was like a bacteria that multiplied itself when exposed to human blood cells." He strokes his beard, looking distant. "It was terrifying. We attached you to the machine so that you would receive nutrients. It also helped remove any foreign entities in your body, or so we thought. We wanted to remove you from the machine after a while, but we had to wait for you to come out of your coma first. We couldn't force it. I needed to make sure you were okay before taking you off it. But some new techs had surfaced and were trying to penetrate our defense shield. We had to remove all devices that gave off any electronic signals. We shut down the lab and hoped that the noise from your machine was too far underground to alert anything or anyone. After the first year and a half without any changes to your condition, all we could do is leave you in the dark and move on. I set up a system to inform me of any changes so we could take you off the machine, but I never received anything. How *did* you detach from the machine?"

"You didn't tape the device to my hand?"

"What device?"

"It was a remote that detached me and reformatted the machine, but I had to enter the command myself. It was the most painful thing I've ever felt." Violet cringes.

"I would imagine so, but you survived that too. I'm so sorry. If the removal had been executed correctly, a serum would have been injected into you so that you would feel nothing and be unconscious." Jack squeezed her hand, wincing at the thought of the pain she must have experienced.

"The lab was busted up pretty badly. I'm not surprised it malfunctioned. Who had access to it? Glass shards were littering the floor. It was like someone had come in with a bat and destroyed everything. Even the monitor for the capsule was destroyed."

Jack's expression turns dark. "Charlie's the only one with the access codes. We would occasionally bring Nathan down to see you. He wouldn't have done this, Charlie would never."

"Did Jenna know Charlie was visiting me?"

Jack says nothing, staying quiet for a moment. Violet isn't sure he even heard her question. She waits for him to come out of it. "Sorry, I had a thought."

"That's apparent. Care to share?"

"Not yet." Violet is about to argue but, seeing the look on his face, she decides to let it go. If he's holding back, he would have a good reason. "Keeping secrets, Wiseman?" she says teasingly.

"You kept secrets from *me*," he says crossly.

"I suppose I did. Though, I don't remember." Violet looks at her hands tracing the dark veins. "I have memories of making a life with Charlie. It was a happy life. Now, I can't make physical contact with him without feeling like something's off. Like a nagging at the back of my mind. Can you explain that?"

"That *is* strange." He stares into her eyes as he strokes his beard.

"I remembered an argument with Charlie. Or perhaps it was a dream. It felt very real, though. He said I needed to forget about the man who killed my father. I couldn't, though. I was disgusted with Charlie. He kissed me and I felt nothing but vile hatred for him. I find it hard to believe I could feel love towards him after that. Something's amiss, when I feel hatred for Charlie yet I have all of these fond memories together." She watches Jack carefully as he avoids eye contact and folds his arms. "Now, I know the original purpose for that machine is to remove unpleasant memories, so that a troubled person can live in peace. This isn't my first time being connected to it, is it, old man?"

Jack sighs, rubbing his eyes. "When your father was murdered you became depressed. In order to keep your depression from doing harm to you and... others, we adjusted your memories with the Anamnesis Manipulator to remove the part that was causing the pain. You agreed to it."

"Okay, I understand memories being removed. What I don't understand is why Charlie needed to be involved," Violet complains. "Why was I depressed in the first place? I hated my father. The only thing I felt about his death was relief. Wait... Did I have Nathan before or after the memory wipe? Was I depressed because I was having Charlie's child?! That would make more sense..." Violet feels her stomach churn, and for a moment the food threatens to surface.

Jack doesn't say a word. He watches her carefully, allowing her to draw her own conclusion. "Aw blast it, is Nathan Charlie's or not?" Violet becomes impatient. Jack falls silent and looks away.

"That is sick. You... oh... I think I'm going to be sick..." Violet puts her head between her knees and breathes deeply. "I doubt I would've agreed to it if I knew you were going to make me believe I was in love with someone I hated."

"For a little while you seemed like yourself again. Then you started disappearing for long periods of time again. That brings us back full circle to your accident." He strokes his beard and continues looking off into the distance.

Violet looks at Jack with narrowed eyes. Still something is missing. "Who killed my father, Jack?"

"A murderer not worth mentioning." He sighs. "You can sleep in the ship tonight. I hear they have officers on search." Jack collects his leather bag and sneaks away into his office.

Violet sits silent, head clamped between her hands. Her memories had been changed. Knowing something wasn't right, she thought she was losing her mind, so she went searching for answers. What could have helped her outside of town? No memories of leaving town came back to her. There was the memory of Charlie arguing with her. Jack is keeping secrets—he basically admitted it when becoming uncomfortable after her father's murderer was brought up. Violet would need to find the records of the criminals shipped out of town after his death. But knowing Jack and his endless resources, those documents were probably destroyed. *I would have needed to leave town to find the murderer.*

Violet realizes she needs air, so she grabs her bag and goes out the side door. The bricks have shifted over time, making the ground uneven. Walking through his garden, she finds a bench in front of the fountain. The smell of roses reminds her of Clara. Sitting down, the tin in her bag shifts, reminding her it is there. She takes it out and rinses the soot off in the fountain. Sitting back on the bench, she pops the lid open. Her head aches as she sifts through the items. A few agate stones, and a pocket knife slid to the side under some old cards and photos. There is a black and white photo, a picture of a young boy not yet in his teens. He has dark hair and a sweet smile. He holds the hand of the girl beside him. That girl is Violet, around the same age. In the photo she wears a lace dress, no smile. Pain shoots through her head, so intense she sees spots. Before she realizes she's doing so, she is screaming out, and then she's plunged into darkness. She doesn't faint but only sees darkness.

Minutes pass. The pain subsides and the darkness fades into light. When she can see again, she realizes she is on her hands and knees, with Nathan, rubbing her back. Tears drip from her eyes, splashing into what used to be the contents of her stomach. Violet looks up at Nathan, and he also has tears in his eyes. He is scared. She quickly moves away from him just as Jack pulls him into his arms. Violet covers her mess with dirt.

"I'm sorry, Nathan. I'm sick and I don't want you to get sick too." Grabbing her bag, she runs down to the dock and hides herself away in Jack's ship. Sliding the large heavy hatch open, she throws her bag in the corner of the cargo hold. With no ventilation besides the small portholes in the side of the airship, it acts as an oven. Folding herself into a ball, she takes deep breaths to calm and soothe her mind, as sweat beads on her neck.

Not long after, Jack comes down with bedding. Violet sits on a stool next to an open porthole. Her long thick braid drapes over her shoulder. "Nathan is okay," he says. "I explained what was going on and he understood. He'll bunk with the girls tonight. I assume you're quarantining yourself until I find out more." Violet nods, twisting her arm out the window, studying the black veins. "I'll know more tomorrow," he says as he sets up her cot.

"Okay."

"Get some sleep, sweetheart." Jack kisses her forehead and heads out.

"Old man," she says with a chill in her voice, but does not make eye contact. He stops in the doorway. "I know there was someone else. I found our picture in the burnt down shed. I *will* find out the truth eventually." Jack shakes his head and keeps walking. The heavy metal door slams shut, leaving her once again to her own thoughts. She opens her clenched fist, revealing the crumpled picture from her childhood. Unable to look long as the pressure in her head builds, she shoves the picture into her pocket.

CHAPTER

3

The water turns crimson as he rinses his hands in the river. Sitting on his heels, he scrubs at his right hand, trying to remove the blood and hair caught in his mechanical parts. His sleeve hides it well, but his entire right limb has been replaced with artificial pieces. Dark brown, chin-length hair falls in his eyes, and he blows at it in frustration. With his left hand he pulls his dripping fingers through his hair. The water helps it stay in place for a short time. Satisfied with the cleanliness of his right hand, he shakes off the excess water. Worried that the parts will rust before he makes it back home, anger flares.

Stacy drapes a handkerchief over his shoulder. On the right side of her head there are two braids tucked behind her ear, and the rest of her silver hair drapes over her left shoulder. Killian glares up over his shoulder at her, before snatching the cloth up. The three white triangles tattooed under her left eye gives her a wild look, especially with the drab clothing she has been collecting since they've started their journey together. Though sometimes revealing and somewhat impractical, he doesn't feel it is his place to tell her how to dress. Winter will soon befall them, and she will have no choice but to wear more clothing. It will be easier to have a conversation without trying to avert his eyes; though currently there is no temptation, as she had almost gotten them both killed. He finishes drying the joints in his hand, stands up straight and takes a deep breath.

Turning to face Stacy, she cowers from his scowl. His dark brown eyes are like a black abyss that barely reflects the light. She knows better than to speak, so follows him silently as he passes. She stumbles over one of the bodies of the four men that had attacked them. One of them looks to be a teenager caught in a bad situation. Though if Stacy had only followed Killian's instructions, then no one would have died today. Unfortunately for everyone, Stacy knows little of obedience. Instead of staying by the skyriders, she had crept after Killian, longing to stay by his side. Killian moved so swiftly, she had lost him and was easily caught by other scavengers like themselves. They thought she was alone and an easy target. She tried to fight them off on her own, but with little body strength and no self-defense training she was quickly overtaken. Layering more deaths onto Killian's conscience, those deaths meant nothing to her. She grimaces at the blood splattered on her boots as she trips into a puddle of blood. It doesn't take long before birds circle them in the sky. As soon as Stacy and Killian are out of the way, they swoop down to feast on the corpses. The sound of tearing flesh turns Stacy's stomach, as she quickens her pace to catch up with Killian's long strides.

In silence they load the skyriders with the goods they collected from the corpses and surrounding decaying homes. The sun is high and the heat rolls over his armored shoulders, baking him under his dark layers of clothing. They have traveled much farther north than they ever have before. Mostly mountains, lakes and rivers cover this part of the country, but small ghost towns are hidden away underneath the overgrowth if you know what to look for. Killian had once traveled the land looking for resources when he was very young, and was very fond of the time he spent with the man who had taught him how to survive. Thinking of the old man now fills him with guilt, as he tries to erase the bloodied faces that flash up in his mind.

The trip home is long, but rising high over the trees allows them to make better time. They no longer have to fly low, searching for potential resources. The sun sets behind them as they make their way through the mountainous terrain. The stars have begun to shine by the time they arrive at the towering waterfall. Stacy pulls a hooded mantle coat over her and braces for the impact as they cross through the water. Killian allows the ice-cold water to soak him through. Shocking his mind back into reality, he focuses on what needs to be done. Moving through the large dank cave, his eyes linger on the lonesome tree on the center island. A wave of nostalgia comforts him. The fluorescent orange-gold leaves sway with the wind caused by their entry. To the left they land in the cargo bay. Empty crates are piled high in one corner, and an extra skyrider sits unused next to it. They park on the opposite side and begin to unload the goods into the empty crates. A broad-shouldered man comes through the only entrance, stretching his arms over his head with a great yawn. Without asking any questions, he starts taking the full crates inside and putting the goods in their rightful place.

He comes across a helmet unlike any he has seen before. When he puts it on, the screen on the faceplate lights up and scans the room. "Whoa! This is awesome!" he says. Killian comes into the mess hall. The man is spinning slowly, allowing the helmet to react to different heat signatures. When he turns around to face Killian, the helmet locks onto him and scans his body, locating abrasions on his fists and bruises on his ribs. "I see you got into a scuffle," the man says. Killian sighs. Focusing deeper, it reveals his skeletal structure. Noticing Killian's right arm, it highlights it in red and informs the man that there is no procedure documented to repair the damage done. "This is an amazing tool," he says enthusiastically. "Where did you find it?"

"Took it off one of the men from the scuffle, Alan."

"Where did they get it?"

"We didn't think to ask," Killian says sardonically.

Stacy comes in with the last crate, and Alan takes the box full of medicinal supplies into the infirmary. Killian is sitting on a stool at one of the dining tables, lost in thought. Stacy sits down across from him. When he notices her, he looks away and walks off. Avoiding her is easier than letting his anger out on her. With a sigh, she watches him head for the showers. Alan returns and offers her a meal with a smile. She accepts, not really seeing him. While he heats up the dinner he had made for them earlier, he watches her staring after Killian in the dark hallway. "So, what happened?"

"Nothing."

"Is that why you're staring after him like a scolded puppy?"

"Shut up..." she says awkwardly, looking away. She looks over at him in the kitchen. He is smiling at her with a goofy grin, resting his chin on the palm of his hand. "I'm not a scolded puppy. He hasn't even said anything."

"That bad?"

"Will you shut up, please?"

"But you're so easy to irritate. Where else will I get my entertainment?"

"You're a dick."

Alan shrugs his shoulders, still holding a silly grin. Plating the chili in a bowl, he cuts up an avocado. Fanning out the green fruit over the chili, he brings it over and places it in front of her. She digs in without a word and he glowers at her. "You're welcome."

"Thanks."

"Spoiled brat," he says under his breath as he walks away.

"I heard that," she says, sending daggers at his back.

36

"Oh no, did I hurt your feelings, princess?"

"Don't call me that."

"As you command, your highness," Alan says with a humble bow.

"You are such a dick," she says again, grabbing her bowl and taking refuge in her room.

"You need a better comeback!" he shouts after her.

* * *

Stacy is tossing and turning in her bed, listening to the light hum of the generators against the wall. Her legs feel restless. Though she came here with a purpose, she struggles to achieve her goal. Her weakness and lack of experience is her downfall. With Killian by her side, she doesn't need strength. She may be able to make a difference with his companionship. Killian had gone to bed without a word. Usually when she has done something wrong, he reacts differently—he yells, throws and breaks things—but this silent treatment is like torture. Giving up on sleep, she opens the door leading to the hallway. Hesitating in the doorway, Alan's snoring is a good sign that it's safe to roam around in her intimates. Heading to the center of the shelter, she stops at Killian's door to listen. It's silent. She quietly walks into the mess hall. The motion-sensor lights curiously remain dark, the only illumination coming from the bar behind the shelves. Standing on the bar stools, she leans over the counter, grabbing the first bottle and glass she can reach and pouring herself a generous amount. Sniffing the alcohol, she scrunches her nose, then puts the glass to her lips and gulps. The first gulp burns; the second gulp has her nostrils flaming.

"You're wasting good scotch." Caught off-guard, Stacy chokes on the liquid fire. With it now in her lungs, she gasps for air as she hacks away. Killian is lounging on a sofa, wearing only a pair of loose drawstring pants. He can't help but smile as he watches her struggle, taking a sip from his own glass of scotch.

As she catches her breath, she clears her throat and straightens up. "I didn't see you there," she rasps, clearing her throat once more.

"I noticed."

"Do you mind if I finish it? I'm having trouble sleeping." In answer, he raises his glass and gulps the rest of his down as she had done. This time she sips it, making a sour face. She watches him stand up unsteadily. His metal arm whirrs and clicks as the pieces move to his will. He lazily makes his way to the bar.

Setting his glass on the counter next to her, he grabs the bottle and corks it. "Why's it so hard for you to sleep?" He stares down at her with dark eyes.

"I don't know."

"Could it be the amount of people I keep killing for you? Are they haunting you, like they do me?" he says, swaying towards her. Stacy doesn't respond. "Why do I keep killing people for you?" he asks in disgust. "I should just let them kill you."

"Then why don't you?" Stacy says, unblinking.

He frowns down at her. "Why don't I..." he says to himself while brushing a strand of white hair out of her eyes with his left hand. Studying her face, he turns his hand and slides his knuckles down her cheek and neck. Resting his hand on the crook of her neck, he looks into her eyes. The heat of his hand sends a hair-raising shiver down her spine. "Or I could kill you myself," he says bitterly as he tightens his grip.

"You could," she says, staring him down.

Though his eyes are so dark, a fire blazes in them as he takes hold of her throat with both hands. Her air is cut off instantly. He is pressing his body against hers, making the corner of the counter dig into her back. With instant regret, Stacy pulls at his hands desperately, digging her fingernails into his left hand. His expression falls. Releasing her, she gasps for air as he takes a couple of steps away from her and turns his back. His shoulders hang low from the weight of his guilt.

"I'm sorry," Stacy gasps. Killian is still a statue, as if he is holding his breath. Stacy carefully moves around him so that she can speak face-to-face. "I'm so sorry I've caused you so much pain." He meets her pleading eyes. "I've never thanked you for saving my life. I've only taken advantage of your generosity, and I'm truly sorry for causing you so much trouble." Killian watches her as she gently places her hands on his chest. "I'll do everything in my power to make it right."

Killian grabs hold of her wrists. The metal of his right hand digs into her flesh. "You can't fix this," he says, pulling her hands away and releasing her.

"Let me try," she says as she reaches a hand up to trace his jaw. Killian doesn't see the woman standing in front of him; he only feels the warmth of her skin. Drawn to the warmth, he crushes his lips against hers. Pressing her body into his, there is no resistance. The mixture of alcohol and loneliness allows him to let go of everything. It's been so long since he's been intimate with anyone that he loses all control, but only for a moment. He is frozen by the image of a sweet sun-kissed brunette smiling up at him. Her green eyes sparkle with tears as she reaches her hands out to him.

He shoves Stacy away from him and stalks away, wiping his mouth.

CHAPTER

4

It is morning. Seagulls cry as they search for breakfast. The waves rock the ship in a soothing way. Violet opens her eyes, tired of pretending to sleep. She stares at the iron ceiling and the rivets with its chipped paint. As much as she tries to recover her memories, she only finds darkness. The headaches increase the harder she tries. Instead she focuses her mind on what she has learned.

Nathan, her child. *How could I have a child with Charlie?* In her mind she puts their faces side-by-side. Charlie has small eyes and large lips, his hair sandy red, and so many freckles. Nathan has thick brown hair, thin lips and large eyes. Not even the shape of his button nose matches. Violet realizes Nathan has all of her own features.

Violet knows she loves Charlie; but unlike her memories, that feeling is more of a brotherly love. The argument with Charlie she dreamt about plays over and over again in her head. If it's a memory they missed, Charlie knows who the boy in the picture is, and he knows who killed her father.

The sun peeks over the horizon, shining brightly through the portholes. Violet covers her head with a pillow. Her eyes are swollen from lack of sleep. With footsteps upon the docks she groans, curling into a ball. The airship door clanks as it unlocks and creaks open. Nathan comes bounding in, dragging a giggling little girl behind him. Her hair is braided over her shoulder, with tight curls at the ends and around her face. Violet peeks out from under the pillow and the little girl gasps. No longer smiling, she stands stiff. Nathan climbs onto the cot and hugs his mother before she can protest. Welcoming the comfort of someone's arms, she hugs him back. "Nathan, you shouldn't be in here," Violet says gently as she strokes his cheek.

Jack stands in the doorway leaning against the wall. "Let him be; he's in no danger." His beard twitches as he smiles.

Violet smiles in return, rubbing Nathan's head gently. The little girl's shoulders relax. "My name is Violet. What's yours?" she says.

The little girl blushes and runs back to hide behind Jack's legs. "This is Lilly, the youngest," he answers for her.

"Hello, Lilly. It seems we have something in common." The girl peeks around Jack's leg. "We were both named after flowers." Violet smiles kindly. The girl looks up at Jack with a smile.

"Well, golly me. You two are fated to be kindred spirits," Jack says playfully. Lilly wrinkles her nose but smiles shyly at Violet. Two more girls walk in, the oldest with a tray of food. "Jolene made breakfast, and that one is Ember." The oldest doesn't smile, but stares emotionlessly. Violet shifts uncomfortably. Ember places the tray next to the cot, then smiles timidly and stands next to Lilly. She has a similar hairstyle with a light curl, but her features are not as soft, with a thin line for an upper lip and light freckles.

"You look particularly wild this morning, old man," Violet says. "Did you sleep at all?"

Jack smooths his unruly hair down, smiling. Dark circles make him seem older. "You should talk. I'm doing more tests, but your samples are extraordinary. Your saliva is harmless, but for now try not to cut yourself," he says while chewing on an empty tobacco pipe. He had run out of tobacco ages ago, but never nicked the habit of chewing on his pipe, especially when he is deliberating. "Eat up and we'll talk." He shoos the children away.

Nathan stays and watches her as she picks the tray off the floor; omelet, toast and bacon, with fresh orange juice. Jack only grows Valencia oranges, which must mean it's the end of summer, which explains the heat. Nathan watches as she eats, but keeps eying her bacon. Violet notices and holds it out to him. He splits it in half and hands her the other piece with a smile. "Thank you." She says, watching him as he chews on the strip of crispy meat. Tears well up as she admires the beautiful boy sitting next to her. She rubs his head and pulls him in for a hug. He wraps his arms around her waist, and she rubs his back. She wonders how she could have left this boy to search for someone, a murderer. He continues to nibble on his bacon while holding onto her waist, staring out the door.

Violet quickly eats the omelet and toast, leaving the plate clean. She gets dressed with the other outfit stuffed in her bag from Clara, fresh trousers and blouse with a vest. After lacing up her boots, she gulps the orange juice down while walking with Nathan hand-in-hand back to the house. Lilly runs past and stops to smile at them, and Nathan looks up at Violet. "Go play, I'm not going anywhere," she replies, smiling. Nathan runs after her while Jolene watches over them silently.

Jack calls to Violet from inside. She finds him in his office, sitting on a high stool, looking through a microscope and writing his findings down in a leather-bound book. He has moved some of his favorite lab equipment here. The office is cluttered with terrariums, books, vials, beakers and an intricate chemistry set. Music is playing on the record player in the corner. His desk is layered with sheets of paper, drawings and photos. Something is illuminated underneath. Violet moves the papers, revealing a piece of glass that looks similar to a clipboard. A video plays and repeats. An airship used to transport criminals from town is hit midair. The ship catches fire and people jump from it as it falls out of the sky. The camera zooms onto the ship before it disappears into the trees and explodes, leaving only black smoke behind. The ship's tag number was painted onto the side of the ship, 327. The video is familiar. When Violet draws closer to see what he had been researching, a stack of paper falls to the ground, drawing his attention. He quickly turns around, snatching the screen and turning it off. "Sorry," she says, helping him pick up the papers. He piles them on top of the screen.

"I wanted to talk to you about these." He traces the veins on her arm. "You've been underground for the past few years. Your skin is very translucent. If you get out in the sun, I believe the smaller veins will not be so noticeable. For the more prominent veins, there's a simple procedure that can help. I'd make a small incision and insert a tiny catheter. With radio waves, I can shrink the walls of the vein, and it should re-absorb. The blood will redirect to other veins. There's no telling whether new veins will show up, but it might help you look a little more... yourself. With anesthesia it would be painless, although there'd be mild bruising."

"If you think it'll help others to not be afraid of me, then let's do it." Looking in the mirror above his desk, she studies her spiderwebbed face. The bruise on her cheek is already fading.

"Just so you know, it'll have an itching or burning sensation until it's fully healed."

"When can we start?" Violet says impatiently.

Jack has her lay down in one of his guest rooms, in her undergarments. Before getting started, he checks the stitches in her neck, sees that they're no longer necessary, and removes them. "You're healing impeccably fast. It may take less than a week if the procedure works. It wouldn't be long before you'd look more... you."

44

He brings in a machine. After administering the general anesthesia, he works on her for about two hours. When he finishes up, he uses a compression wrap on the areas he worked on, then wraps her from the waist up. She doesn't wake for another hour. Jack leaves her to rest while he puts lunch together.

When Violet wakes up, she's very groggy. The confinement of the compression wraps makes her feel somewhat claustrophobic. After getting dressed, she throws her cloak over her shoulders and goes out to the yard. Taking a deep breath, the cool breeze is refreshing. Nathan, Lilly and Ember chase each other in the field beyond the garden. Jolene is watching them from the bench near the fountain. Her short dark hair is thin and cut into a perfect bob. She is very pretty with light brown eyes, but she never has any expression on her face. Her eyes seem dead. She watches the children, but does she see them? She's sewing a patch into a pair of pants and rarely looks down at her perfect stitches. Violet sits next to her. Jolene adjusts so that Violet has more than enough space. Jolene doesn't look away. "Do you need any help?" Violet asks, though she knows her sewing skills are lacking.

Jolene pauses. She looks at Violet, but it's as if she's staring through her. "I do not need assistance. Thank you for asking." Jolene continues working, looking back to the children. Violet decides to take her leave and sit atop the hill where the children play, with the woods at her back. Nathan runs up to her with a tackling hug. Before she can get up, he is off running again.

Watching the children play reminds Violet of when she was a child. She would come to Jack's house as often as possible to play with the orphaned children he took in. They were the closest thing she had to a family. Her mother passed away when she was very young, and her father quickly became the town drunk. When he would become violent, she would run through the woods. He would tire out before catching up with her at the beach. She would spend as much time as possible at the dock, watching the inky sea come and go. For some reason she couldn't remember how she came to meet Jack. She could recall the stories he would tell her, but not how they met.

Jack delighted in reading and teaching others what he's learned. He used to be a pilot and engineer for the military. When he retired, he taught himself how to build homes, and how to work with glass and metals. He began building Safe Haven with people who had escaped the fallen cities. He helped them learn to work with their hands. With all of the technology in the other cities, most people had become used to things being provided for them, but eventually people learned to take care of themselves. Jack continued inventing machines that didn't take away from the skills they learned, including a shield system that would alert them of any threats to the community. Bio-scouts, which had been taken over by other cities, couldn't pass through the shield, like when magnets repel.

A maven wouldn't need to search the woods unless the bio-scouts alerted them to human existence. Everyone's home was installed with a monitor that would only become active if one of the bio-scouts came through the shield. Otherwise people have reverted back to water-fueled generators and steam engines. All electricity from outside of town had been cut off. Fossil fuel is seen only when a refugee happens to have some on them when they pass through the shield. If they happened to leave it outside the boundaries, it was lost, since no one had been allowed to leave ever since a form of government had been put into place.

After the town had grown into a good-sized community, they voted for a leader. Even though he had helped build them up from basically nothing, Jack was too easy-going to be the leader, plus didn't want the responsibility. Russel Banner is currently the leader, and he's always asking Jack's advice anyway. Jack finds it more irritating than anything.

He comes up the hill with two bowls of shepherd's pie. Violet is unconsciously humming 'We Own the Sky,' and he says, "I haven't heard that song in a very long time." When he brings it to her attention she stops. He hands her the bowl and sits next to her.

"Nathan seems very happy," Violet says.

"He hasn't been this energetic in a long time."

Her chest tightens at the thought of him being unhappy. "Is that why he doesn't talk?"

"Oh, he speaks when he has something to say. When he has an opinion, you can't shut him up. Just give him time." Jack wraps his arm around her.

Violet rests her head on his shoulder while they watch the kids chase a dragonfly. "Did you speak with Clara?" she asks.

"Ah... Clara. She's a woman after my own heart. She's well, more concerned for you than herself. I received an earful for the state she found you in."

"When did you meet her?"

"You were there. You don't remember?"

"Apparently not. There are many things I don't remember."

"It'll come back. Patience is a virtue."

"Regardless, she's definitely a keeper. Don't screw it up."

"Yes ma'am," he says with a salute. They eat silently as they watch the children play.

A mild rumble comes from the distance, then a sleek vehicle comes down the path, with red and blue lights flashing on the roof and a billow of steam rising into the air. "Get into the trees, Violet," he suddenly warns. "Don't come out until Nathan comes for you." He doesn't have to say it twice. Violet hides in the woods while he meets the suits at the front porch, just as they knock on the front door. Nathan watches them from the garden. He searches the yard for his mother and becomes nervous when realizing she is gone.

Jack is very animated as he speaks with the officers. Violet's surprise visit to Jenna's Tavern has everyone talking about a sick woman who has abducted a small child from his family. Nathan comes to the porch when Jack calls for him, reassuring the officers he wasn't harmed and that the woman is gone. Nathan agrees with everything Jack says without hesitation, knowing that if Violet was found, she would surely be drafted out with the rest of the criminals, without being given a fair trial.

The suits look around the house and in the airship before finally leaving, kicking up a cloud of dust. Not long after the dirt settles, Nathan goes running up the hill to Violet. "Good to go?" she asks, peeking out from the trees. Nathan takes her hand and drags her back to the house.

Jack waits for them in the dining room. "If you keep making appearances, Violet, you won't have much time here."

"I don't plan on going back to town."

"Good. Clara will be joining us for dinner. She wants to bring you more clothes and such."

The children gather at the table as Jack unrolls maps and blueprints. He is searching for something and seems rushed. Everyone but Jolene seems unnerved by his behavior. He finds what he needs and scans it with a handheld device. When it's complete, he places a stand in the middle of the table and connects the scanner to the base. After it's clamped in, a holographic screen displays the entire town in a glowing green shade. Nathan reaches through it with his hand and Jack swats him away. With a special glove he is able to move the images on the screen around.

Certain areas in town are highlighted in red, stemming out like veins. "What's that?" Violet asks.

"Underground sources of electricity. Someone's tapped into them. They may have given our location away long ago. I don't know how long it's been."

"How did you find out they're using it?"

"They're using the suits, which send data to headquarters in the middle of town, and they have to take energy for them from somewhere. I haven't been alerted of any shift in the shield's strength, so they have to be drawing it from somewhere else. Seems my years of being a hermit have consequences."

Jack zooms into the main location. The headquarters is located in the town hall in the center of town. Jack slams his fist on the table. This is the first time he has lost his temper in front of any of them. Everyone flinches but Jolene. Violet watches her curiously. "I need to go into town. It seems Mayor Banner has taken it upon himself to screw us all," he says bitterly, gathering his jacket before walking out the front door. It slams behind him, shaking the frames on the walls and making the hanging plants sway. He opens the door and peeks his head back in. "I don't know how long I'll be gone, Violet. Take care of the kids until I come back. Everyone stays here!" he says, slamming the door behind him once again.

Lilly, clinging to Ember, begins to cry. "Shh, don't cry, sweetheart," Violet says, coming around the table to rub their shoulders. "Everything will be okay. Jack isn't mad at us. He's just going to fix an issue in town, and then he'll be right back." A machine starts to rumble outside and a dust cloud chases after Jack on his makeshift steam scooter.

Jolene turns to Ember and Lilly. "Do not worry. He will return very soon. Everything will be fine." She smiles but it doesn't reach her eyes. It's the first time Violet sees any emotion on her face, but it looks more menacing than comforting.

For the rest of the day the children play quietly inside. Waiting for Jack to return is proving to be a struggle for Violet. Jolene insists on making dinner. She seems more content keeping busy with work. The girls pull out a toy Jack had created a long time ago. It was one Violet used to play with as well. A model airship is connected to a rod, and at the base is a box with a crank. As you turn the crank, music plays and the ship rises and falls as its finlike wings flap up and down. The tune is a comforting sound. It is the same song she was humming earlier on the hill. The music makes her feel nostalgic.

To keep herself busy, Violet familiarizes herself with the house again. At a certain point, she trips on a toy and falls into the wall in the hallway. When her shoulder hits the wall, a small recessed door opens. Inside is a small compartment in which four weapons are hidden—matching pistols, a tesla rifle, and a hand cannon. She quickly closes the cabinet, making sure no one noticed. She enters his office, hoping to find the rest of his research from earlier, but it looks as if he cleaned up. Violet searches all of the drawers, cabinets and boxes, but it's nowhere to be found. Eventually she gives up and moves on.

Looking through Jack's books, she comes across one that has no title, leather-bound and very worn. She pulls it out and flips through it. It's not Jack's handwriting nor Charlie's. There are many sketches and diagrams. She stops at a page with a drawing that covers two pages. She is surprised when she recognizes herself in the drawing. She is sleeping with a subtle smile about her lips. The sheets are wrapped in a way that shows the curve of her body. No detail was spared, even the beauty marks on her shoulder and above her eyebrow. She looks for a name of the owner but there is none. Flipping further through the book, she discovers that the writing and drawing end before it runs out of pages. Reading through some of the passages, she finds that the author is an inventor like Jack. Some of his creations are beyond her understanding. Nonetheless, she feels a connection with the person by the way they write. She slips the book into the back pocket of her trousers.

A rap at the door makes Violet nearly jump out of her skin. She crouches as she sneaks up to the window. Seeing a frizzy-haired woman in a long bustle skirt and white blouse instantly relieves her. Violet opens the door timidly.

"Oh, good heavens!" Clara is startled by Violet's appearance, her face still covered in compression wraps. She holds her heart and smiles when she realizes who it is.

"Sorry, I forgot about the wrap," she says, scratching at the irritated skin beneath.

"Don't be. Sorry for my inappropriate reaction. I brought you more things," she says excitedly, dragging a large suitcase on wheels into the house.

"Jack had to go into town," Violet informs her.

"Oh, he told me. I came to see you anyhow," Clara says as she rubs Violet's arm. "Come on, let's play dress up!" Clara's excitement is contagious. Soon Ember and Lily are giggling as they try on fancy hats and dresses that are excessively large for them. Violet chooses the more practical items and packs them away into a larger shoulder sack Clara has brought along. She sneaks the leather-bound book in. Setting it aside, she watches Clara help the girls secure hats with pins upon their head. The girls begin acting out a scene of a proper lady breaking wind. Clara is laughing so hard she's in tears, Nathan and Violet laughing alongside them.

Jolene enters the room with a blank look. "Dinner is ready. Please set the table." The girls stop what they're doing, leaving Clara dripping in tears on the floor. Opening the cabinets in the dining room, they grab plates and silverware and Nathan joins in. Clara, wiping her eyes and panting, recovers with a deep sigh.

"You're really good with them," Violet says.

"Oh, it's easy with those two. They're so silly." She laughs again, and Violet nods. "How long do you need to wear that wrap?"

"I don't know. It doesn't hurt, it's just itchy."

"May I take a look?" Violet crawls next to Clara and sits on her legs with her head bent. Clara unwraps the bandages. Violet stretches her jaw and scrunches her nose. "That's miraculous," Clara says in awe.

"Are they gone?"

"The veins? No, but the cuts he made are already closing up."

"Did he make a miracle healing spray or something?"

"No dear, whatever happened to you has changed you."

"Somehow, that's not comforting."

"It'll be alright." Clara wraps her arm around her and Violet rests her head on her shoulder.

"If my mother were alive today, I wonder if she'd be like you."

"That's sweet of you. What happened to your mother, if you don't mind me asking?"

"She died giving birth when I was around five or six. The baby died too."

"I'm so sorry. That must have been very hard at your age."

"It's alright." They both become quiet, thinking of what to say next. "You said you knew me before my accident," Violet says, finally breaking the silence. "What was I like?"

"Oh, you didn't speak much. You kept to yourself. It seemed there was always something on your mind. You were always lost in your own thoughts. When you did speak, you were always very polite."

Violet nods. "Was I a bad mother?"

"No, sweetie, you loved Nathan more than anything. He was the only thing that could put a smile on your face. When you were with him, it was like you came to life." Violet nods again with tears in her eyes, as her throat tightens.

Jolene brings out a pot of chicken pasta with red sauce and a side of garlic bread. It smells delicious and everyone sits at the table. There is lively chatter as they consume their dinner. When they finish, everyone helps to clear the table. Clara and Violet offer to clean up the kitchen, but Jolene insists on doing it on her own, so the two relax in the living room instead, getting to know each other. Violet learns that Clara did once have a daughter of her own. She had grown up and started a family, but they perished in a bombing several years back. Her husband died of blood poisoning when he was cut badly that same year. Clara had had a hard life, living on her own. According to her, finding Safe Haven and Jack was the best thing that had ever happened to her. She has felt safe and welcome ever since.

Before long, the sun sets. Violet has a feeling Jack won't return tonight. Nathan retrieves Violet's bag from the ship so that she can stay in the house. She helps the children get ready for bed and tucks them in. Lilly, Ember and Nathan cuddle together in the queen-sized guest bed, falling asleep almost as soon as their heads hit the pillow. She admires their sweet faces as they sleep, and kisses each of them on the forehead. Jolene finishes up the kitchen and goes to her own room, shutting the door behind her.

Violet and Clara share Jack's bed. Clara falls asleep quickly while Violet stares at the ceiling. Now that the house is silent, she hears everything. The wind swaying the bushes against the house makes an eerie sound. Feeling more paranoid every second, she pulls a blanket over her head. Closing her eyes, the more she focuses on the sounds the clearer they become. Branches scratch against glass windows in the living room. The ocean waves rush onto the sand. An owl calls out in the woods. There is a crunch close to one of the windows by the side of the house. Her heart begins to race. It could be an animal searching for something to eat. Another crunch, but this time the sound is closer.

With the third crunch she jumps out of bed and goes to the hallway. Bumping the wall with her fist, the hidden cabinet pops open. She pulls out one of Jack's pistols. Quietly closing the cabinet door, she slides along the walls, peeking out the window through the heavy drapes. Seeing a small figure move through the garden, she quickly locks the doors and checks all the windows. She grabs the blanket from the couch and sits on the floor with her back against it, facing the door. She waits and listens. The gun is propped on her knee, ready to fire should anyone break in. Her ears buzz as the adrenaline pulses through her. The door handle jiggles. In learning the house is locked up tight, it becomes silent once more.

CHAPTER

5

The sun has just peeked over the horizon. Jack unlocks the front door and quietly enters, hoping not to wake anyone. He sees Violet on the floor sitting up against the side of the couch, asleep with a pistol in her hand. His foot finds a loose board as he reaches out to the pistol, and she awakes in a panic. In a blink of an eye, she is crouched on one knee and ready to shoot. Jack yips in fright with the sudden movement, throwing his hands up in the air. "What the blazes?! Are ye trying to give me a tachycardia?!" Jack yells.

Violet sighs and puts the safety back on. "Seriously, old man? Just call it a heart attack like normal people," she says, exasperated. Ember comes out from the hallway rubbing her eyes.

"Why do you have my pistol?" Jack says angrily, snatching it out of her hand and tucking it into his belt.

"I saw someone outside last night, after everyone went to bed."

"So you're going to track him down and shoot him?! How did you even know where these were? Snooping little devil," he grumbles to himself.

"Him?" Violet asks, raising an eyebrow. Jack curses himself, stomping off and grumbling something unintelligible. He checks on Jolene, who is already dressed and on her way to the kitchen. Lilly and Nathan are still sleeping, as it is still too early for them to get up.

After a frightening wake-up call, a cold shower is just what Violet needs. Looking herself over in the mirror, the smaller veins are already starting to fade. There is no pain. Though her body is still very thin, she's beginning to feel more like herself. Feeling more confident, she finishes up in the restroom and changes into a loose-fitting dress. She hand-washes the clothes she has worn and hangs them on the line from the back porch.

Clara, after making the bed, joins Jack in his office. In passing, Violet hears her arguing with him. "You can't be angry at her Jack. She was scared."

Violet peeks in and sees Jack fuming in his office chair, while Clara stands over him with her arms crossed. "She could've hurt someone, Clara. What if it had been one of the children and she accidentally pulled the trigger?"

"I understand. But she didn't hurt anyone, and she's no longer in possession of a weapon. You need to calm down and look at it from her perspective. She has no memory of what's happened to her. You have no idea what she's been through. She's scared."

"So am I," Jack sighs. "I'm scared that she might not be herself. You didn't see how quickly she moved."

"If you're worried then you need to talk to her. If you don't communicate with her, she'll start to feel alienated."

"You're right," Jack says.

"I know." Clara smiles and bends down to kiss him on the forehead.

There is a rumbling outside as another vehicle drives up to the house. Violet sneaks to the front window, peeking out the front as she waits for the visitor to become visible. Jack comes stomping out of his office grumbling. He swings the front door open and slams it behind him. He stands firm with his fists at his hips. The vehicle comes to a stop at the front porch. It isn't a suit but a man. He climbs off the vehicle and removes his helmet and aviator goggles.

"Go home, Charlie," Jack growls at him. "I don't have the patience to deal with your shenanigans today."

Charlie smiles wryly. "I know she's here, Grandpa. I need to speak with her."

"No, she doesn't want to see you. Go home to Jenna."

"The only way I'm leaving is if you call the suits to remove me. And I have a feeling you won't risk a visit from them just to get rid of me." He spins the helmet in his hands.

"Get off my property, boy!" Jack howls as he reaches for the pistol stuffed into the back of his trousers.

Violet quickly steps out, "It's fine, Jack."

Startled by the touch of her hand, he lets go of the pistol. If you cause any trouble, boy..." he says, waving a threatening finger in Charlie's direction.

Jack returns to the house, leaving Charlie and Violet alone. Charlie looks her over and tilts his head with a smile. He sets the helmet on the seat of his vehicle and stands in front of her. Violet is internally struggling with her emotions. Looking at him, she sees the man she loves. His freckled face is more lean than before, and you can see every muscle as he clenches his sharp jaw. His face relaxes and his blue eyes glisten.

He smiles as he tucks a loose curl of hair behind her ear. Tilting his head again, he studies her expression. "They've faded," he says with a breathy voice. Unable to speak, she nods. "Still so beautiful." A chill runs down her spine as his fingertips gently trace the lines on her face. She takes a step backwards and watches Charlie's jaw clench. He scowls for only a second before his expression becomes light again. "I wanted to apologize," he says, tucking his hands into his pockets.

"For what?"

Charlie glances behind her. Jack is in the window, watching them with folded arms. He smiles and holds his elbow out to her. Violet takes it reluctantly and he leads her away from the house. "I wanted to apologize for Jenna and her hostility. I'm sorry she called the suits on you as well. It won't happen again." They slowly walk towards the dock. "I hadn't told her about your situation. Jack and I thought it best to tell everyone you had died. I didn't want to leave you behind and start a new life with her, but I did it for Nathan. He needed a mother figure in his life. He needed stability. I hope you can understand and forgive me."

Violet doesn't know how to respond. "You tried to replace me?" Violet says, feeling hurt.

Charlie stops her, holding her shoulders tightly.

"No one could ever replace you, Violet O'Daire. I love you more than you could possibly understand."

"But you did replace me, Charlie."

"Jenna and I are over."

"Charlie, imagine how that would make Jenna feel. She's loved you for years. You can't leave her just because I came back to life."

"If she really loves me, she would want me to be happy. I can only be happy with you by my side," Charlie says, gently holding her face in his hands.

"Can't you see how selfish you're being? You haven't changed at all." Violet pulls his hands away from her face.

"You won't take me back?" His expression turns dark.

"How can I? You made a new life with Jenna. You can't just abandon her."

"I don't love her," Charlie says coldly. "I only dream of you." Tears well up in his eyes. "I've missed you so much, Violet." Stepping closer, he closes the distance between them. She closes her eyes, avoiding eye contact. The emotions he displays don't match his tone. He grasps her shoulders and his full lips gently graze hers, but his fingertips dig in. The shock of pain brings her back to reality, and a wave of fear washes over her. Violet remembers Charlie's harshness from the dream she had at Clara's.

"No," Violet says, pushing him away. Charlie sighs. She turns away looking out to sea, wiping her mouth with a shaking hand.

"Violet, please."

"Do you remember the day my father died, Charlie?" Violet asks nervously.

"As clear as day," he says dryly.

"We were near the waterfall. Do you remember? That day, you were so angry with me."

"I remember."

"So, it wasn't a dream." Violet turns to face him. Staring him down, he straightens his shoulders, holding his head high. "You told me to forget him, the man who killed my father." She steps forward, watching his expression carefully. "Who is he, Charlie?"

"He's of no consequence. He's dead. He can never hurt you ever again," Charlie says sincerely, as if she needs to be consoled.

"The only person who hurt me that day was you." Charlie's eyes become dark. "I don't need you to tell me. I only wanted to confirm it as a memory. Thank you for the clarification. Go home to Jenna, Charlie."

"You asked us to remove him, Violet. You can't be angry at me for doing as you wished. I can tell you're upset, so I'll leave you for today. We can talk more later." Charlie steals a peck on the cheek and walks away without looking back.

* * *

After dinner that night, Jack invites Violet back to his office. Distracted by her own thoughts, she follows silently. Jack leans up against his desk with a mighty grin.

"Why are you smiling like that?"

"I have something exciting to show you," Jack says proudly. He scoots down and points to the microscope, "Take a look." She does as she is told as Jack snaps on some rubber gloves.

Looking through the scope, she recognizes red blood cells. "My blood?" she asks.

"No, it's mine," Jack replies. "Keep watching." He takes a dropper and adds a black substance to the petri dish. She looks back in the scope. The black liquid turns out to be another form of blood cells, dark blue in color. As the blue cells begin to mingle with Jack's blood, they pulse and stretch as if reaching out. When it touches the red blood cells, they melt into each other as if being devoured, and the cell splits in two. In a matter of minutes, the petri dish has been taken over by the dark cells. Violet feels the blood leave her face and she begins to feel sick to her stomach. Jack pulls the petri dish from under the microscope and drops the entire thing into a jar with a light purple liquid.

"Was that *my* blood?"

"That was maven blood."

"Why the hell would you keep that around? Especially with kids around?"

"They know better than to come into my office. Anyway..." Jack prepares another dish and sets it under the lens. "Watch this." The dish has another sample of Jack's blood cells. From another dropper with dark liquid he adds a drop. Violet watches closely. These blood cells are a purple shade. They don't stretch or reach out, but mingle with the red blood cells. The red cells stay intact.

"Nothing happened."

"Keep watching." He adds one more drop. The maven's blood is dropped on the opposite side of the purple. Instantly the purple stretches out as the blue touches the dish. Though some red cells had been taken, the purple cells quickly devour the blue and multiply, leaving the rest of the red cells to themselves in half the time.

"What was that?" Violet can't take her eyes away.

Jack takes the petri dish and dumps the petri dish into the purple liquid again. "The red blood cells are human. The blue, maven. And your blood looks like a mixture of the two, hence the purple hue. For some reason, your blood reacts to Maven as if it were a virus and kills it, leaving the human blood untouched. It's a mutation."

"I'm a mutant," she says reconfirming.

"You're a mutant!" Jack says with excitement. "It's incredible! Do you understand what this means? Your blood is like a virus to maven. Their exoskeleton is extremely difficult to penetrate, but if we can get the tiniest bit of your blood into them it would be game over! Your cells have adapted in a way that may benefit all humanity."

"Great, a mutant weapon."

"At least you're not poisonous to humans. This could help in reversing your banishment." Jack shakes his finger at her. "You'd be welcomed back into the colony with open arms."

"And you'd be banished for letting me back in. Also, I still look like a monster." Violet rubs at the fading veins that remain.

"They're fading. You keep looking at this negatively. This is a good thing. You should be happy." Jack pats her shoulders before bringing her in for a hug.

"Thank you, Jack."

After sharing the good news, the children are put to bed and Jack brings out his rum to celebrate. Clara, Jack and Violet share a couple of glasses. With less weight on her shoulders and a bit inebriated, Violet is able to sleep a little better that evening.

CHAPTER

6

Violet is beginning to get her strength back. No longer is she sickly thin. Over the next few days Charlie returns to speak with Violet, trying to win her over. When Violet refuses to speak of anything but her father's killer, he leaves. Jack has not informed the people of Violet's return, or what her blood is capable of. Not wanting to risk anyone else's banishment, they keep this secret. Jack spends most of his time in his office, monitoring the barrier and the town's activity. Violet keeps hearing things outside the house, and can only sleep with a glass or two of rum.

One evening the rum runs out. Violet lays on the couch, staring at the ceiling as shadows dance across it. The heat from the day forces them to keep the windows open, so the breeze can flow through the house. The curtains rise and fall as the house breathes. The sound of a branch cracking has Violet on edge. She sneaks over to the wall and peeks around through the curtains. The moon is full and its light blankets the land. There is movement near the woods. Violet holds her breath as a small figure runs down the hill. Crouching low, they sneak into the garden. Violet sits below the window, still listening and waiting. The person is growing nearer to the window. She can hear their breath. Peeking out once more, she sees another figure quickly moving down the hill. She watches as the figures collide with one another. A scream is cut off and the figures struggle back up the hill. Though the air is warm, Violet shivers. *What was that?* she asks herself.

In the morning, she asks Jack and Clara if they heard any noise the night before. Violet tells them what she saw and Jack becomes uneasy. Clara tries consoling Violet while Jack once again shuts himself up in his office. His breakfast remains on a tray in front of his door, untouched.

It is almost noon and the children are playing quietly in the living room. Jack's office door swings open. "Violet!" he yells. She's making the bed in the other room when Jack calls for her. She comes to him immediately. "Get the children and the emergency packs. We need to leave." Violet, seeing the fear in his eyes, doesn't question him.

Opening the closet door, she grabs all the packs available. Handing one to each person, she helps strap them on over their chests. "Grab a change of clothing," she tells them, "and don't pack anything unnecessary." The children become frightened with the urgency, but they do as they are told. Jolene and Clara assist the children. They move quickly. Grabbing the bag Clara gave Violet, she checks to make sure everything, including survival rations, are there before throwing it over her shoulder. Jack hands her the pistols and an earpiece. Her stomach drops, but she straps on the holster with the weapons and places the piece into her ear. Jack has two large cases in his arms, leading everyone to the dock.

A vehicle comes up the path and skids to a stop as everyone is leaving the house. Charlie climbs off his ride and takes his helmet off, confused by the commotion. Relieved it's not the suits, Violet ignores him and follows Jack. Charlie runs after them. He catches up to Violet and quickly grabs her arm.

"Wait, I want to apologize," he says. "Jenna isn't a problem anymore, She'll leave us alone from now on."

"What are you talking about, Charlie? We don't have time for this."

"Last night she was lurking around the house. Is that why you're leaving?"

"Go get Jenna and get out of town!" Jack barks. "We don't have much time!"

The sirens began to wail. Everyone is frozen by the chilling sound. Jack rushes them to board the ship. He doesn't even strap the cargo down before starting up the engines.

"Why are the sirens sounding!" Charlie asks nervously.

"Because ye dobbers have been usin' city energy," Jack spits angrily. "Our town's been discovered. A fleet is comin' fur us now. We don't have any trained fighters, nor ships." You know Jack is serious when the Scottish brogue in him comes out.

"I'm coming with you," Charlie demands, running back towards the house.

"We don't have enough provisions to include you," Jack bites. Violet helps him load up the rest of the supplies as Charlie runs back full speed with a pack on his shoulders. "Ye can't just leave Jenna to fend fur 'r self. She's not the brightest!"

"She needs you more than we do," Violet adds patiently, but Charlie shoves himself through the opening as the door slides closed. "What about Jenna?!" she yells, outraged by his selfishness.

"She knows what she's doing. She can take care of herself," Charlie says. His eyes shift once and she immediately knows he's lying, but Jack doesn't have time to shove him off or argue. They must get as much distance between them and the town as possible.

"Selfish... pure selfish wallaper," Jack snaps. Charlie shakes off Jack's comment. The bitterness in Jack's voice is surprising. For a man who has always been gentle and sweet, no one would know he can have such a bite. Jack escapes up the ladder to the upper deck, and the door to the cockpit slams shut. Clara helps Violet strap the children into seats as the ship roars to life and soon starts rising out of the water. Charlie holds onto the straps hanging from the ceiling to maintain stability. Jack calls Violet to the upper deck through the earpiece, and she climbs up. "Keep an eye out for ships and bio-scouts," Jack says. Violet nods.

The ship rises high into the sky and Jack's house quickly shrinks out of sight. They fly west towards the fallen city. Within two minutes of their takeoff, Safe Haven is up in flames and smoke. A sleek pointed ship can be seen faintly in the distance, but only when the light catches it. No one could have escaped in time, unless they were at the edge of the border already on their way out.

Once the ship is at the right altitude, Jack turns on autopilot. Everyone is able to walk about. They climb to the upper deck to watch their hometown fade into the distance. Jack sits in his chair in the control room, holding Emery and Lilly on his lap, comforting them. Jolene stands portside, staring off into the storm hovering over the fallen city. For a while no one speaks. Charlie stays close to Nathan. With arms folded, Violet leans against the railing at the bow, watching them, wind blowing her hair free from the loose braid. Nathan's lips are pinched tight. He pulls away when Charlie pats him on the shoulder and runs to Violet, wrapping his arms around one leg. She smiles down at him and rubs his back.

Charlie comes to lean against the railing opposite Violet. "You're looking so much healthier," he says with a smile. Nathan glares and goes back to the cockpit with the girls.

"Thanks." Violet nods her head, not making eye contact.

"Are you going to forgive me already?"

Violet doesn't want to talk about it now, but there's no escape on a ship a thousand feet from the ground. "For which part, Charlie? For finding a new girlfriend while I was in a vegetative state? For leaving your current girlfriend to be slaughtered while you chase after your old love interest?" She shakes her head and scoffs, stepping closer so that his face is inches from hers. "Or should I forgive you for wiping my memories and replacing them with ones of you, so that you could play house?" His eyes become wide with realization. "I know you created our relationship in the anamnesis manipulator. It wasn't real. If it had been, I wouldn't have felt the need to leave in the middle of the night to find whatever was missing," Violet says calmly.

Charlie's expression turns sour. "Your memories are returning," he confirms.

"Little by little."

"How much do you remember?"

"Enough to know that our past is a lie and I don't wish to continue it. You know what I think?" She doesn't wait for his response. "I think I knew all along that you weren't the one for me. Maybe that's why I risked everything, including my own life... to get away from you." The look of awkwardness is quickly replaced with indignation.

Charlie's head falls and the corner of his mouth curls up. He laughs to himself, shaking his head. Violet leans back, holding onto the rail with both hands. "You didn't have any complaints when we made love," he says in a loving way as he moves closer.

"Well, I wouldn't have even let you into my bed if I had known you wiped everything I hate about you out of my mind." Violet smiles back at him sweetly.

He laughs, stepping forward, pushing his hips against hers. Violet's back digs into the railing. He leans in so that his lips brush against her ear. "You're the most ungrateful wench I've ever met," he says, speaking only loud enough for her to hear. "I gave you everything you asked for. I took care of you. I even took care of your illegitimate *bastard* son all this time. And what do I get for it?" He rests his hands on her waist.

Inside Violet is seething, but she holds a smile as she looks into his icy blue eyes. "Thank you... for letting me know Nathan isn't yours." She pats Charlie's arms. "Now I can move on free of guilt, maybe even find his real father."

Charlie guffaws. "Let me remind you, he's dead, I made sure of that... twice, in fact." He brushes her cheek with his knuckles, a wry smile on his lips.

Suddenly there's the sound of a loud click next to them. They turn to see Jack standing with his blaster cocked, aimed straight at Charlie's temple. Clara stands close by, watching them with a hand over her mouth. "Give me one reason not to blow your head off," he says. Charlie looks back at Violet as she taps her earpiece. Jack had been listening to their entire conversation. Charlie steps back with his hands up.

Out of the corner of her eye, Violet notices Jolene moving slowly towards the cockpit. Something is wrong. Jolene is changing. "Jack?" Violet draws his attention. Her hair is growing as the color changes to a purple hue. Her movements are strange and twitchy. The children scream and begin crying from the cockpit. "It is alright, Lilly, it is Mama," Jolene says, her voice growing deeper in pitch. "Come to Mummy, Lilly." Jack turns his weapon on Jolene and takes a shot; but when the bullet hits her shoulder, sparks fly. She isn't fazed and continues to pull at the cockpit door, the handle bending as she pulls at it. In the children's panic, they hit the control panel, and the ship veers off-course.

"Jack!" Violet yells, pulling her pistols from the holsters. With the first shot she hits the side of Jolene's face. Her flesh rips to shreds, revealing a metal interior and mechanized parts.

"Get down!" Jack yells to the children. As they crouch down, Jack shoots the glass out on the opposite side of the cockpit. He knocks sharper pieces out with his elbow. Violet continues shooting Jolene while the ship is losing altitude. Jumping through the open window, Jack hands the children off to Clara. They fall back behind Violet, still shooting. Charlie is frozen stiff with fright. Jolene no longer looks human in any way. Most of the flesh has fallen off, exposing her true form. No one has ever seen this kind of technology, not even Jack. Jolene rips the door to the cockpit off. Jack shoots his blaster and hits her square in the forehead. Trying to catch her balance, she steps backwards, only to fall over the side of the ship. Jack hits the thrusters, but they're plummeting too fast. The engines are able to slow the speed of the ship, but they're still on a crash course.

He steers the ship closer to land and yells, "Brace yourselves!" Violet and Clara crouch down over the children and hold tight. Hitting the surface, the ship is almost completely submerged before it comes back up. Water floods the engines and they are stranded. As the water spills off the deck, they gasp for breath. The children are choking on water and coughing. Violet stands up and looks around. They're not far from shore. Jack has gashed his forehead and blood streams down his face. Charlie is portside, hanging from the railing with one arm, when a mechanical hand grabs hold of him. He screams. Jolene is still on the ship.

"Violet, get the kids out of here!" Jack commands. Violet looks around and finds a lifeboat, a flat plank in the shape of a crescent with propellers on either end. Attached are several carabiners and rope. Throwing the board into the icy water, she helps each child onto the wing then slips herself into it, attaching herself to the board first and then each child.

Clara throws Violet's pack over. Pulling it over her shoulder, she looks back at Clara. "Go!" she yells with the rifle in hand. Hearing Jack and Charlie struggling, she wants to help, but she knows she must get the children out. She starts up the board and they quickly move towards shore. Completely soaked, they drag themselves onto the rocky land. Violet squeezes as much water out of their clothes as possible. The packs are waterproof. Looking back at the ship, one of the engines explodes. Lilly jumps at the sound and instantly bursts into tears. Violet pulls the kids into her chest. "It's okay, they weren't on the ship," Violet says, reassuring herself as well as the children.

The ship starts to sink. Through the smoke, Violet sees Jolene fall into the water and begin making its way towards them. "We need to move," she says, taking Lilly into her arms and pulling Nathan and Ember along. Not far into the woods she spots a large building. It looks abandoned, with a lack of maintenance and overgrowth. There is a large revolving glass door. She pushes Nathan and Ember through it first; she and Lilly follow. She wedges a metal sanction post in the door, locking it in place. The structure is built to allow as much natural light in as possible; but with the overgrowth of trees and moss taking over, it's still very dark.

The floors are carpeted in red, worn and faded. They walk down a wide hallway. Hanging from the ceiling is a skeleton of a whale. The metal framing in the ceiling had been painted white at one point, but is now cracking and flaking away with rust. The walls are bare cement, with water damage stains and decaying pictures of sea creatures. The girls are whimpering, and Nathan lets silent tears fall from his cheeks. The room opens up, with large glass aquarium walls from floor to ceiling. Animals none of them had ever seen but in books are on display, some of them horribly mutated. She sympathizes with the creatures.

Violet hears something coming from deep within the aquarium. She stops, halting the children. She hears a strange breath, almost like a hiss, followed by a fast ticking. The hair on her body stands up. Violet crouches, covering the girls' mouths. She holds her finger to her lips. Their eyes become wide in fear. Violet moves low to the ground. She signals for them to follow, and they move as quickly and quietly as possible. They make their way across the wide room and find themselves stuck in a corner.

Violet sees movement through the glass aquariums. Maven. Two of them are coming from a hallway leading deeper into the building. As these otherworldly creatures communicate with each other, they hiss and click through their beaklike mouths. Another sneaks around the corner from which they came, blocking the only exit they know. The pale white creature stands eight feet tall. Its head is sharp, with almond-shaped eyes that are purely black. Black stripes on its chest outline its ribs.

They are surrounded. Without hesitation, a bone shard is shot at them. Everyone ducks but Nathan, scared stiff. Time seems to slow down for Violet as she sees the shard heading straight for his chest. He turns his back just as the shard begins to dig into his skin. He is knocked out of the way just as Violet snatches the shard from its path.

Her blood boils as she locks eyes with the maven. Without thinking, she runs towards the towering beast. She hears nothing but its screeching battle cry as she uses its stone-like limbs to climb. Straddling the creature, it slashes at her arm and waist with its one claw, slicing through her flesh. She feels nothing as her fist bashes into its chest once. The rock-like exoskeleton cracks. With one more swing of her fist and a cry of exertion, she punches straight through. Black tar-like blood splashes her face and spills out of its chest as she rips its heart out. The creature crumples to the ground, seizing, with her crouched over it.

She gets to her feet as the other two come at her full-speed. Shards barely miss her, only to stick into the cement wall. Retrieving one from the wall, she runs at the next maven sliding across the wet floor, and slides through its legs to climb up its bony back. She straddles its head before plunging the spike straight down through its skull. As the maven falls under her, the third runs her through from behind, right below the ribs. She screams with rage. As it yanks free of her, she falls over the maven corpse. Dodging its next jab, she spins, hitting the bloodied spike with her right fist. The spike breaks off and she catches it with her left hand. Just as the beast catches hold of her long braid, she twists, stabbing upwards under its rib cage with full force. As it tries to run her through with its last spike, she catches hold of it and pivots, pulling the arm down over her shoulder. The maven is caught off balance.

Within seconds she is on top of its chest, holding its arms down with her long slender legs. Raising the spear overhead, she brings it down with all of her strength, crushing its throat as it already starts to convulse. Raising it again, she stabs its chest again and again, until it is completely caved in.

The maven is limp. Panting, Violet turns to the children, her shoulders slouched. A thick coating of maven blood drips from her hands and face, her clothes completely drenched. All her adrenaline and energy is used up. The children don't move but stare wide-eyed. She holds her side, trying to hide the blood spilling out of her. She feels her limbs going numb. "It's okay," she groans with her hand out in front of her. She feels herself losing consciousness. Her body goes limp.

Unknowingly, they had more of an audience than expected. A man wearing parts of an armored suit catches her before she collapses. Violet loses consciousness, the person's faceplate being the last thing she sees.

CHAPTER

7

Stacy runs through the flooded hallway in which the two mavens came, splashing water in every direction. Her long, white, almost silver hair is braided intricately. A cropped shredded top reveals her thin waist with armor on one shoulder, knee pads, high top boots and black shredded pants. She stops in the doorway. "Holy tits!" she says, seeing the three dead maven. "How'd you do it?" she asks Killian, who is crouched on the floor.

"Watch your language. There are children." He nods in their direction. She spots Nathan first, shaking and crying. He doesn't take his eyes from the man holding his mother. The other two girls are cowering against one of the aquarium walls across from Nathan. "I didn't do this." His voice is distorted by his helmet. He leaves it on, allowing the helmet to check Violet's wounds. It scans her thoroughly. There are abrasions across her back and arms, and a puncture wound through her back and out her abdomen. Luckily, no organs were damaged, though she's losing blood.

"Well, it must've been the children," Stacy says sarcastically, stepping carefully around the dead maven to reach him. The man sets Violet down gently and rips a piece of his tattered cowl from

73

his neck. When she sees what he's holding, she arms her weapon. It emits a high-pitched frequency. "*She* did this?"

"Put the gun away, Stacy," Killian says as he wraps the strip tightly around Violet's torso. Wiping the muck from Violet's face with his sleeve, he reassures Nathan it will be alright.

"What's wrong with her face? Oh man, she's a lost cause. Look, her blood is turning black."

The man ignores her and continues cleaning her face. He rips another piece and wraps her sliced arm, tying it off. He lifts her up in his arms. "Get the kids," he says, walking past her.

"You can't be serious. Killian? Kill... Hello!! They'll slow us down. Are we not going to check out the crash site?" He continues down the hallway they came from. Stacy sighs, turning back to the kids as Nathan stomps past her, splashing the puddle of maven blood onto her legs. "What the hell?" she yells, jumping away. Lilly and Ember follow suit, splashing her again, mucking up Stacy's boots. "Ugh, I hate children." She spots the bag Violet dropped and grabs it before stomping after them.

When she catches up to them, Nathan is holding his mother's dangling hand while Lilly and Ember hold hands on Killian's other side. Stacy watches them disdainfully, arms folded. Outside the building sits two skyriders. At one time they may have been beautiful vehicles, one red and one blue. Now they are blackened and rusted, easier to hide. Killian sits Violet in front of him, resting her head back on his shoulder. Nathan climbs up behind him. Killian starts to protest, but stops himself when he feels the boy shaking. "Hold on tight, okay?" Killian says to the boy. Nathan holds onto Killian's jacket tightly.

"Killian, why are you bringing the dead girl?" Stacy says, catching up with him.

"She isn't dead."

"Okay, dying, same difference," she says, exasperated. "She's obviously on her deathbed. Look at her veins."

"Not dying either. Could you be a bit more sensitive? Again, there are children."

"Sensitive? Since when are you sensitive?" she says as if she has tasted something bitter. "No one can survive a maven attack. Why risk our lives for her? Could she be contagious?" While securing her helmet, Ember climbs up behind her, and Killian knocks his knuckles on his helmet. "What is that supposed to mean?" she says sarcastically. Lilly struggles to climb up, then struggles to pull Lilly up, but Stacy shows no interest in helping either of them.

"Don't let them fall off," Killian warns. Ember pulls Lilly up to sit between her and Stacy. He revs his engine and starts ahead. Nathan holds onto Killian tightly.

"You can't make up for your past by trying to save lost causes!" she yells, knowing he won't hear her.

They travel some distance through woods and a few ghost towns. They leave behind the ocean and head into the mountains. No longer can you smell the salt in the air, nor hear the seagulls fighting over food, replaced instead by the scent of pine trees and the sound of rushing rivers. Following an old road, the blue river runs alongside it. After some time they leave the paved road. Still following the river, it leads them to a large waterfall. Nathan gasps as they fly straight under the falls and are quickly soaked once more by the frigid water. The girls shriek in surprise as they hit the ice-cold falls. Beyond the falls is a large dark cave. An orange-colored tree growing from an island at the center of the cave glistens. Its yellow leaves and fruit glow brightly.

Killian turns left into a tunnel, dimly lit by the cargo bay. He parks and holds Nathan's arm as he climbs down. He lifts up unconscious Violet and leads them through a corridor as Stacy pulls in, Nathan staying on Killian's heel. He brings them into a sterile infirmary, containing a countertop with a sink, and many cabinets with glass doors, so that you can see the supplies inside. Laying Violet on the steel sickbed, Killian removes his helmet, armor and gloves. His right hand has Nathan on edge, having just had a bad experience with a cyborg. Killian's scruff looks messy on his slender face. His dark brown eyes match his hair. It just brushes his shoulders, sweat making it stick to his forehead as it falls in his eyes.

Killian washes up before handling Violet further, then pulls open a cabinet. Grabbing an injection gun, he fills the syringe with a serum. Nathan holds Violet's limp hand to comfort her, as much as comforting himself. "This will give her her strength back," Killian reassures him as he swabs her neck. The smell of rubbing alcohol permeates the air. Nathan nods, eyeing Killian's right arm as he pulls up a stool. He injects her and rubs the spot once more.

"Is this your mum?" he asks. Nathan nods. "You look like her. What's your name?" Nathan ignores his question, trying to nudge her awake. "Let her rest, she's been through a lot. Can you help me treat her wounds?" Killian asks, seeing the tears well up in his eyes. Nathan agrees and washes his hands. Killian hands Nathan gauze and ointments to set on the tray at Violet's bedside. He removes Violet's harness, placing the pistols at her feet, then removes her clothes, leaving on her undergarments and draping a warm blanket over her legs. He shows him how to clean the wound appropriately and disinfect it, before stitching up the hole in her abdomen. He continues to ask Nathan questions, but to no avail. Lilly and Ember come in and help with the cuts on her arm and back. He works mostly with his left hand, keeping his right arm on his lap, seeing that it's making them uncomfortable.

"Now I get why you kept the kids," Stacy says, coming in and leaning against the cabinet with a smirk on her face. "You wanted little slaves! Maybe one of them can cook."

"Jolene cooks… cooked. She tried to kill us," Ember responds, remembering what happened on the airship. Her eyes fill up with tears.

"Uh...okay?" Stacy looks away uncomfortably. There is an awkward silence.

"I'm sorry you had to go through that," Killian says. Directing his attention to Stacy, he says, "We couldn't leave them to fend for themselves. As for helping, it's good for them to learn this early on."

"Why are you wasting meds on the dead girl?"

"Not dead," he sighs. "Special blood type. Look for yourself," He hands her the helmet.

Stacy rolls her eyes. "It's so sweaty!" she complains, popping it onto her head after wiping it down and keeping one hand on her weapon. On the inside of the faceplate you can monitor the vitals of every living thing in view. Violet is alive and healing as they patch her up. The hole in her abdomen is already healing from the inside-out. Looking closer, she is able to see her blood type, and determine if there are any foreign entities or infections. "She doesn't have a blood type? What the blazes is she, a mutant?"

Violet gasps awake, ripping the gun from the holster at her feet, seeing only Stacy in the helmet. Stacy, a lot slower in her reaction, pulls her weapon. "Whoa! Weapons down!" Killian yells, shoving Stacy back and stepping in front of her, knocking her weapon out of the way. Violet is struck with a throbbing headache as she stares into his brown eyes. They are so dark they seem to stare into her soul. The pistol is still cocked and aimed between his eyes.

"Where is my son?" Violet demands, pressing her palm into her temple, hoping to relieve the pressure, it doesn't subside. Nathan, who had ducked below the bed, pops his head back into view. She sighs in relief as she wraps her free arm around him, hugging him tight. She grunts from the pain but ignores it, comforting herself in knowing he's alright.

Killian reaches for the gun still aimed at his skull. She twitches her hand, a warning. "Where are the girls?"

"Right here," Ember says from the other side of the table.

Violet turns, trading the gun to her left hand and hugging them just as tightly. "You two are okay?" They nod in unison. Killian moves to reach for the gun while she's distracted, but she hears the movement and reacts instantly. Swinging her legs off the table, she slides off carefully. Killian reaches out to catch her if she falls. Groaning, she holds onto her side.

"You should rest. You're going to tear your stitches."

"I don't have time." She turns to Nathan. "Where's Jack?"

"We left them behind. We're in the mountains," Ember answers, choking on her words as she tries not to cry.

They come around to Violet's side, and she rubs Ember's shoulder. "The mountains... Damnit." She scrunches her hair with one hand at her temple, trying to think of what to do.

"I knew we should have blindfolded them," Stacy complains.

Glancing down at herself, Violet realizes her clothes have been removed. Her white undergarments, still wet, are sticking to her body, revealing too much to these strangers. She tries to reach for the blanket crumpled on the floor, but it causes a sharp pain that shoots through her abdomen. Violet slams her fist on the table in anger, and an impression of her fist is left behind.

"Okay, freakishly strong veiny girl is creeping me out," Stacy shifts, readying her weapon once more.

"Go prep something in the mess hall, Nox," Killian replies. "I'm sure the kids are hungry."

"I'm not their mother, *honey.*" Killian glares at her as she pulls off the helmet, the silver hair that came loose from her braids sticking to her face.

"They'll also need some dry clothes, *dear.* Find Alan, he'll help."

"Fine. But if you start asking me to wash the laundry and give them baths, I'm going to throw them out to the wolves," Stacy grumbles as she leaves the room.

Violet glares her down, still aiming her pistol at her until she disappears behind the swinging doors. Adjusting her aim back to Killian, he watches her carefully, hands still in the air. "Why don't you kids follow Stacy," he says. "She'll introduce you to Alan, who's much nicer. He'll help you get cleaned up and fed." They can hear Stacy yelling for Alan over the loud music playing in the hall.

The children look at Violet. She can tell he wants to speak with her alone, but she doesn't know these people or if they even are people. Killian's right hand keeps drawing her attention. "The kids stay with me," she declares, pressing her knuckle against her temple, trying to relieve the pain. "I don't know you and I don't trust you."

Stacy's voice echoes again as she yells for Alan. "What do you want, you old nag?!" they hear a male voice yell back.

Killian snickers. He's still holding his hands in the air. "You're bleeding," he says, reaching out to her waist. She flinches back. "You ripped your stitches. Please, I only want to help you."

Nathan turns to face his mother, nodding. She can feel the blood dripping down her skin. She tries to lift herself back onto the table with one hand, but struggles. Killian carefully extends his hands to help her up. She allows it and groans in pain. He works carefully, showing her the ointments and tools he's using. He explains the procedure to Nathan, and shows him once more how to stitch properly. When he finishes with the hole through her abdomen, he has her roll onto her side to fix her back. De-cocking the pistol, she sets it down. Rolling over, Killian allows Nathan to do the stitches. He looks at his mother for approval, and she nods encouragingly. Allowing Nathan to do the stitches eases some of the tension in the room. Violet watches Killian as he instructs her son on how to close her up. The pressure in her head becomes unbearable, and she closes her eyes and holds the back of her skull, the pressure easing slightly with the darkness. Killian helps Nathan tie the stitches off and swab the area clean.

The door swings open and another man comes through the door. Violet pulls the weapon out once more. Killian jumps to his feet with his hands up again, stepping into her line of fire. "Whoa, I just came to see if you needed any help," Alan nervously laughs. He is in his late thirties, but is a very handsome man with short messy brown hair, a square jaw, cleft chin and medium build.

The room starts to spin. Just as she begins to faint, Killian snatches the pistol from her hand. Holstering it, he hands the weapons off to Alan, who asks with concern, "Is she gonna be alright?"

"She lost a lot of blood, but she'll be fine if she stops overexerting herself."

Alan smiles awkwardly at the staring faces. He introduces himself, shaking their hands politely with a big smile. He leaves the room with the weapons, assuring them they are in good hands, and that dinner would be ready soon.

Killian covers Violet's wounds in bandages and lays her onto her back so that she's resting comfortably. He goes back to the cabinet and pulls out another syringe. "This will help her stay calm and sleep, so that she doesn't rip her stitches again. Is that okay?" he asks Nathan. He looks back at his mother and agrees. Killian administers the drug. Taking a warm wet cloth, he helps Nathan wipe the blood from her face and arms. When they finish cleaning her up, they cover her with a warm blanket. When dinner is ready, Killian is finally able to convince the children to leave for a bit, so to eat in the mess hall with Alan.

When Violet comes to, she flinches. She sits up quickly, which makes her head swim. "It's okay, the kids are eating dinner," Killian assures her.

"Where are my pistols?" Violet growls.

"You seemed a little hostile with them around, so I had Alan put them away," he says seriously as he holds his hands up in the air, as if she was still holding them. "Do you remember what happened?"

"We crashed into the ocean..." Violet breathes deeply as she tries to calm her emotions. "I'm pretty sure I killed some things..."

"Yup, I'd say you killed all of the things," he laughed, combing his hair back with his fingers, where it immediately fell back into his eyes. "I heard your scream and came to help, but... you're pretty intense," he says, smiling.

"I have anger issues," Violet says, shading her eyes from the light and his gaze.

Killian looks at the dent in the table. "Remind me not to get on your bad side." Violet nods in agreement. "Are you alright?" he asks, showing concern.

"Major headache." She rubs at her eyes.

He goes back to the cabinet and returns to her side. "Let me take a look."

She jumps at how close his voice is. "You're in my bubble."

"Let. Me. Take. A. Look," he says sternly. Squeezing her eyes shut, Killian holds her chin up between his thumb and finger. The heat from his fingers burn her chilled skin. "Open your eyes," he commands. His right arm begins wheezing and ticking as he holds up a small flashlight. Reluctantly she opens them. Shining a light in her eyes, her pupils react accordingly. "I didn't see any swelling when I scanned you. Though there seemed to be some scarring in your cerebral cortex. Besides that, everything seems to be okay."

He turns back to the cabinet and returns with two pills in hand. She looks at his right hand, feeling uneasy about being in the same vicinity as another cyborg. She takes them into her hand and glares up at him. "Painkillers," he says, grabbing a cup and filling it with water. He holds out the cup as she swallows them dry, watching her with a light smile on his face.

"I know I look sick. It's not contagious," Violet says, covering her eyes again. Killian nods, silently watching her. "My name is Violet O'Daire." She pauses for his response, but he just smiles. "Nathan is my son. The girls belong to my friend. Ember is the oldest, Lilly is the one with curls." She waits again for him to respond. "Can I get your name? Or should I just call you Sir Stares-a-lot?" She peeks at him again with one eye.

He drops his head, smiling. "Sorry. Killian Grey," he says with a smirk.

"Thank you for helping us, Killian," she says softly. Killian looks back at her, hearing her throat tighten as she speaks. Taking a deep breath, she fights the tears back, pushing thoughts of Jack to the back of her mind.

"Whomever it is you're looking for, I'm happy to help."

Violet frowns at him, unsure of his intentions. "Thank you, but I'd like to leave now, please."

"I don't think that would be wise. You're still in rough condition. You need to rest."

"I don't have time for that."

"If you want to keep those kids safe, then yes, you do have time," Killian says with a frown.

"I need to find the rest of the people in my group," Violet responds with a growl. "I need to make sure they're safe."

"More kids?" The concern on Killian's face is clear.

"No."

"Then they know how to take care of themselves. Rest tonight. We can find them tomorrow." Killian tucks a stray hair behind her ear. His touch starts a fire in her chest.

She looks up and the throbbing in her head pounds harder. "If we're going to stay here, I will ask that you respect the bubble," Violet says, tracing an invisible circle around her. Killian laughs.

Stacy clears her throat in the doorway. She has changed her clothes; no more armor, instead just a shredded tunic, shorts with thigh high socks, and boots. "If you're done flirting, food's getting cold," she says with malice. Killian smirks, shaking his head, while Violet swings her legs off the bed. Stacy leans out of the way for Killian to pass, then falls back into place as Violet carefully climbs off the table. She waits for Killian to turn the corner before speaking. "I don't care how strong you are, freak. I won't hesitate to destroy you and yours if you threaten what we have here. I like the way things are. This is my home. Don't get comfortable." She stands in front of Violet and shoves a pile of clothing at her before walking out.

"How could I?" Violet mumbles to herself. She removes the sticky undergarments, throwing them into the sink. Stacy has given her sweatpants two sizes too large, and a very chunky sweater. The thick clothing is welcome, as the air is dank.

She follows the corridor down. At the end is the mess hall. It's a very large room with five walls and four long tables in the center, dark hallways heading in every direction. One wall has a long window and a door opening to the kitchen. The two walls opposite have countertops for trays and trash cans, with a machine that is playing music. It is nothing like the old gramophone Jack and Clara have.

Across the room, the far wall is set up as a wet bar. There are shelves with many different types of liquor, and several stools. Against the fifth wall is a long couch and two easy chairs, with a smaller table at the center. The children are already eating, but Nathan scoots down so that Violet will sit between him and Lilly. They are dressed in baggy t-shirts, no pants or socks. Killian is on the opposite side of the table, watching them poke at their food as if it was his evening entertainment. He has changed into a long-sleeved tattered black sweater with extra fabric at the neck that droops. His hair is pulled back and tied off at the back of his head, with a few loose strands falling free. Stacy sits beside him and fills her plate with salad and chicken with a cheese sauce. Alan comes in with a bowl of biscuits, smiling brightly. He sits down a seat away from Stacy with excitement and looks around the table. "Oh... biscuit?" he asks as he holds out the bowl.

Violet takes her place between the children. Alan stands up, holding his hand out to her. "It's very nice to meet you, Violet. It's a pleasure to see new faces."

"Thank you," Violet says shyly, taking his hand.

Each of them takes one biscuit and picks at them. "Let me show you how to make these amazing," Alan announces. He takes a biscuit and cuts it in half. He butters each side and grabs a jar from the middle of the table. Pulling the stick out, glistening amber honey drips off. The children's noses scrunch. They've never seen honey, so they think it's brown snot or something equally as disgusting. He spreads a thick layer of honey over the biscuit, then looks at their horrified faces. "What? What's wrong? This is how you eat a biscuit!"

Violet can't help but smile. "It's honey," she tells the children. "It's sweet, like candy."

"Here, try one," Alan says, holding the two halves out to Lilly and Ember. They hesitate at first; but once they bite into it, their eyes light up. Lilly holds out her plain biscuit to Alan.

"Can you fix mine too, please?" she asks sweetly.

"It would be an honor, m'lady," Alan replies with a flourish of his hand, smiling brightly while taking the biscuit. Ember and Nathan hand theirs off to him as well. Killian joins in helping prepare them. Violet portions her plate and begins eating, feeling comfort from Alan's warm personality.

The children are still picking at their food after the biscuits are devoured. "Thank you for the meal," Violet says politely. Stacy nods, stuffing another bite into her mouth. "When the children are finished, we'll gather our things and go."

"But you just got here!" Alan says with a pitiful look on his face.

"We already talked about this, Vi," Killian says, picking up the empty plates. Violet stares at him wide-eyed. No one calls her Vi, yet it seems natural coming from him. The others look at him curiously.

"Violet," she corrects him. "I think you should speak with the rest of your family before you invite new people to stay." Stacy looks around indifferently.

"It's not necessary. I built this place, therefore I choose who stays and who goes," Killian says curtly, dropping the dishes off in the kitchen.

"Are you holding us hostage?" Violet raises her eyebrows and folds her arms.

Alan leans back in his chair with his arms behind his head as he looks back and forth between Violet and Killian, a large smile crossing his face. "Yeah, Killian, are they hostages?" he teases. Killian glares at him. Alan sits straight again folding his hands in front of him as he bites his lips to hide the smile.

"If I have to hold you hostage to allow you to heal, then yes," Killian says, returning to the table to stand behind Alan. Stacy watches Violet for her reaction, with one arm resting on the back of her chair.

"We don't want to be a burden." Violet smiles sarcastically at Stacy.

"Pffft!" Alan accidentally spits out food and waves his hand. "You're no burden."

"I'm not burdened. Are you?" Killian says, looking over at Stacy. She shakes her head while taking a drink of water, staring Violet down. Killian smiles brilliantly and slaps his hands down onto Alan's shoulders in triumph.

"Ow!" Alan cries as he rubs at his right shoulder. Killian quietly apologizes, holding his hands behind his back. Stacy smiles at Violet with ice cold eyes.

"I just don't think—"

"Mama, I'm tired." Nathan tugs on her sleeve. Violet's words catch in her throat. It's the first time he has spoken to her. She smiles at him. Brushing her fingers through his hair, she bends down to kiss him on the forehead.

"The boy speaks!" Killian says with a surprised smile.

"Let the kids rest!" The room echoes. Alan winks. Nathan tries to hide his grin.

Violet looks back at Stacy as she glowers back, shrugging. "I guess we can stay one night, if there's room."

Alan throws his hands up, waving them at the empty tables in the wide-open room. "Eh..." he shrugs. "Oh! Let's do a tour!"

"He doesn't get out much," Killian says, smiling down at him.

Alan jumps to his feet and comes around the table. He holds his elbow out to Violet. "M'lady." Violet takes his arm and the children stand up with her.

"He's too scared to leave," Stacy grumbles.

"Such a gentleman." Violet chuckles, ignoring Stacy's comment. Stacy snorts, rolling her eyes. Killian watches them leave the table, somewhat envious of Alan. He takes the opportunity to speak privately with Stacy about her behavior, glaring down at her.

Alan insists on starting from where they came in. He leads them back to the port which holds all their cargo and vehicles. He explains what the crates are for and which vehicle is his, petting it like it's a precious treasure. Coming back, the first door on the right is the laundry facilities, the second the sick bay. He opens the first door on the left to reveal a massive garden. Every fruit and vegetable they could mention has its own place. Alan doesn't stop talking. He points out each piece of produce as if they had never seen real food before. They're impressed that the indoor garden is so successful underground. Even fruit trees are growing happily.

Crossing through the garden, they exit on the other side. The hallway is pitch black until he starts walking, then motion sensors automatically turn the lights on in each room. The only lights that have a switch are the sleeping quarters and mess hall. He points out the bathroom at the end of the hall, and the girls quickly run to it. Alan waits patiently before continuing. When they return, his handsome smile makes them blush.

The next room is recreational. A table with black felt and different colored balls stands at the center. A large leather couch backs the wall. The bar from the mess hall extends through into this room. Moving through to the next hallway, they find a room with shelves packed with books. A few more couches and side tables with lamps are in the center. The walls are smothered with artwork she has seen from books. Through to the next hallway are the sleeping quarters, two bedrooms with king-sized beds, each with their own personal toilet. The first one hardly looks lived in, except for the desk covered in mechanical parts, wires and papers. In the second room, the sheets are falling off the bed and clothing is thrown about. Across the hall are yet more sleeping arrangements. This room is more like a roundabout hallway, with bunks lining the outside walls. In the center of the room are two large restrooms, the first with several stalls and sinks, the second just an open tiled room with a drain at the center, with two shower heads on three walls. No privacy whatsoever. The children pull blankets off the beds and wrap themselves up. Alan helps Lilly, who is struggling.

Alan leads them back to the mess hall. "So," he says, "no matter which hallway you're in, everything leads to the mess hall. You can't get lost." Stacy bangs around in the kitchen, cleaning up her own dishes. Killian watches them as they finish the tour. Alan stands proud with his hands on his hips and a large grin.

Lilly trips on her blanket as she reaches up to Violet. "Will you hold me?" She has dark circles under her eyes, as tears start to fall down her cheeks.

"Are you tired?" Violet asks. She tries to pick her up, but feels a sharp pain shoot through her. Killian comes to help as Alan picks Lilly up, wrapping her up in the blanket. They all agree to being tired. Killian takes Nathan's hand, leading them back to the sleeping quarters, while Ember takes Violet's hand. Lilly and Ember are tucked into one bunk and Violet kisses them. "Don't be afraid," she says. "I'll be sleeping in that bunk right over there."

"I want to sleep with you," Lilly says with tears in her eyes.

"Me too," Ember says with a shaking voice.

Violet holds them tightly, and Killian picks Nathan up. "Come on, you can all sleep in my room together."

Nathan raps his knuckles on Killian's right arm, in which he is being held. "Mama, he is a robot? Is he like Jolene?"

"That's something I've been wondering myself."

"I lost my arm in a fight. It's just a mechanical prosthetic," he says, flexing his artificial fingers. Nathan wraps his arm around Killian's shoulder and pats his back gently, as if he were comforting him for his loss. He smiles, patting his back in return. Violet's heart swells with the interaction between the two.

Alan helps Violet gather the girls and follow Killian into the first bedroom across the hall. Killian sets Nathan down while he replaces the sheets with fresh ones. The bed is large enough for all of them to sleep comfortably. Violet looks over the room. A small bladed knife catches her eye. Swiftly she takes the blade and hides it behind her inconspicuously. Killian tucks all three of the children in with a smile. Alan watches in awe and curiosity.

"Good night... sleep tight... don't let the bed... bugs..." Alan was cut off by Killian's glare. "Just kidding. There aren't any bugs," he says, laughing nervously, walking back to the door. Killian rubs the bridge of his nose as he follows him out.

"I'll be right back," Violet tells the children, moving quickly to the doorway. "Killian, wait." Killian and Alan stop and turn back. She awkwardly avoids their eyes. "Jolene. We thought she was a human. The only thing that seemed off about her was her personality. She turned out to be a cyborg. It could change its height, its features, its hair color and length. It tried to kill us. She's the reason our ship crashed. I'm telling you this so you'll understand why I need to see it. Now," she says awkwardly.

Killian nods, pulling his sweater off over his head. For a second, Violet is distracted by his bare chest, but it's his arm that draws her attention. She gently inspects the scarred tissue on his shoulder where the arm is attached with metal plates. He holds out his mechanical hand. She takes it to inspect the construction of it. The arm looks as if it was crafted from scrap parts. "I have to ask one more thing from you," she says.

"What's that?" he asks, smiling gently.

"To forgive me." Before Killian can blink, she swipes the short blade across his chest, just below the collarbone. Bright red blood spills out of the laceration as he flinches back in shock. "I'm sorry! When I shot at her, she didn't bleed." She avoids his eyes as she presses her hand against the wound to stop the bleeding.

"What the hell?!" Alan says. "Can't trust us until we bleed? That's messed up."

"It's fine," Killian says as he winces.

"You're asking me to stay in an underground shelter in which we have no escape, with three strangers, one of whom is making us all uncomfortable and another who obviously doesn't want us here. Please understand. I'm sorry," Violet says seriously.

"It's okay." Though eye contact seems to make her head pound, she struggles to look Killian in the eye. Something about him is alluring.

Trying to distract herself from him and the pounding in her skull, she looks to Alan. "This place looks like it was built to hold a lot of people. Why is it just the three of you?"

"This place was built a long time ago. My father and I built it together in case of an emergency. It was meant for a couple of families. I was separated from them years ago."

"I'm sorry."

Killian shakes his head and smiles. "If you need anything, we'll be across the hall."

"Thank you," Violet says. Killian slides the door closed behind him. Stacy could be heard outside the door. "You can sleep with me," she says playfully. Killian laughs out loud. Then she hears Alan say, "When was the last time you changed your sheets?"

"Screw you, Alan." She slams her door and it becomes quiet.

* * *

Violet is restless as she watches the rise and fall of the children's chests. After an hour of waiting to drift off, she gives up. After making sure their arms have dropped limp, she carefully slips out from between them. She pulls the door open slowly and looks both ways to make sure the hallway is clear. Tiptoeing down the hall, she sees Killian cleaning up after her and the kids through the kitchen window. Moving silently, she slips past and enters the infirmary. She pulls the sopping wet clothes from the sink and quietly moves into the laundry room. There are several large machines with many buttons and settings. She sees a pile of clothing in the corner, the kids' clothing. All their bags are piled in the corner. Not understanding the large machines, she uses the large tub sink to wash all the clothes by hand. When she finishes, she lays them out to dry on the side of the tub and any other surface she can find. She pulls her bag out of the pile. Opening it up, she searches through it to find the leather-bound book. Some of the pages are damp from the dive they took. She pulls it out and holds it to her chest. Coming back, she peeks around the corner. Killian is no longer in the kitchen. She quietly sneaks back into the bedroom. Wrapping a blanket around her, she sits on the floor and flips through the pages, letting them air out.

Later in the night, Killian wakes up to a strange sound. It echoes, so he knows it's coming from the mess hall. Jumping out of his bunk, he pulls his weapon from the drawer in the nightstand. Alan is asleep in the bunk next to him, snoring lightly. Slowly he moves along the walls. Feeling the cold cement along his bare back gives him a chill, and makes him thankful he's still wearing pants. The mess hall is dark except for a couple of floor lights marking each hallway. Turning the corner, he aims in the direction of the sound. Violet is hugging her knees on the couch, crying softly and sniffling. He sighs and puts the safety on before setting the gun down on the table next to the sound system. He sinks down next to her. His hair drapes around his face as he watches her. She doesn't look up to see who it is. "I'm sorry for waking you," she chokes.

"Don't worry about me," Killian says softly.

Violet takes a deep breath to calm herself as the pressure in her head builds. "I think they're dead."

"Who?" he asks, patting her back.

"Jack, Clara and Charlie. They were still on the ship when it exploded." Her voice breaks as she speaks of them. Killian wraps his arm around her shoulder, pulling her in. She sobs into her hands against his chest.

"Tomorrow we'll go back," he says quietly as he rests his chin atop her head. "Try to think positively. If they're anything like you, they'll be just fine."

"They aren't like me. I'm... something else."

Killian pats her shoulder. "I mean your determination. Everything will be alright," he reassures her. She nods but can't stop crying. Killian rubs her back. Violet's head swims, as the drugs are in full swing. The warmth of his body is soothing, and feeling his hand follow the curve of her back and waist stirs feelings she hasn't felt for years. He feels her body tense.

Her breath catches as she tries to speak. "Killian?"

"If you say anything about your bubble, I'm going to leave you here alone in the dark on this cold leather couch." Violet holds her breath, weighing her options. "You're the one who woke *me* up, after all. I'm not going to make a move on you."

After a moment she relaxes. "Sorry," she sighs, wiping the tears from her cheeks onto her sleeves. In the darkness, her head doesn't hurt nearly as much as it did. He pulls the tie out of her braid and plays with her wavy hair as her breathing steadies. It brings a calmness to both of them. It doesn't take long before Violet falls asleep. Killian follows, letting his head rest on the back of the couch.

* * *

It's morning and Stacy is the first one up. She walks into the mess hall, noticing movement from the corner. She focuses her eyes to find Killian asleep on the couch, with Violet draped over his bare chest. As the lights brighten, Killian grumbles, hiding his eyes from the bright light with his arm. Violet isn't fazed, as her hair covers her face. Stacy slams a helmet onto the dining table, making both of them jump. Feeling warm skin beneath her, Violet sits up in a daze, trying to focus her eyes. Slowly the events of the previous night become clearer. Looking down at Killian, she groans as the headache comes back in full force. She tries to stand, losing her balance for a second. The wound in her side sends her a warning not to move so abruptly. Killian moves to hold her elbow, keeping her steady. Violet holds out a hand, letting him know she's alright. She leaves them to check on the clothes in the laundry room. Killian sighs, rubbing the sleep out of his eyes. "That was rude," he says to Stacy.

"Getting cozy with the freak?"

"Don't get jealous," he says in frustration.

"Don't give me a reason to," she says, walking towards him. She rests her hands on his shoulders and pushes him back onto the couch, her silver hair spilling over her shoulder.

He holds her waist away from him. "We've talked about this, Stacy. I can't do it."

"As far as I can tell, the world has ended. Why are you still so morally conflicted? It's stupid." She twists her hips, sitting on his lap. "For all you know, your wife is dead," she whispers in his ear.

Violet comes back down the hall and awkwardly pretends she can't see their quarrel. Quickening her pace, she walks down the next hall with the pile of clothes in hand.

Killian shoves her off. "She *isn't* dead," he growls. "Know your place." Getting to his feet, he leaves her on the floor. Though she's been rejected by him already, this one stings a bit deeper. Even though she has a bruised tailbone and an equally bruised ego, she can't help but admire his body as he walks away. As he stretches, you can see each muscle contract in his back. When he turns the corner, she stands up and adjusts her sweater, then goes back to the table to clean off her helmet and shine her boots.

Violet leans against the door, out of breath. Her heart is racing. The children start to stir, so she comes away from the door and takes deep breaths to calm herself, greeting them as they wake with fresh clothes. After she gets them dressed, she leads them to the dining table and searches the kitchen for something to eat. There's a large refrigerator full of different foods. She picks a few eggs and a loaf of bread, and starts breakfast.

Killian, all dressed in gear, comes into the kitchen silently and leans against the counter, crossing his arms and legs. He watches her reach for a pan that is too high. She stands on her tip-toes and, with a long painful stretch of her body, grabs it off the hook. "What are you making?" he suddenly asks.

Violet jumps, dropping the pan on the floor. It clatters as the heavy pan meets the cement. Killian tries to hide his smile, but feels somewhat guilty when she hisses in pain. "Eggs in a basket?" she says awkwardly, picking up the pan, trying to avoid more pain.

"Make two for me, please!" Alan yells through the window. His grin puts a smile on her face.

"Me too," Killian says.

"And your girlfriend?"

"Doesn't eat breakfast!" Alan yells from across the room.

"It's not like that," He grumbles, taking his leave when she doesn't respond.

Violet finishes and cleans up after herself before serving them. Everyone sits down. She finds herself feeling comfortable for the first time since the crash. Alan jokes with the kids between each bite. When Stacy comes in, she rolls her eyes. Violet notices she is starting to wear less and less clothing. Wearing a sheer grey tank-top, you can see her bra peeking through, and her pants contain holes in strategic locations. "I can patch those pants for you if you'd like," Violet offers.

"They're supposed to look this way."

"Oh... nice." Violet tries to recover from her comment. Alan snorts with laughter but tries to hide it with a cough.

"Why is your hair grey?" Lilly asks. "Are you old?" Killian tries not to laugh, but his shaking shoulders give him away. Alan howls with laughter.

"I'm not old. *Alan's* old," she says, shooting daggers at anyone who makes eye contact.

"She's super old," Alan says, still laughing. "That's why she's so grumpy all the time." Stacy stares Alan down as she cleans her gun.

"Jack is old too," Lilly says. "He isn't grumpy, unless Charlie's around." Killian looks up from his empty plate.

"Not all old people are the same," Violet says with a wink. She takes the empty plates to the kitchen and starts washing.

Killian leans in next to Lilly and whispers, "Why doesn't Jack like Charlie?"

Alan leans in as well. "And who *is* Charlie?"

Lilly, thinking it's a game, whispers back. "Charlie is Nathan's dad. Jack doesn't like it when Charlie comes to take Nathan home."

"Why not?" Killian asks. Lilly shrugs. "Is he a bad dad?" She shrugs again.

"He yells a lot," Ember speaks up. Killian nods and scratches the scruff on his jaw.

"Charlie sounds like a dick," Alan whispers to Killian. Killian grins and Alan leans in again. "And who's Jack?"

"He's my grandpa," Lilly says.

"Not really," Ember interjects solemnly. "He's *like* our grandpa. He's everyone's grandpa. He gave us a home."

"Jack's an inventor," Lilly says.

"Jack's a pilot," Nathan adds.

"Jack sounds cool," Alan says.

Nathan nods in agreement. "He makes amazing machines. He saved my mom."

"Well then, he should come live with us," Killian says quietly so Stacy can't hear.

"What about us?" Nathan asks.

"Well, all of you have to stay if Jack stays, right?" Alan winks at Killian.

"Right. How about I take Stacy and go find him and bring him back?" Killian asks.

"Okay, but you have to bring back Clara too," Ember chimes in.

"What about Charlie?" Nathan asks, looking down at his hands.

"Do you want him to stay with us?" Killian says in a serious tone. Nathan thinks for a moment before shaking his head in shame. "Then don't worry about him." Alan looks at Killian curiously.

Violet finishes cleaning the dishes. As she's putting the dishes away, something catches her eye. She spots her holster and pistols hidden in a large pot in one of the cabinets. She straps them on. When she comes back, she looks at the children. They stare at her like she's going to abandon them. Violet avoids their eyes.

"Where do you think you're going?" Alan laughs.

"You said we're going to the crash site today," Violet says.

Killian glares at Alan, seeing the pistols strapped to her hips. Alan hangs his head, knowing he failed to hide them well enough. "I don't think that'd be wise," Killian says. "Why don't you stay behind while Stacy and I check out the crash site."

"You don't even know who you're looking for. I have to go with you," Violet says in frustration. Her fists clench.

Killian stands up and walks towards her slowly. "If you get separated from us, you won't know how to get back. I'm not risking that. Besides, the kids need you here." Violet is unable to look away from the darkness in his eyes as he closes the distance between them. "You stay here. We know how to track people." Violet hears the snap on her holsters as Killian tries to disarm her. The pounding in her head was distracting her from how close he had come. Before he can flinch, she has one pistol aimed at his chin and the other at Stacy.

"Killian?" Stacy says through clenched teeth. Killian slowly raises his hands.

"Oh shi…iiiin splints," Alan says, trying to correct himself in front of the kids. He's never seen anyone move as quickly as she just did, except for mavens.

"Batting your pretty eyes may work on racy Stacy over there," Violet says tensely, "but I'm not so easily manipulated."

"Watch your mouth, mutant," Stacy hisses. Alan snickers.

"The children and I will join you. We will not be held captive here." Violet quickly glances around the room. The children are watching calmly. Alan is covering his mouth, trying not to make a sound. "I may have seemed weak last night, but I assure you if you move one more inch towards your gun, I won't hesitate to blow your pretty little brains out," Violet says, looking away from Killian. Stacy freezes when her eyes are on her. "I heard you talking to the kids. Why are you trying to convince them to stay here? Promising to bring back people you might not be able to find?"

"Whoa, easy, sweetheart," Alan says. "No one wants to hurt you or the kids." Killian holds a finger out to Alan, silencing him.

"I don't know that. I don't know any of you. I don't trust *her*, most of all." She nods in Stacy's direction. "We appreciate the hospitality, but I need to find my family. You're hiding something. I can tell by the way you look at me. The way you touch me, as if we're all good friends." She glances at Killian. "You're nice and all, Alan, but I can't trust any of you. You could be murderers, rapists, cannibals." Violet catches Stacy's nervous glance at Killian and presses the other pistol against Killian's skin without looking away from Stacy.

"Cannibals? Really?" Alan grasps the hair at the top of his head, unsure of what to do.

"Vi," Killian says, so low only she can hear. Hearing that name turns her head. The throbbing turns to a sharp pain in her skull.

"Violet," she says through clenched teeth.

"You know deep down we have no ill-will towards you or the kids."

Violet steps back, stretching her arm out so that there's distance between her and Killian. Her head pulses and her eyes glaze over. "No, I don't. I couldn't trust my father, I couldn't trust Charlie, and I can't trust you."

"I could have left you and the kids at the crash site. I brought you here to help you." Killian steps closer to her. The pistols shake in her hands. "What are you really scared of?"

"Pain," she chokes as tears fill her eyes. Everyone else around them seems to fall away. She only sees Killian. Everything around him fades into darkness, matching his eyes.

"I promise, if they're alive, I will find them and bring them back." Killian reaches his left hand out slowly. As he cups her cheek, his fingers slide to her neck.

"It hurts," Violet chokes out. Killian tenses. The pain becomes so severe that her eyes roll in the back of her head. Killian catches her as she goes limp. Alan jumps to his feet, as well as the children.

"Mama?" Nathan's voice cracks.

"Not easily manipulated, my ass!" Stacy pulls her weapon, aiming at the unconscious Violet. "What'd you do to her, anyway?"

"I didn't do anything," he says with worry in his voice. "She said she was in pain." Lifting her up into his arms, he transports her to the couch. "Alan, get the med kit." Alan was on his way before Killian could finish the sentence.

"Please tell me we're kicking them out! You know she was ready to kill me, right?"

"Violet wasn't going to kill you; she was just scared. She doesn't understand what's happening. Put the gun away. You don't know what she's been through."

"Neither do you! Why are you taking her side, Killian?"

Killian pulls one of the pistols out of Violet's hands, pointing it at Stacy. "Stop questioning me. If you don't like how I run things, then *you* can leave." For a moment everyone is on edge. Finally, Stacy puts down her weapon. Killian removes Violet's holster and puts it behind the bar.

"I'm telling you, this is going to blow up in our face," Stacy complains.

"Wait for me in the cargo bay," Killian says as Alan comes back with the kit. "I think she just fainted from the pain. I'll check in when we get to the site." Killian synchronizes Alan's watch with his. "Be careful. She dented the metal table in the infirmary with her fist. If she puts up a fight, play dead." He pats him on the back.

Alan stares after Killian as he walks out of the room. Shaking off the chill that has rolled down his spine, he shines a light into her eyes. Her pupils shrink. "She'll be alright," Alan says to the children. "Looks like she just fainted." Turning, he realizes he's been left with three frightened small people to take care of. "Ooookay... I can do this." He claps his hands and rubs them together.

CHAPTER

8

Violet wakes up to Alan blasting music, twisting his body in such a way that just looks silly. The children sit in a half-circle watching him flail about, laughing. Violet sits up, holding her head. It still aches, but only mildly now. Her holster has been removed and weapons hidden away once more. Alan's movements are so ridiculous that Violet, even though as angry as can be, can't help but laugh too. When he hears Violet's laughter he stops, combing his fingers through his hair nonchalantly. He is embarrassed but pretends not to be, laughing at himself. The children wait for him to continue. Instead he grabs Ember's hands, pulling her to her feet for the next song. They start dancing together. Nathan and Lilly start dancing, twisting their hips like Alan.

Killian's voice comes over the speaker next to the sound system. "*We arrived at the aquarium. Over and out.*" Violet rushes over to respond. Alan beats her there and stands in front, guarding it. "Okay," he says, "I know you're really badass and strong, so this is me asking you politely. Please don't hurt me? I'm just doing what I'm told. The comms are for incoming only, unless there's an emergency," He closes his eyes and winces, ready for abuse. When she doesn't react, he opens one eye. She's watching him with arms folded. Alan realizes she isn't going to react harshly and stands straight again.

"I'm sorry," Violet says, grabbing a seat at the bar. "I wasn't going to hurt anyone." She rubs her temples. "I just don't trust him. There's something off about him."

"He's an alright guy," Alan shrugs. "If he wanted to hurt you, though, he would have tried already." He bites his lip, hoping it doesn't come off wrong. "Also, you're terrifying. I don't think he'd even try." Alan winks. "So, what was with the fainting episode?"

"I don't know. Ever since arriving here, I've had this massive headache. It spiked the moment he touched my cheek. My mind went blank, overwhelmed by a loud buzzing." The pain was unbearable. Though there was more to it, it wasn't really something she could explain.

"That sucks," Alan says when he can't find anything better to say.

"Indeed." Violet half smiles. "Just because you say he's a nice guy, though, doesn't mean I can trust him that easily."

"Well, he'd probably understand your situation better than anyone. A few years back he was drafted. Forced to leave his wife behind to fight a war for a nation that no longer exists. The aircraft was attacked close to Fallen City. His ship went down. He was smart enough to jump before it exploded. Making his way home, he met Stacy. She's cool and all, just very bitter and selfish. It took him a year or two to find his way back home. Found me on the way. Supposedly his wife thought he was never going to return, and tried to off herself. Vegetable status. While he was trying to see her, they found him and tried to kill him for abandoning his duty. Lost his entire arm in the fight. That's when I saved his life, you know. Stopped the bleeding, helped him attach his prosthetic. Works better than new... because I am awesome. Anyway, I guess his dad is a crazy genius with lots of secrets. He showed us this place and we've been here ever since. He can relate to you losing your husband and stuff."

"I don't have a husband." Violet tilts her head curiously.

"Oh, I thought Charlie, being Nathan's dad..."

"He's not Nathan's father, either." Violet frowns, tightening the folds in her arms. Nathan looks their way, matching her frown in confusion.

"Oh, the kids said he was." Alan straightens up.

"They're mistaken." Violet thinks quietly for a moment. "Charlie... is a worthless human being. Though I don't wish him dead, he means nothing to us." Alan stands there awkwardly. "So, what's Stacy's story?"

"I think her dad was rich. Hence the attitude problem. Stacy's not really one to share, though." Alan rubs his chin curiously.

"Well, what about you? Where's your family?"

"Killian and Stacy are my family. Most of my blood family died of disease. Some were lost to mavens. It was a long time ago, though." He shrugs. "I'd been in hiding for several years in an abandoned hospital. Not much to do there but read."

"I'm sorry about your family."

"Me too." He smiles, quick to change the subject. "You want to play a game to pass the time?"

"Um... sure?"

The children follow them into the recreational room. Alan introduces her to the game pool. Not knowing anything about it, he shows her how to play. He stands behind her, positioning her arms in an intimate way. The kids giggle when she accidentally hits him in the gut with the pool stick. There are several board games the kids pull out. Alan gets excited, because Killian and Stacy refuse to ever play with him. He sets up one of the board games and starts teaching them the rules.

* * *

Killian lets Stacy lead. She drives ahead of him at an alarming speed. He follows close behind. After leaving the mountains behind them, her temper has finally cooled off. Slowing her speed, she aligns her skyrider with Killian's, glancing over at him focused on the path. She pulls in closer to him, almost to the point of touching. He glances over and nods. Knowing she's forgiven, she feels relieved. Soon they will be back in the ghost town in which they found Violet.

Before long, the aquarium is in sight. The smoke behind it has dissipated. Killian turns on his com, updating Alan on their location. They leave their vehicles hidden in the brush. Slowly and cautiously they make their way through the building, weapons armed. Making it out through the revolving doors, they see the wreckage protruding from the ocean. Paying close attention to the ground as they come closer to the water, they find markings of something being dragged.

As they silently follow the markings, they find a portion of a bionic being in the sand. Carefully closing the distance, they make sure the being is not alive before touching it. It's missing its lower half. Pieces of purple hair and fleshy pieces stick to the metal. The cables and wires hang from its frame, ripped and scorched.

"This must be Jolene," Killian says, studying the body.

"Okay..." Stacy plays uninterested. Beyond the biotic corpse they see tracks leading into the trees. They follow the broken branches, one of them with dried blood. The tracks lead them to a path. They return for the skyriders before moving on.

"I used to think we had a lot in common," Stacy says, breaking the silence. Killian rolls his eyes. "Something's changed. I don't understand why you care about these people. I understand that you can relate to her because she lost her family but... you've never been the comforting type." Killian sighs. "If she didn't have children, would you be acting the same?"

Killian chooses his answer carefully. "There are plenty of reasons. When I saw her killing the maven, I watched through the practitioner's helmet. I saw her move with terrifying speed. I saw her crush through the maven easily. She's a mutant, but when the blood dripped from her arm into the maven, it was like acid to them. Her blood could wipe them out. She's a weapon. We need to keep her on our side for now."

"Thank the stars! I thought you were going soft," Stacy laughs. "Maybe when we get back we can drain her dry. We don't need her, just her blood, right?" Killian doesn't show any emotion or speak any further. Putting their helmets back on, they start up the skyriders and start back to the path. Killian sets the practitioner's helmet to highlight any blood tracks. The helmet works better than he could have imagined. Following the blood trail, they are able to find fresh tracks.

They come deeper into town, now traveling on paved roads. The streets are lined with different shops. The trail ends at a grocery store. Pulling around to the back, they check the perimeter. Stacy leaves her helmet behind before they enter through the back. Walking into the store with weapons in hand, they listen for any sign of activity, but it is absolutely silent. They separate, checking each aisle. They've been picked clean, aside from the pet food.

Just as Stacy passes the pharmacy counter, she hears the click of a gun being cocked. She freezes and slowly turns her head. Charlie is crouched behind the counter, ready to shoot. The right side of his face is scraped up, and his copper-toned hair is disheveled. He holds his finger to his lips. She knows she wouldn't be able to move fast enough to escape a bullet this close. He slowly comes to his feet and takes the weapon from her hands. She holds tight but he rips it from her grip. Her lips purse. Charlie turns her away from him and uses a plastic zip tie to tether her hands behind her back. He wraps his arm around her shoulders and keeps his back to the wall as they move, gun pressed against her ear.

Killian comes into view with his back turned. Charlie points in Killian's direction and pulls the trigger, just as Stacy shoves into his arm, causing the bullet to shift. Killian falls to the ground, the bullet hitting his helmet, making the screen crack and short out. Sparks scorch his face as he throws the helmet off and it spins on the floor. Spotting them, he positions himself out of harm's way, lining himself with the shelving.

Charlie kicks Stacy in the back of the knee. She falls to all fours, yelling in pain. He yanks her hair back so that the pain on her face is visible. Holding his gun up to her head, he calls him out. "Come out now, or your pretty girlfriend will have a hideous hole through her skull," Charlie calls. Killian comes out with his gun aimed at Charlie's head. Charlie curses. "You've got to be kidding me. Why won't you die?!" Charlie screams. Killian smiles, still moving closer.

"You know each other?" Stacy says with contempt.

"Don't come any closer. I'll blow her away."

"I don't doubt it." Killian responds. Stacy eyes Killian.

"Drop your weapon," Charlie commands. Killian shakes his head slowly. He doesn't look away from Charlie, like a panther stalking its prey. "Drop your fracking weapon, you damned fool!" he yells impatiently.

"So you can try to kill me again?" Killian scoffs.

"Why shouldn't I kill you right now?" His eyes are blazing with hatred.

"...Hello?!" Stacy yells.

"Ouch. That's cold. The oh-so-wonderful Killian Grey has become heartless." Charlie laughs. "Never thought I'd see the day."

"What do you expect? Losing everything does that to you. You took my arm." He flexes his mechanical fingers. "You took my *wife.* You took my life and made it yours," he spits.

"Your *wife,* if you can even call her that, couldn't handle the loss of her beloved murderous *husband,* so she wanted to forget. I obliged," Charlie sneers.

"It was an accident. He would've killed her and you know it. You just wanted me out of the picture!"

"Accident? And yes, I did want you out of the picture," Charlie laughs.

Stacy yanks her head, hoping he will loosen his grip. "It's not worth getting killed over," she growls. "I don't want to die because of your stupid vendetta." Killian ignores her, stepping closer. Charlie smiles wickedly. Killian lets off a shot. The bullet hits the shoulder Charlie is using, making him drop his weapon. His shoulder thrown back, he falls backward in shock. Stacy throws herself to the floor. Within seconds Killian closes the distance, kicking Charlie's cannon across the floor and standing over him. Stacy pulls her hips and legs through her arms, so that her hands are in front of her. She grabs her weapon and aims at Charlie, who is gripping his shoulder and crying out in agony.

"Where are the rest of them?" Killian growls. Charlie ignores him, moaning. Killian kicks him in the ribs. He cries out again, still ignoring his question. Killian crouches down, pressing his knees into Charlie's shoulders, putting most of his weight onto the wound. Charlie stares up at Killian, gasping and clenching his teeth.

"The boy is scared of you, you know. Your own son is scared of you," Killian says in a low voice.

Charlie's expression changes. Ignoring the pain, he starts to laugh hysterically. "You found them." His laughter is cut short as Killian's knee digs deeper. "That bastard child isn't mine." The pleasure in Killian's expression is undeniable; but Charlie, fuming, will not allow Killian such pleasure. "You know that kid probably isn't yours either. That whore was always sneaking off in the middle of the night." He spits in Killian's face as he speaks.

With his metal hand, Killian squeezes his throat. Charlie's face starts to turn red, and his eyes bulge as he becomes desperate for air. Clara comes out from behind the pharmacy counter with her hands up, begging him to stop. Stacy takes aim at Clara. Killian releases his grip as he notices the woman with a white blouse stained with blood. "You must be Clara," Killian says, taking to his feet as Charlie gasps for air.

"Please don't hurt us," she begs, tears streaming down her face.

Killian wipes his face on his sleeve. "I won't hurt you. Where's Jack?"

"Here!" Jack yips. Killian signals Stacy and she takes aim at Charlie. Clara steps away, giving Killian a wide berth as he rounds the corner. Jack is on the floor, stretched out, with one hand holding his bleeding ribcage. His face is white from blood loss. Killian is at his side instantly. Pulling Jack's hand away, he reveals a broken rib sticking out of his flesh.

"Damnit, we have to get him home!" he yells to Stacy.

"Uncuff me," she demands to Clara. Clara carefully comes up to Charlie and digs into his pocket. Pulling a knife out, she holds it carefully, making sure Stacy is aware of her intentions. She cuts her wrists free. Stacy holds her hand out and Clara hands over the knife, returning her hands to the air. "Are we seriously bringing these people back with us?"

Killian helps Jack to his feet as gently as possible. "Stacy, Jack Wiseman... Jack, Stacy Nox."

"Nox," Jack breathes with a nod. They make eye contact and for a moment Stacy hesitates.

"Pleasure," she says sarcastically.

Killian pulls Jack's arm over his shoulder helping him walk. "You can put your hands down, we won't hurt you," he repeats to Clara. "Are you wounded?"

She shakes her head, though he notices the cut on her eyebrow and the bruise forming around the swollen area. "No, this isn't my blood, but Jack's been in and out of consciousness."

Killian is on the comm, telling Alan to prepare the infirmary for one severely injured man.

"What about this jackass?" Stacy kicks Charlie in the thigh. He glares up at her, breathing heavy through his teeth. Killian steps in front of him, drawing his weapon once more.

"Don't!" Jack pants, reaching for his arm weakly. Killian looks at Jack. Not looking to argue, he moves past them, Clara following.

"Leave him!" Killian calls over his shoulder.

Stacy cracks a smile. "Your lucky day, pretty boy." She picks up Charlie's cannon on the way out.

"You can't leave me here!" Charlie wails. He continues to yell and curse them as they move out the back. He tries to get up, screaming in frustration and pain as he tries to get to his feet. He bursts through the back door as they take off on their skyriders. He roars with rage as they disappear into the distance.

* * *

Violet and Alan are cooking dinner when Killian comes on the comm, telling them to prep the infirmary. The children are playing a game together. She takes care of the food while Alan moves quickly to prep. He sterilizes the equipment and lays it out on trays, setting them aside for when they arrive.

Everyone is on edge at dinner, waiting nervously for their arrival. One hour later they hear the rumbling of the vehicles. Alan meets them as they burst through the door. Stacy and Killian are hauling an unconscious Jack into the infirmary. They lay him down on a table as Alan washes his hands thoroughly. "Can I get the helmet?" Alan asks.

"It was damaged," Killian replies.

Alan sighs, pulling down a screen from the wall. No time for complaints. He uses a tool to scan Jack. His X-ray is displayed on the screen. The damage is highlighted, along with recommended procedures to fix it. Alan scrolls through until he finds one they have the tools for. "Everyone out!" he shouts as Killian helps remove Jack's clothes.

"Let me help, I have experience," Clara begs. Killian nods, letting her take his place as he pulls Stacy out of the room.

Stacy turns on Killian, holding him back. "I need to know the truth," she whispers. "What that guy was saying... is Violet your wife?"

"She's the person I left behind, yes." Killian looks into her eyes.

"You lied to me."

"I didn't lie to you. I just left out some details."

"You didn't think that was something you should've shared with me?" Stacy angrily asks, pushing him against the wall. "And she acts like she doesn't even know you."

"She *doesn't* know me... anymore. Her memory was wiped. When we found the underground entrance back into my hometown, I found her as well. She was attached to a machine capable of wiping anyone clean and giving them completely new memories. I rigged it so that she would come out of it, but Charlie caught me. And now you're caught up."

"Does she know her memories have been wiped?" Stacy asks. Killian shrugs. "Well, that's messed up." Killian gives a weak smile as he pushes past her.

Violet and the children wait anxiously at the dining table. Violet is standing, unsure of what to do with herself. They've already finished their meals. Killian and Stacy come to the table, sitting across from them. Violet sets clean plates in front of them and sits back down, looking past Killian into the dark hallway.

After taking a deep breath, Killian smiles at them, studying their sober faces. "Jack will be fine. He's a little beat up, but Alan

110

will fix him up, good as new. Clara's helping." The children's faces relax, but Violet doesn't believe him, considering the urgency over the radio and Jack being carried in. Killian watches her as Stacy serves herself some food.

"And Charlie?" Nathan asks. Violet turns her attention now to Killian, waiting for an answer despite the headache coming back in full force.

Killian glances at Nathan and down at his empty plate. "Charlie stayed behind. He didn't want to come." He shovels food onto his plate. Violet glares at him, knowing Charlie would never have chosen solitude over a shelter and the only family he has left. He's too much of a coward. She's not about to talk about it in front of the kids now, though. Looking for a distraction, she asks the children to take a seat on the couch, while she grabs a book from the library.

Violet reads to the children as they huddle together on the couch. A wail comes from the infirmary and Violet cringes. Nathan, Ember and Lilly look to the dark hallway in concern. Killian puts on some music before heading to the kitchen to clean up. Stacy lingers in the recreational room, shooting pool. Alan emerges a few hours later. He has blood on his sleeves. He doesn't say a word but locks eyes with Violet and gives her a wink and a smile, letting her know that everything is alright.

Alan heads to the showers, and Violet asks the children to stay put while she checks on Jack and Clara. Clara is already patched up and has changed into a fresh blouse. Wiping Jack's forehead with a cloth, Clara kisses him and combs her fingers through his wild white hair. Violet watches with relief. With teary eyes, Violet and Clara hold each other tightly. Happy to be together again, a weight is lifted from her shoulders. Having three lives dropped into her lap is an overwhelming responsibility. She hadn't realized it was weighing her down until it was lifted.

Killian enters the room with a couple plates of food. Violet leaves, allowing them to rest. She avoids looking Killian in the eye as she passes. He follows her out. Grabbing her hand in the hallway, she flinches away. "Thank you for helping us," she says, keeping her eyes low and walking away.

Killian rubs his face in his hands with frustration. "You're welcome," he says to himself, as she is already gone.

Violet assures the children that Jack will be alright. Alan has taken Violet's place reading to the kids, with Lilly on his lap. Violet takes a seat next to Nathan, kissing the top of his head as he wraps his small arms around her waist. Trying to ignore the envy bubbling to the surface with the picturesque scene, Killian takes a deep breath and walks away.

No tours are given this evening. Clara is given one of the bunks. After Alan says goodnight to the children, he takes to his bunk as well. Violet tucks the kids into the large bed before checking on Jack once more. He is in good condition but still sleeping. Killian leans up against the wall in the hallway, waiting outside the infirmary. Violet comes out. Seeing him waiting, she tries not to make eye contact, but he steps in front of her as she tries to pass. "I know you're upset with me for not bringing you along, but I kept my word," he says.

"I'm not upset. I already thanked you for keeping that promise."

Looking around the hall, not wanting anyone to eavesdrop, he gently pulls her by the sleeve into the cargo bay. This gesture has her heart pounding. *Is this fear of being alone with him?* The island with the orange-colored tree glowing at the center catches her eye. Drawn to it, she walks to the edge of the platform to get a better view. Her heart pounds as she recognizes it.

"You're not upset about Charlie?" Killian says expectantly.

Drawing her attention back to him, she keeps her eyes low. "No, but I don't believe you. Charlie would never have chosen to go on alone." She folds her arms as she comes to stand before him. He folds his arms in turn, leaning against some of the crates lining the wall. "What did you do?" Killian avoids her eyes now. "Did you kill him?"

"I didn't kill him. He threatened us and held Stacy hostage. I did what was necessary to keep everyone safe. I just... maimed him." Killian watches her. Her expression doesn't change. "It wasn't safe to bring him here. Nathan made it clear he was not good to him. People who threaten and hurt women and children are not welcome in my home," he says sternly.

"You maimed him?"

"In the shoulder."

"Did he cry?" A slight smile escapes her face.

"Just a little bit." He smiles back.

He did bring Jack and Clara back safely, but Violet still feels uncertainty with him. Killian reaches his left hand out in concern when she rubs at her temples with her eyes closed. His fingertips brush her cheek. She jerks away and her breath comes short. Her heart pounds in her ears, making the pressure unbearable. "Bubble," she whispers, tracing a circle around herself. She looks into his dark brown eyes for a second and looks away. Tucking his hands under his arms, he stares down at the floor. "There's something about you... I don't know. Ever since we got here, it's been like a hammer bashing my skull in, and it seems to get worse when you're around." She closes her eyes, rubbing at her head. "Maybe it's just stress."

Killian watches the pain in her face and sighs. Pulling himself away from the crates, he opens the door for her. "I'll show more respect for your personal space," Killian says without looking her in the eyes. "Go get some rest."

"Thank you," she says before turning away. "For helping us." For reasons unknown to her, she feels guilty. She walks out of the cargo bay, letting the door swing closed behind her. Not five steps down the hallway, her legs start to tremble. Willing herself back to her room, she keeps walking, holding onto the walls. Before entering her room, she wipes tears on her sleeve and clears her throat.

Upon entering, Nathan is very perceptive. He comes to her with open arms. "Is Jack okay?"

"Oh yes, he'll be good as new before you know it. Everything's going to get easier from now on." She pulls him in for a hug. The girls, who have been sitting tensely on the bed, relax their shoulders. Violet hugs them as well, and tucks them back into bed. With no desire to sleep, she sits at the desk, pulling out the leather-bound book from her bag. Flipping through the water-stained pages, she comes across a drawing. The whole page is colored in black except for an orange and yellow tree. *I knew I'd seen that tree before*, she thinks to herself. Curious, she flips a couple pages back. There are words written, though on some of the pages the ink has started to bleed from water damage.

June 20

We're almost finished. The atrium is stocked with fresh soil and seed. We just need to find some mattresses. Hopefully we can find some art. The walls are cold. There are still a few rooms that are big and empty. I don't know what they're for. Jack says it's for fun. I don't see the point. It's a shelter. It's not meant for fun. It's here to protect us. I wish we had something like this back home. Maybe they'd still be here. I miss them. At least Jack found me. I have family again.

Jack has taught me a lot. I'm excited to help him install the new equipment we found. I've never seen an oven with 8 burners before. This place is made for so many people but it's just the two of us. I wonder what it's like in his hometown. I bet he has a lot of family. I hope he's rich. What kind of food will we eat? I'm sick of squirrel meat.

114

August 28
I don't want to leave. This cave is beautiful. I love what we've made.
Why go back to the city? Jack has made it clear I don't have a choice.
All this crap about needing social skills. I don't need other people,
just Jack. The old man is stubborn.
I will miss this tree most of all.

Remembering how Killian had said he helped his father build the shelter, she looks back at the book. He couldn't be someone from her past. He would have said something. What if he killed the person who really helped build this place? He could have been taken in by the man from her past and stolen his identity. *I wish Jack would wake up.* Flipping through the rest of the book, she makes her mind up.

When Stacy hears Violet return to her room, she sneaks down the hallway. Hearing something crash, she quickly moves past the infirmary. It sounds like a struggle. Stacy opens the door to the cargo bay. Killian is sitting on the floor with his face in his hands. His shoulders are shaking as he sobs. His knuckles are bloody, and shattered pieces of a wooden crate are scattered about him. Quietly, she walks in and crouches next to him. Resting her hand on his shoulder, he flinches, realizing he is no longer alone. He wraps his arms around her waist, pulling her into him tightly. Feeling pity for him, she kisses the top of his head as she cradles him to her chest. She can't hold back her smile as she combs her fingers through his hair.

Killian pulls himself together, pulling her away from him. She helps him to his feet. She holds his hand as they walk back down the hall. "You go on to bed," he says to her. "I'm going to clean up my hands and check on Jack." He doesn't wait for Stacy to respond, closing the infirmary doors behind him. Stacy sighs and mumbles under her breath as she heads back to bed. She checks on the others in passing. Clara and Alan are fast asleep. The door to Killian's old room is closed. She presses her ear to the door. It's quiet. Feeling content, she goes back to her room.

She hears a quiet ping resonating from somewhere in her room. Quickly shutting the door, she begins the search. Clothing and bedsheets are tossed to the corner of her room. Underneath the bed is an old bag she once used a long time ago. She pulls it out and searches the pockets. There's nothing, but it's still sounding off. She feels around, and inside the walls of the bag there is something hard and rectangular. Grabbing a knife, she cuts it open, pulling out a device. Realizing what it is, she tosses it across the room. It crashes to the cement floor and then there is a voice coming from it. Her heart is racing. *Have they been tracking me this entire time?*

"Eustachia? I can't see anything, John. Are you sure it's working?" Stacy curses herself, recognizing the voices. Dragging herself off her bed, she reluctantly picks up the device, propping it up on her desk. Sitting down in the chair, she takes a deep breath, folding her arms indifferently.

"I thought you agreed to let me go," Stacy says, staring at the glass screen.

A woman comes into view. She is older but still beautiful, with the same white markings across her high cheekbones. Her white hair is pulled back smooth and tight; her simple dress, a crisp white with geometric cutouts. "Darling, we hoped by now you would realize what you are giving up."

"I know exactly what I've given up." Stacy looks away in protest.

The woman sighs. "Your father wants you to come home. You have a responsibility to this family and to the company. He's done everything possible to keep you off-screen, but the people you've collected are criminals. You've even become involved with one of them. That's extremely inappropriate and dangerous."

"I never asked you to protect me. Let them see! I'm not going to be tied down to your stupid responsibilities. Give the position to someone who actually wants it."

"I'm protecting this *family* by keeping you out of sight, you little wretch. Letting them see will ruin us all." A man with dark hair and stripes of silver on the sides of his head comes into view. "Stop being a selfish little brat and come home. If you continue refusing, I'll send someone to drag you back kicking and screaming, like the child you are!"

"Hello, Father," she says with a falsely bright smile. "Oh yes, I've missed you too. I'm doing well, thank you for asking."

"I'm not playing your games."

"Why not? I've been playing your games since I got here. Now I understand these people a lot better. If only they knew these 'wars' are nothing but an extermination of a lower class, to provide safety for a population of ridiculous people who think themselves more important than the rest. What do you think would happen if they found out the truth?" Stacy covers her mouth, her voice dripping with sarcasm.

"If you tell them anything, I'll have them killed."

"I doubt that would go well for you, since I'm in their company."

"I'm sending an extraction team for you in 24 hours. That's plenty of time to say your goodbyes."

"I'll come willingly on one condition."

"I don't think you're in any position—"

"If you want me to take over the company, you'll allow me to make a recruitment."

The man guffaws. "Tell you what. If you can convince that man to leave everything behind for *you,* I'll help you get a voice on the council. In fact, I'll give you six days to win him over without letting the others find out the truth."

"Deal."

"You won't like the consequences if you fail."

Before she can respond, the screen goes black. Biting her fist, she slams the blank screen down on the desk. Quickly sweeping her room for cameras, she finds none. Giving in to her tired body, she strips down, dropping her clothes onto the floor, and crawls into bed. Though drained, she knows she won't sleep easily tonight. Laying under the covers, she stares at the ceiling, trying to figure out a plan of action.

CHAPTER

9

It is dawn, but the lights in the shelter begin to brighten as the hour passes. Jack awakens. Looking around, he recognizes the infirmary he built ages ago. There have been improvements since his departure, but surely it's the same one. Killian sits on a stool, resting his head upon his arms on Jack's bedside, his dark hair shading his eyes. His shoulders shake as a whimper escapes his lips. Jack rests his hand upon his quivering shoulder. With a jerk, Killian raises his head. His eyes are bloodshot with dark circles. Killian rubs his palms into his eyes, wiping away the sleep with a sigh. Jack pities him. Moving to the table next to him, Killian holds his hands between his knees. Unable to make eye contact with Jack, he looks solemnly down at his own hands. It is still early, and no one has risen from their beds. "What happened to you, boy?" Jack says warmly. "You've changed."

"What would you expect?" he says, rubbing at his stiff neck.

"I expect you to respect life as precious. In a world full of death and destruction, I raised you to have mercy."

"Henry didn't deserve mercy, though I wasn't aiming to kill him. And Charlie... I could've done a lot worse. I was merciful enough."

"If I hadn't said anything, you would've shot him dead. Instead, you left him wounded and unarmed. You might as well have put a bullet in his head."

"He deserves to suffer," Killian grumbles.

"I know he's a lousy excuse for a man, but how can you have so much hatred for him?"

With a deep breath he thinks back and begins telling his tale, starting with the death of Violet's father.

* * *

Violet told him to meet her at the dock of the dark sea, promising him a surprise. He was almost to the edge of the woods when he heard Henry's voice. He was yelling at someone, but they weren't responding. A pang in his chest told him something was wrong. When he saw Henry on top of her with his hands about her throat, there was no thinking. No logic. No hesitation. Picking up the largest rock around him, he ran as fast as he could. With one swing he could hear his skull crack. Even though he knew the back of his skull had caved in, he was unable to stop himself. He never wanted to stop bashing the rock into what once was a human skull. Only when Violet's voice broke through the buzzing in his ears was he able to stop.

Violet pulled him off Henry with tears streaming down her smudged face. Seeing the red marks around her neck, he felt himself crumble. Touching his hands to her neck, he smeared her father's blood. It was then that he came out of it, and shock and panic had set in. He knew there would be consequences for what he had done. Violet was speaking to him, but he didn't hear a word until the crank sirens came. She was screaming at him. She begged him not to let them catch him, to run. She was pulling him by his clothing, but he was unable to move. Her voice still rang in his ears.

120

Charlie came then, separating them. By the time Killian realized he would have to leave town and start over, it was too late. Charlie fought to keep him there until the suits arrived, regardless of how much Violet tried to interfere. There was no trial. Charlie acted as a witness. Killian was drafted onto the next flight. He was not given any rights or visits before being shipped off with the rest of the criminals. Watching his home disappear behind him, he knew there would be no returning. It was a death sentence. Heading to the fallen city was to face certain death.

Before they reached the city, the ship came under attack. It caught fire and the next thing he knew, he was jumping into the ocean. Those who survived scattered. Finding shelter in a small urban home, he was able to find dry clothing and food. Eventually he found his way back to the shelter he and Jack made, but he needed to get back to Violet. He started the garden with the seeds stocked in the atrium.

Seven months after the accident, he met Stacy. She needed him more than he needed her. For a while he helped her, out of fear of guilt for leaving her behind on her own. Stacy seemed a helpless fool who lived a sheltered life. Eventually, she became more independent and even helpful over the next year, as they made the shelter livable. They stocked the rest of the stores with whatever they could find, looting abandoned towns. Stacy didn't know that their trips for supplies were also for the purpose of finding the way back to Safe Haven.

A little over a year later, while checking out an old hospital, they happened upon Alan. He was very knowledgeable when it came to medicines and procedures, but it took some convincing to get him to join them. The promise of a safer shelter helped ease Alan's mind.

Eventually they came across the border of Safe Haven. Killian found the underground entrance he and Jack had closed off with bricks years before. While he broke through the wall, Stacy and Alan acted as lookouts, but he was thankful Stacy didn't listen.

When he entered, he saw that one of the rooms was still active. That's when he found Violet. Finding her in that state was insufferable. He attached the release apparatus to her hand and told her he would wait for her as he started the process to bring her out of a coma, but Charlie interrupted. He was checking on her and reacted poorly, attacking him, throwing everything within his reach at him, until he was able to retrieve a weapon hidden in one of the drawers. Killian evaded the first shot, but it hit the monitor of the anamnesis manipulator. The second shot took his arm. The blast ate at his flesh like fire spreading across paper. Running out of the room, Stacy met him in the hallway as Charlie sent off more shots. His bad aim only scorched the walls, lighting the way out.

They escaped; but Killian, being in excruciating pain, didn't get far. Alan had medicines that lessened the pain. His skin and muscles at his elbow had been eaten away to the bone. Tying off the wound, Alan ended up having to remove the arm entirely before the burn spread into his shoulder and chest. With all the pain relievers Alan provided, nothing could remove the feeling of metal grinding at his humerus. Alan cauterized the wound and made him as comfortable as possible. Killian designed his arm later on, and Alan helped him build it onto his body, which was a pain in itself.

* * *

Jack rubs his chin after Killian tells his side of the story. "I had no idea you had found your way back into town," he says. "I had a vague suspicion that maybe you were the one who had released Violet, but I didn't allow myself to indulge in the idea."

"There are two things I must know," Killian says after a moment of silence. "Does Violet know her memory has been wiped?"

"Yes, but we haven't told her about you," Jack says solemnly.

"Fine. And second, is Nathan mine?" Killian looks Jack in the eye with a hard expression, awaiting his response.

"He does look so much like his mother, doesn't he?" Jack says, then sighs. "'Tis true, he is yours. She was pregnant and was going to tell you that day at the dock."

Killian stands briskly, turning his back on Jack. He pulls his fingers through his hair with a deep breath, and suddenly boisterous laughter resounds in the room. He turns to Jack with tears in his eyes and a grin reaching ear to ear. Pulling Jack into a fierce hug, he wails in pain. Killian releases him, apologizing, but nothing would remove his smile. "He's mine? He's really mine?" Killian repeats over and over in disbelief. He isn't sure if he wants to cry or laugh, so ends up alternating between the two, covering his face with his hands. Kissing Jack on the forehead enthusiastically, he leaves the infirmary, another laugh echoing down the halls.

Clara passes him, giving him space as he almost skips down the hall. He turns on some music and dances into the kitchen. Clara watches him curiously as he pulls out bowls and pans. She brushes off his peculiar behavior to check on Jack.

Alan comes out, rubbing his eyes and squinting from the light. Music playing so early in the morning is unusual enough, but dancing about the kitchen as he preps breakfast has Alan dumbfounded. Never has he seen Killian so elated. He strolls into the kitchen with his hands in his pockets. Killian spins around singing the lyrics. Catching Alan watching him, he winks and continues dancing around, spinning a pan in his hand. It puts a smile on Alan's face. "What's got you all chipper?"

"I'll tell you a secret, my friend," he says, cracking eggs into a bowl.

"Proceed."

"That woman sleeping in my bed is my wife... though she doesn't know it yet. That part is complicated." He frowns, though still doing a little jig.

"Killian," Alan interrupts, "you can't just claim whoever steps foot in this place! That's not how marriage works."

"What?" Killian tilts his head as he whisks the eggs together. "No, she already *is* my wife. She just can't remember. They wiped her memory." He laughs.

"You're kidding me." Alan looks at him incredulously. Killian shakes his head with a wide grin, still singing along to the song. "Why didn't you say anything when she first arrived? Does Stacy know?"

"She knows," Killian says uncomfortably.

"I can't believe this. We finally have another gorgeous single woman in the house, and she turns out to be your wife? Why do you always get the girl? You should've told me before I got all crushy on her."

"Um, sorry?" Killian laughs. "But let's face it, wouldn't you have gotten a crush regardless?"

"Yeah, but it's different now. Man, you suck." Killian sets the whisk down and comes to stand in front of Alan with a large smile. "Okay, you're creeping me out now." Alan shifts back, but Killian puts his hands on Alan's shoulders, and gets so close that Alan thinks he might kiss him. Tilting back as far as he can, he scrunches his face expecting to be violated. His left shoulder slants down under the weight of Killian's metal arm.

"I have a son," he whispers.

Alan's eyes blink and then open wide. "Whaaaaat?! Is it Nathan?" Alan whispers back. Killian smiles in response. "Congrats, man!" Alan smiles but also doesn't know what to do with this information. Killian pulls Alan into a bear hug and releases him when he squeals in pain. Alan stretches his back, trying to pop it back into place. Killian returns to the food, whistling along with the music as he cooks. Alan sighs. Watching his friend, he laughs to himself. After all these years, he deserves this happiness.

After assisting Killian with breakfast, Alan sets the table. Killian ventures down the hall to wake those still sleeping. He knocks on his bedroom door before sliding it open. The room is very dimly lit. The girls facing the doorway wake up to the light from the hall. He whispers that breakfast is ready and they wriggle out of bed. Nathan wakes up to the movement and follows suit, rubbing his eyes and giving a big yawn. Killian smiles and rustles his hair as he passes. Nathan smiles in return and hurries after the girls.

Violet is still asleep on her side. Her shoulder peeks through the neck of her sweater. She is dreaming. The muscles in her neck tense and release. Mumbles escape her lips. He carefully sits upon the bed next to her and leans in close to hear better. "You, gin," Violet whimpers.

Ignoring the strange sounds she made, he gently rests his hand upon her shoulder. Leaning in he quietly speaks. "Vi…" He is cut short when her arm jerks and she screams. Her elbow meets his cheekbone hard, and he falls back onto the bed. "Argh!"

"What? Oh! What are you doing in here?" Violet yells, scrambling away, falling off the bed.

Killian is laughing and crying once more. "Agh! I'm sorry. Are you okay? Ow," he says, holding his face.

"What's going on in here?" Stacy is at the door. Flipping the lights on bright, she stands in the doorway in a bra and small shorts. Killian sits up and touches the split flesh below his eye. "What did you do?" Stacy runs to Killian's side as blood streams down his face.

"It's my fault. I popped the bubble," Killian says, still laughing. "Breakfast is ready by the way. I didn't want it to get cold."

"I'm sorry," Violet says, hiding her laughter behind the sheet she's pulled from the bed.

"I know you don't know your own strength, but learn some self-control, mutant," Stacy chides. Heat rises in her chest at her words.

"Don't be rude, Stacy," Killian says, brushing her hands away. He gets up off the bed and Stacy throws daggers at Violet while escorting him out of the room.

"Ow," Violet says to herself as she rubs at her elbow. It is still tingling from hitting her funny bone. Violet pulls herself together and walks out to the mess hall. Jack and Clara sit at the table staring her way, snickering. The children are confused. Alan is trying his hardest to hold in his laughter but fails. His guffaw becomes contagious as Jack starts to rumble as well, but then cries out in pain as it disrupts the stability of his broken rib. Violet, blushing, tries to wipe the embarrassed smile from her face, biting her lip. Sitting next to Alan, he makes her a plate, still giggling to himself. Nathan sits on the other side of her.

Killian comes out of the infirmary. Seeing Violet next to Alan, there is a flicker of jealousy. His smile returns, though, when he sits next to Nathan. White strips of tape hold together the gash below his eye. He's no longer wearing the black sweater but a tank-top. Stacy comes out wearing Killian's missing sweater. She slides in next to him, though there is less room on that side of the table. She pulls up the long sleeves before making herself a plate. Alan and Killian stare at her as she fills her plate full of food. Spotting the attention on her, she stops. "What? Sometimes I eat breakfast," she says awkwardly. They shrug off her peculiar behavior.

Killian starts a conversation with Nathan, asking everything he can to get to know him. Nathan at first answers shyly, looking back and forth at Jack and Violet. Jack smiles when Nathan answers.

Violet listens, curious of his answers as well. Both of his parents learn for the first time that his favorite color is green, his favorite food is bacon, and his favorite pastime is playing with Lilly and Ember. Stacy interrupts the many questions to ask about their next venture out for supplies. Killian gives her a look that has her eating in silence.

Eventually Nathan is sharing stories that have them all laughing at Charlie's expense. Before long, all but Stacy is sharing stories and laughing. Stacy is studying the room as if she hadn't seen it before. She finishes her food quickly and leaves, hiding herself away in her room. When the children finish their food, they ask to be dismissed. With Jack around they are all manners. Jack waves them away and, after taking turns hugging him and Clara, they run off to play in the atrium.

"Not to dampen the mood, but we have some things to discuss, Wiseman," Violet says, folding her arms.

"I'm in trouble," Jack sighs. He begins to stand and Clara helps him to his feet. Violet watches him suspiciously. "If you want to talk, you can't expect me to sit on those awful metal benches, can you?" Violet smiles and meets him on the other side, helping him to one of the leather easy chairs. Taking a seat on the couch, Killian takes the seat next to her. He smiles at her, but she doesn't make eye contact. Violet shifts in her seat, making more space between them, attempting to ignore the never-ending pain in her skull. Alan clears the table and takes a seat at the bar. His seat squeaks as he turns to face the conversation. Clara takes to the other easy chair. Trying to keep her mind off Killian, Violet stares straight ahead, waiting for Jack to get comfortable.

Stacy comes out in her own clothes, her hair wet. With everyone watching her uneasily, she pours herself a glass of bourbon.

"A bit early, isn't it?" Alan says quietly.

"It's going to be a long day," she complains, taking a seat next to Alan at the bar.

"Alright, Violet, what's on your mind?" Jack asks with a smile, though he squirms from the pain in his ribcage.

"Jolene. What was she and where did she come from? How did she get into town without setting off alarms?"

"It was a cyborg. The shield didn't work because of the organic matter she was disguised with. The girls accompanying her may have assisted with guiding it. It must have been watching those girls for a long time. It may have killed the real Jolene in order to take her place. It knew what their mother looked like, and tried to take that form. An error in programming, perhaps."

"Where would someone even find the parts for it?"

"The fallen city, maybe?" Killian interrupts. "I've found high-tech equipment close to that city before."

"Do you think there are more of these disguised cyborgs?" Violet asks, ignoring Killian's input. Jack looks back and forth between the two of them.

"Yup," Stacy chimes in as she stirs the ice in her glass. Everyone looks her way, but Stacy keeps her eyes on her glass.

"They're here to hurt us, like the maven," Clara says, stroking Jack's hand.

"Or to observe us," Stacy contradicts.

"If their purpose is to observe, then why did it become violent?" Violet asks, rolling her eyes.

"A glitch?" Stacy shrugs.

Violet glares at her inquisitively. "Why would they be observing us? To what benefit?"

Stacy shrugs again in response, waving her hand without looking away from her glass, indicating to Violet that she would say nothing more. She continues looking about the room curiously, as though she's admiring the structure, tilting her head occasionally.

"What I'm worried about," Violet says to Jack, "is how you of all people couldn't tell something was wrong with her. She wouldn't look me in the eye. She wouldn't talk to me unless responding to a question. She never watched her hands while she worked. She kept her eyes on her surroundings at all times. No one is capable of sewing a straight line without looking at it."

"She seemed to act like most children who have gone through a traumatic experience," Jack replies. "I never noticed the way she worked."

"She was creepy. I think we should find more information on these cyborgs."

"How?" Killian asks.

"Government buildings," Violet says. "They log footage from city cameras that are still active."

"How do you know that?" Jack asks.

"I remembered something. Or I think I remembered. It could have been a dream. I… I remember leaving town. I had a solar powered cruiser hidden in the woods. I don't know how far I traveled before coming to one of the abandoned cities. There was a large building. Its walls were made of glass with metal framing. I remember I had been there before. I knew my way around the building. I was meeting someone there. He's a friend and he was helping me find something."

"He?" Killian asks. "What's his name?" Alan watches Killian with a smirk.

"I don't remember, it's beside the point. That room had at least ten large screens lining the wall. In the middle of the room was a desk with a lot of buttons and switches. I didn't know what they were for, but he knew. He knew exactly what he was doing. That room had access to cameras; not just ones from that city, but from any city with an active camera system. We were able to locate video feeds stored years ago. We should be able to find something on these cyborgs."

"What were you looking for?" Killian asks.

"None of your business," Violet snaps. "It has nothing to do with what we're discussing right now!"

"It might have something to do with it. Did you find what you were looking for?"

"I don't know, we had to leave. Maven found a way into the building, as well as a Seeker. We got separated... I think that's when I was injured. I set off a detonator... then you woke me up from my dream. Maybe I'd know more if you hadn't woken me." Killian is puzzled by her sudden animosity.

"We should take a look at that control room," Stacy chimes in, playing at indifference.

"It can wait. Right now we should lay low, heal up," Jack says. Everyone agrees but Stacy. She sighs and walks away after finishing off her drink. After their meeting ends, there is an awkward silence. Violet offers Killian's room to Jack and Clara. Killian agrees and offers to prep the room. He leaves them to their small talk and cleans up the room, fixing the bed with fresh sheets. After prepping the beds, he heads to the showers. Something catches his eye, passing the doorway. He stops and takes a couple steps back. Stacy is on a stool with a screwdriver and hammer in hand. She presses the screwdriver into a dark corner and hits the handle with the hammer. Sparks fly and she steps down, sweeping her feet along the floor, trying to hide whatever has fallen.

Stacy looks up and down the hall before picking up the stool and walking away quickly. When she is out of sight, he crouches next to the pieces on the floor reflecting light. Tiny pieces of glass and metal bits are scattered. Curiously catching up with her, she is in the next hall doing it again. Another spark and she moves on to the next. Just as she hits the third one, he confronts her. "What on earth are you doing?"

She drops the screwdriver and it crashes to the floor as she catches her balance. "Hell, you scared me, Killian," she whispers.

"What are you doing?" Killian repeats, sternly snatching the hammer out of her hand.

"Nothing to be angry about."

"Oh?" Killian says, sweeping at the broken glass on the floor with his foot.

"I'll clean it up." She shrugs nonchalantly.

"Don't make me ask you again, Nox."

She looks up and down the hallway before taking his hand. She drags him into the sleeping quarters and brings him into the shower room. She begins stripping and he tries to stop her. She hits his hands and holds a finger to her lips. Signaling to him to start stripping, he hesitates, and she turns on one of the showers. Seeing as he is still standing fully clothed and averting his eyes, she comes to stand in front of him. She still has her bra and underwear on, but he still doesn't understand, so she helps him out of his clothes with a struggle, but leaves him in his briefs. Pulling him under the steaming water, she puts her hand around his neck and pulls him close to her. She feels his muscles tense as he becomes uncomfortable by their close proximity. Bringing her lips up to his ear, she whispers, "There are cameras hidden throughout this shelter. I don't know how long they've been there. We don't have a control room, so I'm assuming you didn't install them." She looks up at him for a response, and the concerned look in his eyes gives her the answer. "Someone could be listening now." Killian is no longer holding her away from him, but listening intently.

"How long have you known?" he whispers in her ear.

"I noticed them this morning. We need to locate and destroy them quickly. Someone knows where we are." Killian pulls away slightly to look into her eyes. She isn't fooling around.

The door to the showers opens. With the sound of the showerhead blasting water, they don't hear the creak as it opens. Stacy looks over Killian's shoulder and covers her mouth with her dripping fingers. When he notices her attention has gone

131

elsewhere, he turns his head. Violet stands in the doorway with a towel in hand. When Killian sees her, he curses himself. Before he can think of what to say, Violet averts her eyes and backs out of the room, closing the door behind her.

"Damnit. Find them all and destroy them. I'll find the voltage detector," he says quietly, pushing himself away from her.

Stacy catches his hand before he finishes getting dressed. "She doesn't know who you are, Killian."

"She'll remember at some point. I don't want her getting the wrong idea."

"If that's the case, you need to tell her about us anyway." Stacy shoves his hand back to him. "You wouldn't want your relationship to start up again with secrets lingering." His face turns pale as he realizes the truth in her words. He wraps a towel around his waist as he chases after her.

Killian catches up with Violet in his old room. Violet sits at the desk looking at the leather-bound book. Her heart is racing. She looks back at him and frowns. Violet is confused by the pang of jealousy. What is there to be jealous of? She has no feelings for this man she barely knows. Looking back at the book, she tries to calm her heart that is beating against her chest.

He closes the door behind him so they will be alone. She hears his footsteps coming closer. "I'm sorry I interrupted you," she says. "I'll knock next time."

"It's not what you think."

"I don't care, it's none of my business," Violet says, flipping pages.

Killian is at her side and leans over to see her face. "Your attitude says otherwise. You're flushed," he says, kneeling down beside her.

"Maybe it's because I'm embarrassed about walking in on… that. Or it could be that you're kneeling next to me in nothing but a towel."

"I'm wearing underwear…" he says as he secures the towel.

"Look, I don't know who you are. Yet you keep butting in on conversations that have nothing to do with you. You seem to show plenty of interest in my son, but you haven't asked much about me. You keep touching me and getting in my space. Even though you've promised to honor the bubble, you keep breaking that promise. Though you seem to be in Stacy's space all the same, so maybe you're just a touchy-feely guy. Either way, you make me uncomfortable." She stares angrily at the blank pages of the book.

"I'm sorry," Killian says.

Violet shakes her head incredulously as she flips the pages in the book. "You know, Alan told me that you and your father built this shelter when you were young. I know for a fact that Jack was the one who built this shelter. He doesn't have any children. There was a young man that Jack took in and he helped with this place."

"Is that so?" Killian smirks.

"It *is* so." She holds up the book, open to the page of the glowing tree. Killian smiles and covers his mouth with his hand. Violet glowers at him. "I also know that boy was close and important to me." She turns to the drawing of her sleeping in bed. "I don't remember him," she says through clenched teeth as her eyes glaze over. "But if you were him, you would've told me." Killian starts to say something but she cuts him off. "Did you kill him?"

Killian pulls the chair she sits in away from the desk and turns her to face him. "I know this must be very confusing for you, but I assure you I have not killed that man."

Violet, becoming uncomfortable, folds her arms over her chest and stares at the only exit. "Then where is he? How did you find this place?" Fighting through the pain, she looks him in the eye. Killian reaches his hand out to touch her face. "What happened to respecting my personal space?" Violet says breathlessly.

"I can't help it when you cry."

"Where is he?" Violet asks desperately. Though she doesn't want him to touch her, her limbs feel weak as the pressure in her head builds.

"He's right here."

"You're lying!" she cries.

"I'm not lying." Killian tucks a lock of hair behind her ear.

"Please stop…" she says as tears spill from her eyes. The pounding in her head has her swimming, but she can't look away from Killian's abysmal eyes. "Alan told me about your past. You were married, you got drafted, she tried to kill herself."

"You and I were never officially married. Someday you'll remember things. I'll help you in any way I can."

Killian lifts his hand to wipe her tears. She catches his wrist. "So, you lied to Alan and Stacy? How can I trust anything you're saying?"

"You've always been stubborn." Killian laughs off his frustration.

"You don't know me," Violet growls.

"I know you better than you know yourself right now."

"I can't do this." Violet stands, though her legs feel like jelly, shoving the chair backwards.

"You can trust me, Vi," Killian says as he gets to his feet. "You can trust me."

In the mess hall music is still playing. The song changes to a familiar tune. Her breaths quicken.

I know you have to leave me
It's only for the best
I beg you to be careful
Now's not the time to jest

I watch you turn away and
You walk on out the door

134

I'm holding my chest tight
As I crumble to the floor

"Turn it off!" she gasps. Killian doesn't understand as she clasps her hands over her ears.

Now here I am waiting for your return
But it's been so long, I beg, remember me
When the sun's shining
When the rain falls and soaks in
Remember me
When you lie awake
When it aches, when your heart aches so

The song plays on. *You can trust me.* The words resound in her head over and over. She sees the Dark Sea, the dock. She is running and jumps off the dock into the water. Hiding underneath, holding onto the barnacle-covered pillar. Behind her a boy surfaces from underneath the water. He looks concerned and touches her swollen lip. It stings. Violet shivers against the pillar, frozen in fear. "I can help you. You can trust me. My name is Killian." The name resounds in her head like an echo of her own voice speaking, laughing, whispering, crying, screaming his name. His face flashes in front of her with so many different expressions, from when he was younger to an adult.

The name screams in her head again, and now she is laying in the sand in Safe Haven. She can't breathe. On top of her is her father, his face bright red and scrunched like an angry dog. His hands are wrapped tightly around her throat. So much pressure in her skull, it feels as though her eyes will burst out of her head. Just as everything is going black, the hands disappear. For a second, she forgets how to breathe. Then, she is gasping for air, choking on her swollen esophagus. The weight of him is lifted.

Rolling over, she pushes herself up. Looking around, Killian is on top of her father with a bloodied jagged rock. His face and clothes are covered in blood. He screams as his rock comes down again and again. Henry's limbs twitch. As his rock rises again, she reaches him and he is frozen. He is breathing heavily and crying.

She pries the rock from his fingers. "Killian," she rasps, "You killed him."

She holds his bloodied face in her hands and his eyes begin to focus on her. "I thought you were dead." His voice breaks. "Vi, I killed him?!"

"It's okay. You saved me, it's okay." Her eyes begin to blur. He reaches up to touch the red marks around her neck, smearing blood. His hands begin to shake and tears begin to spill from his eyes again. Sirens wail in the distance. "Killian, you have to go. Run!"

"I can't leave you! They'll think you did it, Vi! I can't let them send you away!"

"If you don't go, they'll send *you* away! They won't send me because I'm—"

"No, I have to stay with you!" His lips crash into hers.

She tries to pull away. "No! No! Leave! Everything will be okay if you leave now!!" She staggers to her feet, pulling him up with her. "Leave, you idiot!!!"

He starts to run just as Charlie collides with him. The suits pull out onto the path. It is too late. She tries to pry Charlie off Killian, but it is no use. The suits take over and they quickly drag him into the vehicle. She starts after them, screaming, "No! It was me! I killed him!!!" Charlie denies her involvement, claiming her a victim. "Leave him alone!" she yells. Killian turns, staring at her out the window with a weak smile. *I love you*, he says. She screams and fights Charlie to get to him as they pull away.

More and more memories flood her mind until everything goes black.

CHAPTER
10

"Vi? Violet, can you hear me?" Killian waves his hand in front her as she stares blankly. Her body goes limp and he catches her before she hits the ground. Her eyes slowly roll to the back of her head as she starts to convulse. "Alan!" Blood starts to drip from her nose. "Alan!" Killian screams desperately. "Violet, come on!"

Alan throws the door open. Killian holds her tightly to his body. Her limbs go limp once more. Lifting her up and carrying her out of the room, Alan is at his heels, checking her pulse. "She isn't breathing," Killian says, terror coating his voice. Laying her down on the table in the infirmary, she gasps and some color comes back to her face. Alan brushes Killian aside as he scans her. She coughs and gasps for more air. "Violet, can you hear me?" Alan asks. No response. "Look at her brain activity." Alan is panicked. The screen is showing colors fluctuate and expand in her brain in a strange way.

"Do something!" Killian yells, but Alan doesn't know what to do. He can only watch as her body writhes. He dabs at the blood spilling from both nostrils.

A scream escapes from her chest as she arches her back. Her eyes open and she covers her ears. "Make it stop," she yells.

"Make what stop? I can't help you unless you tell me," Alan says.

"The music!" They become quiet, listening. In the mess hall a song is playing.

I come home from the work day
Relax and have a soak
I eat alone and start to cry
Because my heart has broke

And here I am waiting for your return
But it's been so long, I beg, remember me
When the sun's shining
When the rain falls and soaks in
Remember me
When you lie awake
When it aches, when your heart aches so

Clara is already at the player, switching off the music. When the music is interrupted, Violet is curled into a ball, shaking. Killian wraps his arms around her, trying to soothe her. Her hands are still clasped over her ears.

"What just happened?" Alan asks.

Clara comes in to check on Violet. "This happened before with the same song. She didn't have this severe of a reaction, though. I thought she just hated the song."

Violet groans as the pain begins to subside. Alan holds the towel up to her nose. Her hands shake as she reaches out to hold it herself, and Alan continues helping. Killian stomps out of the room to find Jack in the easy chair, waiting impatiently and biting his cuticles. Killian briskly crosses the room, grabbing hold of his tattered shirt, leaning in close. "When you wiped her memory, did you have music playing in the background?" Jack looks apologetic.

He rubs his hand over his face and nods. "Did you know this would happen!?"

Jack nods again. "A fail-safe. If we needed the memories to come back, the song would trigger them."

"Did you know it would cause her pain?!" Killian yells.

"I didn't think it would cause damage if the memories would return."

"You brainwashed her! It might not have even recovered her memories. It may have even done more damage. Whether she agreed to it or not, it was wrong!" Killian spits disappointedly. Jack silently nods, tears filling his eyes.

Killian pushes himself away from Jack and walks back towards the infirmary. Stacy catches his eye. She is still clearing the rooms of cameras. She makes eye contact with him and smiles sympathetically. He ignores it, continuing on to Violet and lingering in her doorway. The bleeding has stopped and beads of sweat are making her hair stick to her face. Alan is asking her questions while petting her hair back. *Do you still feel pain? Do you know what happened? What's your name? Do you know where you are?* She answers without hesitation in short shaky breaths. Alan assures Killian and Clara she will be alright, and prescribes her rest. She still avoids looking at Killian, tears soaking her cheeks. He watches Clara as she takes a wet cloth and wipes away her tears and sweat.

Violet refuses to sleep, afraid of the memories or nightmares that might linger behind closed eyes. Alan gives her a sedative while Killian is getting dressed. It doesn't take long before she is out cold. Killian touches Clara's shoulder when he returns. She hands him the cloth hesitantly with a timid smile. He sits on the stool next to the bed and watches her chest rise and fall with each breath. He combs his fingers through her damp hair and kisses her pale lips.

He watches her as she sleeps, brushing his fingertips across her soft, pale skin. Alan scans her again, checking her brain activity. "Look at this," he says, pointing to the screen. "It was like her brain was destroying and healing itself at the same time. Now there's normal activity. If it were anyone else, they'd be dead. The mutation in her blood saved her life." Killian pats Alan on the back and returns to Violet's side.

"Can you watch her for a bit?" Killian asks, Alan agrees. "Thank you." Alan knows he is thanking him for more than just watching over Violet.

Killian searches for Stacy and finds her in the game room through the bar. He crosses the room quickly. Stacy slides under the pool table with her feet sticking out. He looks back down the hall before closing the door and shoving a heavy chair against it. He crosses the room and barricades the other exit. Wrapping his hands around her ankles, he drags her out from under the table. "Can I help you?" she chuckles.

"I have questions."

Stacy holds her finger to her lips and wriggles back under the table. There is a sizzle and the aroma of burning plastic fills the air. "All clear. That was the last one, I believe."

He drags her back out by the ankles, this time with more force. Before she can react, he is on top of her, with one hand about her mouth and the other holding a blade against her aorta. His knees ground her arms to the floor. The pressure is cutting off her circulation. His eyes are cold and sweat beads his forehead. "You're going to tell me everything you know. I helped build this place. We never installed equipment like this. Yet you knew to destroy them. You've been acting suspicious all day." He removes his hand from her mouth.

"I don't know what to tell you. I found these things by chance. I knew it wasn't your doing."

"Why did you think you should take care of it without informing me?"

"I didn't want to burden y—" The blade cuts her off as she feels it break the skin. She squeals.

"Tell me what you know."

"If I tell you, they'll kill you."

"They…" Killian waits for her to answer.

"I refuse to put your life in danger."

"You'd rather lose your own?" Killian digs in deeper and a drip of blood slides down the side of her neck.

"There's the ruthless man I know." Stacy smiles. "I'm not who you think I am."

"A spoiled brat who's used to getting her way?" Killian strikes a nerve and she frowns, pursing her lips. "Someone who knew nothing on how to navigate, fend for herself, *survive.*"

"You didn't have to help me."

"I was brought up to help the weak."

"I wasn't. I was brought up to exploit the weak and control people. To tell people what they need and how to live. I was brought up to teach people that they're expendable unless proven otherwise."

"Who are you?"

"Stacy Nox, from the Stratos Development, Station 6." Killian stares at her blankly and she smiles. "You people have no idea." The blade is pressed deeper and she gasps. "I am Stacy Nox, heir to the Nox Company. Basically, royalty to you. The fallen city you all are afraid of is protected. Any unauthorized personnel are executed upon entry. The constant storm is there in order to keep the precious station out of sight from the bottom dwellers. Each station is occupied by the geniuses, the politicians, and their workers. Living on the station is a privilege."

"If this is true, then why are you on the ground with us bottom dwellers, *your majesty*?"

"I was tired of watching innocent people be destroyed. Watching your people kill each other for nothing. They started the program over a century ago, originally to reduce overpopulation. Now it's used to keep bottom dwellers from becoming a threat. We could have ended the program years ago, lived on Earth comfortably and rebuilt a civilized society, but it continues while the higher powers live in pampered comfort. I came down to show them that bottom dwellers are human like the rest of us, and should be treated with more respect. But I was an idiot. My plan to throw it in their face failed. My father's been filtering the surveillance footage so that no one would see royalty reminiscing with the bottom dwellers. It's all for naught," she says, looking up angrily.

"This is ridiculous."

"You don't believe me." She smiles. "Unfortunately, my father has been manipulating the system this whole time. In six days, he plans on sending an extraction team. He wants me back under his precious control. He wants me to take over his stupid company so he can retire. He knows about us as well, and isn't happy about it. That's how I knew about the cameras; he's been watching us the entire time." She giggles. "I wish I could've seen his face when he saw his precious daughter being defiled by a bottom dweller," she says with a sneer.

Killian becomes silent. He climbs off her and sits cross-legged. Stacy rubs at her arms as the blood rushes back into circulation. Blood still drips down her neck as she sits up and leans against the legs of the pool table. Killian still holds the bloody knife in his fist. He flips it and holds the blunt end to his lips as he thinks. Stacy watches him curiously as she sees the cogs moving in his mind.

He blinks up at her and stares. "Your Father is sending an extraction team, so he knows where you are. You spoke to him from the fallen city. How?"

"I found a communicator sewn into a hidden pocket in my bag."

Killian climbs to his feet and pulls her up by her shirt. Holding her arm tightly, he drags her to the door, kicking the chair out of the way. Hiding the knife against his leg, he keeps her in front of him. Though he's drawing attention to them, he ignores everyone as he moves quickly through the halls. Shoving her into her room, he slams the door shut behind him. "Show me."

She quickly slides under her bed, retrieving the sack, and pulls out the communicator. Handing it over to him, he looks at her incredulously. Seeing the shattered screen, he looks for a way to turn it on. Stacy places her hands over his. "It isn't broken, but if you turn it on and they see you, they'll know I told you. I won't be able to protect you then, or anyone else here for that matter."

Killian wipes the blood from his blade on his pants before folding it into his pocket. He plops onto Stacy's mattress, ignoring the lumpy disarray of the covers. He holds his head in his hands and rubs his palms into his eyes. Stacy puts the communicator in her back pocket. Crouching down, she sits at his feet and wraps her hand just above his knee. "It'll be okay."

Killian folds his hands into each other and watches her for a moment. "What position does your father hold in your society?" Stacy cocks her head. "Is he the leader of the station?"

"There's the magister, Bellamy Sinai, and then his subordinates. My father's one of those subordinates. Why do you ask?"

"If you want people to be treated equally, you should take your father's place and be that influence."

"No one would agree with me. It would change their way of life too much."

"How can you say that when you're standing here with me? If you want change, others do as well."

"You can't become a subordinate just by inheriting your father's company. You need the people to look up to you and vote. Also, you don't retire from subordination; you have to be voted out or die."

"Why are you wasting your time here with the bottom dwellers, when you could be making a difference where it matters?"

"I can't do it on my own. I have no influence."

"Have you even tried? Or have you just been throwing tantrums and running away from home to prove your point? Go back to your station. Fight for us. Otherwise you're no better than them." Killian brushes her hands off and walks out of the room. The door slides shut behind him.

Alan is waiting for him in the hallway. Killian sighs and pretends not to see him as he walks down the hallway, but Alan grabs hold of Killian's arm, pulling him back. "What happened to your good mood, man? I don't know what's going on between you two, and frankly I don't want to know, but you're losing yourself, Killian. If you don't straighten up, you'll lose everything."

Killian nods and starts to move past him, but Alan steps into his path again, holding one hand out. "The knife." Alan waits as Killian contemplates. Finally, he hands it over and brushes past him.

Killian returns to the infirmary to find Clara sitting with Violet, reading a book. Standing in the hallway, he looks around and his eyes meet with Jack's. Shaking his head, Killian hides himself away in the atrium. Nathan, Lilly and Ember sit quietly under a tree, twining flowers together. They chatter and giggle as he prunes and picks ripe fruit and vegetables. The sound of their laughter lightens his mood, and soon he's smiling along with them as he works the soil. After rinsing his harvest, he sits under the tree with them, eating a bowl of raspberries and strawberries. Delighted, they all share in eating the juicy treats.

Evening comes and Alan calls everyone to dinner. The table is unusually quiet, with little chatter between the children. Violet is still shut away in the infirmary. Sitting next to Nathan, Killian watches him curiously as he holds Lilly's hand under the table. He tries to hide his smile without success. Jack keeps his eyes low during dinner and eats very little, before retiring to the room Killian set up for him and Clara.

"We should leave tomorrow to investigate that government building," Killian says.

"Everyone agreed we should wait," Alan says without looking up from his plate.

"Stacy has found and removed some equipment installed in this shelter that wasn't put there by any of us. Someone knows we're here. We need to find out who that is and what kind of threat they are to us. We don't know how long they've been watching us." Stacy looks up at Killian. He moves his food around his plate before taking a bite.

"We don't even know if Violet will be functional tomorrow," Alan says.

"She isn't coming. Vi can tell us how to get there or show us on a map," he says, taking a gulp of water. He makes eye contact with Stacy as she rubs at the bandage on her neck. Alan glances at Stacy, knowing he's missing information. The table goes quiet again. Killian wipes his mouth and stands up. He makes another plate of food and excuses himself. They watch him as he heads back to the infirmary with both plates of food.

Stacy finishes quickly, leaving Alan with the children and the cleaning-up. He sighs and starts collecting dishes. Ember, feeling uneasy, helps clear the table. He pats her on the head when she offers to help him with the dishes, while the others get ready for bed.

* * *

Killian closes the door behind him. Violet has turned to her side, with her back to the door. He sets the plate down on the side table and sits on the stool at her bedside. Leaning his elbows on the edge of her bed, he holds his head up at his chin, watching her body move with each breath. "Are you awake?" He waits for her to say something or move. Her breaths are shallower than when he left. "I brought you dinner. Alan made it, so it's a little over-seasoned."

He waits again for some response, then leans back and rubs his eyes before pulling his fingers through his hair. "I'm sorry you've been through so much. It was all my fault. If I hadn't... I have a lot of regrets. If your memories come back, I hope you can forgive me for what I've done, and for leaving you when you needed me most..." He bites his lip as tears overflow, and shakes his head. "Our son is beautiful." His laugh turns into a sob.

Pulling himself together, he takes a deep breath. "I messed up, Violet. There was a time I had given up on us. In a moment of weakness I... I messed up. You'll probably hate me for it." He sighs and looks up at the ceiling. "I've become another person, Vi. I don't feel like myself anymore. I've hurt so many people. Now that I have you back, I feel like I can be myself again. I need you, Vi." His shoulders crumple as he weeps into his hands.

Violet is holding her breath now. She can hear the hatred in his voice when he speaks about himself. Her throat tightens. When she hears him breaking down, she can't hold back the tears. With all her memories back, she recalls the mistakes she has made herself. She is just as guilty as Killian. Turning over, she sits up slowly, crossing her legs.

He wipes the tears from his eyes and tries to look indifferent. He takes a deep breath. "Sorry if I woke you." Killian stares at his hands, laughing nervously but the smile doesn't reach his eyes.

Violet grasps his hand, still avoiding his face. "I've also done things I regret. You have nothing to be ashamed of."

"You can't say that until you know the truth."

146

Taking a chance, she braces herself for more pain when she looks up at him. A sigh of relief; she's able to look him over without the jackhammer bashing into her skull. "If you can look past my faults, then I can look past yours." With her thumb, she wipes at the tears still spilling from his eyes.

He looks up at her and, seeing the tears in her eyes, he feels his heart tearing. "Are you in pain?" Killian asks, the fear reflecting in his face. Violet shakes her head and draws her face closer. He stares into her glistening blue eyes, holding his breath. Her gentle lips meet his. "Vi?" he asks when he takes a breath. Her eyes are closed when she pulls back. Opening her eyes, there is a slight smile on her lips. Fresh tears fall and he sees the woman he fell in love with. Wrapping his arms around her, he grasps at her skin as if she will disappear. "Violet, my beautiful Violet," he croons as he threads his fingers into her hair and kisses her as if it is his last.

Managing to wrap her arms around his neck, he lifts her off the table. She wraps her legs around him. Killian breathes in, consumed by their love for each other. As their kiss deepens, regret and guilt is erased. Killian sets her back onto the table as they impatiently start to pull at each other's clothing. "I'll never leave you again," Killian says breathlessly against her chest. "Never again." Articles of clothing are thrown about the room as they embrace intimately.

CHAPTER

11

Violet wakes early in the morning. Killian's left arm is draped over her. Letting out a sigh, she reminisces in her memories, thankful to know the truth. She had been lost for so long. Finally having these memories back proves she wasn't losing her mind, chasing after nothing. Though, with the good comes the bad. Remembering the mistakes she has made brings a new feeling to the surface. Her stomach aches with anxiety. Reluctantly she leaves the warmth of his body.

She makes a feast for breakfast—eggs, potatoes, flapjacks smothered in jelly, sliced fruit, and salted pork belly fried to a crisp. She has the table set before anyone rises. Not wanting to wake anyone, she sneaks into the bunk room. Peeking in, she sees Alan twitching with a quiet snore. Nathan sleeps on his stomach in the next bunk, with his arm dangling off the edge of the mattress. Quietly, she tiptoes into the shower room. Though they have been there for a few days now, her hygiene has been lacking, and Killian and Stacy are partly to blame for that. Heat rises in her chest as she recalls their embrace in the shower.

Once in the room, she looks to lock the door, but it's a simple knob, no locks of any kind. Violet strips down and peels off the few remaining bandages from her body. She turns on the closest showerhead and it shoots out ice cold water. The sudden freezing blast forces a squeal out of her. She quickly covers her mouth, hoping not to have woken anyone. Occasionally testing the water with her hand, it finally begins to heat up. After unraveling her braided hair, she ducks under the hot water and is covered in fresh goosebumps. Steam starts to fill the room. Grabbing a spritz from the soap dispenser, she quickly washes her hair and body. Her hair is down past her hips as the curls loosen. She sits under the faucet as it massages her scalp and her newly formed pink scars. Killian had helped remove the stitches earlier that evening. Dried blood and grime swirl down the drain at the center of the room.

The hot water is so refreshing and comforting. Examining her body, she notices there are a lot less visible veins. Though there are still a few left, she's looking much less alien than before. Unable to wash away her anxiety, her mistakes are still fresh in her mind. Like Killian, she has her own regrets. Killian... his regrets... how many people has he hurt? Is Stacy one of those regrets? Her chest feels hot at the thought of them together. She bites her lip, trying to remove the sting of jealousy invading her heart. Squeezing her eyes closed, she lets the showerhead dump water over her face.

The shower next to her sends a blast of cool air towards her, as the water rushes to the floor. Sending goosebumps across her body, she gasps. Violet covers herself as she opens her eyes. Killian is soaking his head, facing the wall, all the muscles in his body contracting as he rubs his hands over his face in the water. Killian peeks out of the corner of his eye. Her skin flushes and her heart begins to pound against her chest. "I woke up and you were gone..." Killian says to the wall. He is tense with worry.

Violet moves in close, wrapping her arms around his waist. "I remember... everything," she responds. Killian's muscles relax and his smile reaches his eyes. His hands reach up to cradle her face, and his fingertips reach around to the nape of her neck. Chills run down her spine. He kisses her, but unlike last night it is gentle and calm.

"Aww, isn't that sweet. Someone must be feeling better." Stacy stands in the doorway with a nasty smile on her face, arms folded. Violet pulls Killian's hands down and they separate. "Yeah, let's not defile the showers," she jeers. "Other people need to use them as well."

"You're one to talk," Violet says. The memory of Killian and Stacy embracing in this room makes her stomach tighten, and she clenches her fists. She openly walks in front of Stacy to grab a towel. Stacy's smile slowly slides from her face into a grimace as Violet wraps herself up. Killian watches Violet dolefully. "Excuse me," Violet says politely. Stacy steps out of the doorway and Violet briskly walks out. Killian washes quickly, ignoring Stacy as she undresses.

As Violet passes the mess hall, she sees that Lilly and Ember are already helping themselves to breakfast. Her feet leave wet prints as she walks across the cold cement to the bunk her sack sits upon. Distracted by her emotions, she dries off, drops her towel, and starts to get dressed. Alan, waking up on his stomach, is shocked to see the bare backside of Violet as she pulls up her drawers. Thick veins down her spine are as dark as tattoos. He is mesmerized as she pulls on tight leather pants. She throws a pink lace tunic over head as she turns to walk out. She stops, seeing Alan with his jaw hanging. "Oh, I'm sorry, Alan," she says. "I forgot you were there."

"What? Oh... no, it's cool. I mean, sorry... I wasn't expec... that is, that lightning tattoo on your back is pretty sweet."

"I don't have a tattoo, Alan." Violet smiles.

"Well, still... Neat," he says, throwing a thumbs-up.

Violet brushes off his fumbling. "I made breakfast. Are you coming?"

"Yah, for sure." He starts to get up. "You know what? I'll meet you out there."

"Okay," Violet laughs, walking out.

Stacy, though she doesn't usually eat breakfast, sits down across from Killian, who is seated between Nathan and Violet. She complains that the eggs are cold and the flapjacks are too sweet. Alan wraps the pork belly into the pancake and eats it. Nathan sits there giggling and follows suit. Manners were always important in Jack's home, though now he just sits quietly, not paying much attention to those around him. As Violet begins to eat, Jack looks over with glossy eyes. Seeing the look of grief on his face, she leans over the table, patting his hand. He flips his hand and squeezes hers. Killian watches them from under a furrowed brow. Violet catches his eye. Though her lungs feel heavy when their eyes meet, she feels the cold breath of jealousy lingering. Breaking away from his gaze, the blood leaves her face. She tries to eat, but loses her appetite before finishing her plate. Reminding herself of her own unfaithfulness, she buries the ache in her heart.

After several seductive glances from Stacy in Killian's direction, Violet excuses herself to the library. Admiring the art on the walls, she stops at one she can't take her eyes from, depicting a lighthouse at night next to rough waters. The moon shines through the clouds onto the water, and a ship in the distance careens, and someone in the water watches it gain distance. Something about it strikes a nerve. Taking a deep breath, she tries to hold back her tears. Attempting to distract herself, she walks among the shelves, looking at the titles of the many books they have stored.

She hears the door open and someone walking quietly. Looking over her shoulder, she sees Killian with a sheepish smile. Violet smiles in return and looks back at the books. Coming to stand behind her, he wraps his arms around her shoulders and kisses the top of her head. She closes her eyes and revels in his embrace for a moment.

"I need your help, my love," Killian says in a low voice. Violet turns, letting his arms fall to her waist. She smiles, happy for the distraction from her own mind. "I need you to tell me where that building is. The one with the control room." Her smile falls.

"Why?" Violet asks.

Killian laughs. His smile is warm and his laughter melts her heart. "I want to take a look. Whatever information it may hold would help us a great deal."

"When do you want to leave?" Violet shifts awkwardly.

"I'll leave as soon as you tell me."

"I'll be with you, so I'll be your map." She smiles.

"I know you want to help, but I think it'd be better if you stayed here. Nathan needs you here."

"If there are still maven roaming that building, *you* need me."

"We'll be fine. I don't want to lose you. You barely escaped your last maven attack."

"Killian." Violet pulls away, pushing his arms to his sides. "Taking your girlfriend along for the ride again and leaving me behind is not in your best interest." She walks past him.

"Violet," he says with a sigh. He follows her as she walks quickly through the mess hall. Stacy is sitting upon the cleared table with one leg propped up on the bench. She is waiting impatiently. Alan is sitting on a stool next to her, and they watch as Killian follows her into the bunk room. Stacy scoffs, and Alan can't help but snicker along with her as Killian glares at his audience.

Violet is lacing up her boots when Killian comes through the door. Leaning against the doorframe, he holds his arm out, bracing himself. "Violet. I don't want you to come."

"I really don't care," Violet says as she throws on a frock. She walks up to him and waits for him to move out of the way. "Let's go," she says, shooing him with her hands. Killian rolls his eyes and shakes his head. Violet, becoming impatient, shoves him.

Though Killian had been bracing for impact, he underestimated her strength. Falling into the hallway, Violet walks past him as she pulls on her gloves. Killian, cursing himself, gets back on his feet quickly, but Alan is already bursting with laughter. Even Stacy can't hide her grin.

Violet, making her way to the cargo bay, signals Alan to follow. He jumps to his feet but gets a glare from Killian that has him tilting back on his heels and back in his seat. Stacy smiles, looking at her nails. "Stubborn as always!" Killian complains as he catches the door after Violet.

"Killian, nothing will change my mind. I need to go back."

"Why do *you* need to go back?"

Violet almost blurts out her reason, but the words don't come out. She stands there with her mouth open for a moment.

"Mama?" Nathan comes out from behind a crate.

"Nathan? What are you doing out here?" Violet chides.

"Playing hide and seek."

"You can't play out here. What if something fell on you, or you fell into the water?"

Nathan's eyes are glossy and his cheeks are bright red. "Mama... I don't feel good."

Violet drops to her knees next to him and holds her inner wrist to his forehead. "He's hot," she says, looking up at Killian. Nathan wraps his arms around her neck as she picks him up. Killian follows her back in. Feeling Nathan's forehead himself, he holds his hand to his son's burning cheek.

Bringing him into the infirmary, Violet lays him down on a bed. Killian covers him in blankets and takes his temperature. Wetting a cloth, Violet rests it upon his forehead. The thermometer beeps. "100.3 degrees," Killian says, relieved. "It's high, but he's not in real danger. We need to keep an eye on him. We don't want it to get much higher. Make sure he's drinking enough liquid." Violet nods as she removes her frock. Noticing that Nathan is watching him, Killian smiles kindly. "Try to sleep as much as you can, okay?" He pats Nathan's foot and he nods.

Killian opens the door to leave. Stacy is waiting with arms folded. "Did you get the location yet? We're wasting time." Violet watches Killian's shoulders slump as he closes the door behind him. He says something in a low voice but the door muffles his words.

"What can I do?" Violet asks Nathan as she lays her head down next to his on the pillow. Nathan reaches his hand out and strokes her cheek. Violet smiles and climbs into the bed with him. She wraps her arm around him and combs her fingers through his soft brown hair. Soon enough he falls asleep. Watching him quietly sleeping, he looks so serene. Though now with the calm sound of his breathing, there's nothing to distract her from her own mind. Her chest is heavy with thoughts of Killian, his hypnotic brown eyes and beautiful smile. Lurking in the back of her mind is lingering guilt. She holds tight to her little boy.

Violet, half asleep, realizes she is dreaming; though not really dreaming, but reviewing her memories. She cringes when the bomb explodes and the ceiling comes down onto her. The door creaks open. She opens her eyes. Nathan is still sleeping, but his hair is damp and sticking to his forehead. She hears someone quietly coming closer. A hand touches her shoulder and grazes her arm down to her fingers, sending goosebumps up her spine.

She turns and sees Killian, looking so serious at first. Looking into her eyes, a smile lightens his expression. "Lunch is ready. Go take a break and I'll stay with him." Violet looks back at Nathan. She wants to stay, but her stomach protests with a loud gurgle. "You didn't eat much for breakfast. Go. I'll let you know if he wakes up." He sets his mug down on the table to help her up. Violet removes the towel from Nathan's forehead and kisses him. Still too warm. She hands Killian the compress and slowly moves towards the door. Killian goes to the sink, rewetting the towel before returning it to Nathan's forehead. Seeing them together makes her heart ache and her throat tighten. She never thought she would see them together like this.

Violet washes her hands in the kitchen before sitting at the table. Sandwiches were made with a warm broth for dipping. "Where do you get the meat?" she asks Alan as he stuffs his face full of bread and meat.

"Hunting," he manages to get out.

"So, it's not beef?"

Alan shakes his head, "Deer."

Violet pushes out her bottom lip. "Poor deer," Violet sympathizes. Stacy snorts. Violet dips the sandwich and takes a bite. She doesn't hold back the moan. "This is really good."

"Killian made it." Alan smiles. Violet smiles in return, glancing over her shoulder towards the infirmary. "Nathan is sick?" he asks. Violet nods. "It's probably just a cold," he says, trying to comfort her.

"It's the first time I've had to take care of him while he's sick. I feel helpless and paranoid."

"Killian's broth will make him feel better." Alan winks.

"It's not fair that you're keeping him here when he has things to do," Stacy mutters. "Why don't you give him the location of that building so we can stop wasting time?"

"He wants me to stay here. If I give it to you, he'll just trick me into staying."

"Your trust in him astounds me."

"I know him better than you do. He'll do whatever he thinks is best to keep me safe. What he needs to get through his thick skull is that I don't need his protection."

"Well, we don't have time to wait for your spawn to feel better. You need to decide what's more important," Stacy says while picking up her empty plate. Violet watches her as she rinses her dishes in the kitchen. Stacy's eyes shift about constantly. The others don't cut into the conversation. As Stacy comes out of the kitchen, she hesitates before deciding to sit at the bar.

Everyone seems to be in a rush to find this place. "What is the hurry?" Violet asks. Stacy ignores her. Reluctantly she leaves her sandwich to stand beside Stacy's stool. "I *said*, what's your hurry?"

Stacy rolls her eyes and stares blankly into Violet's. "People die every day because of this war thing. Waiting means losing more lives. There might be information there that can help everyone. Help with the cyborgs, help with the maven..."

Violet watches Stacy. There is truth in what she says. There is definitely information in that database that could help a lot of people, such as where the fleets are coming from. Angry with her own selfishness, being exposed by someone like Stacy hurts her pride. She quickly moves to the library. Searching the shelves carefully, she finds an atlas. Flipping through maps, she finds the one she needs. Grabbing a pen from the desk in the corner, she marks the location, and adds instructions on how to enter. Returning to Stacy's side, she slams the atlas onto the countertop and the ice in her glass clamors. "Here's your map. I need you to do something for me in return."

"What's that?" Stacy glares at her.

Violet doesn't look her in the eye. "Search the building. If you find a body, a human body... or what's left of one, bury him for me." Violet walks past her.

"What the hell?" Stacy watches Violet as she returns to her seat.

Violet returns to her food, but it has gone cold. She eats in silence as she watches Stacy sip at her drink. When Violet finishes, she returns to the infirmary. Glancing through the porthole in the door, she sees Nathan is awake. Killian is helping him sip broth from the mug he brought in. Nathan's hands are shaking as he lifts it to his mouth and gulps it down. Killian tries to slow him down without success. He sets the empty cup on the table and grabs a jar. Lifting the blankets, he pulls one of his feet out. Pulling his sock off, he massages some cream into the sole. When finished with both feet, he returns his socks and rubs some on Nathan's chest as well. Nathan gives a weak smile. Killian starts to get up, but Nathan reaches out, his arms open wide. Killian sinks onto the bed, wrapping Nathan into his chest. Violet opens the door slightly to hear what they are saying.

"I will always be here for you," Killian says gently. "And your mom." He pats Nathan on the back while rocking back and forth. "Get some more rest, okay?"

"Can I have more first?"

"Yes, of course," Killian laughs. Laying him back down, he tucks him in.

Violet pulls back, leaning against the wall. She wraps her arms around herself. Grabbing the cup, Killian turns and heads straight for the door. "Killian," she says. He stops with a gentle smile. "I gave Stacy the map. Do what you will with it."

Killian's smile turns sour, glancing down the hallway. "What made you change your mind?"

"Your girlfriend helped me get my priorities straight."

Killian looks down the hallway once more, his face twisting angrily. He steps closer to her, pressing her back flat against the wall. "She's not my girlfriend. We kissed once. It meant nothing."

Even before he finishes his sentence, the blood has already left Violet's face. She laughs. "It doesn't matter. You have what you need. You can go." She doesn't mean for it to come out in such a harsh tone, but she can feel herself losing control. She folds her arms tighter to her body and looks down the hallway, trying to fight back the loathing.

"I'm not going anywhere," Killian says. "It can wait. I need to take care of my family first." Violet looks into his eyes. His words seem sincere. Seeing the tears welling up in her eyes, he shakes his head. "Violet, it meant nothing," he says, leaning in closer.

"Then I feel sorry for her. Something tells me it meant something to her." She swallows the knot in her throat.

"I'm going to get more food for our son. We'll talk more later." Killian sweeps her elbow as he walks away from her. Not wanting to give anyone else a cause for concern, she squats to the floor, holding her face in her hands. *I have no right to be jealous.* Scrunching her hair in her fists, she takes deep breaths.

Killian returns with a full cup of steaming broth and a small sandwich. He walks past her into the room, letting the door swing closed behind him. Hearing their muffled conversation, she gets to her feet and watches them. Nathan is holding a photo out. Killian laughs and rubs his face, as if trying to hide his happiness. He nods. Nathan rests his hand on Killian's with a weak grin. Killian hands the picture back to Nathan and helps him with his broth.

With a heavy slap on her shoulder, Violet nearly jumps out of her skin. Her skin still stinging, she turns begrudgingly. Alan is peeking over her shoulder. "Who are you stalking? Or should I ask *why*?"

"I'm just keeping an eye on my son."

"You don't have to worry. You should've seen how giddy he was when he found out Nathan is his. He won't let anything happen to him."

"Was he happy about that? Or just happy to know he isn't Charlie's?"

"No. I've never seen his face light up like that."

Violet smiles and turns away to walk back to the mess hall. Alan walks alongside her with his hands in his pockets. He continues to follow her into the library. She sees him out of the corner of her eye. Alan watches her as she touches the titles of the many rows of books. "What do you want, Alan?"

"I want to know what's going on in that head of yours." He knocks a knuckle on the side of her skull.

"Nothing's going on."

"I beg to differ. Something's bothering you. I think you remembered something you don't want to share. Could it be something that would make you feel guilty? You can always tell me. I'm good at keeping secrets."

Violet turns to him. The look he sees has him rocking back on his heels. "Some things don't need to be spoken of. I told Stacy everything that needs to be said."

"If it's really important that you come along, we can wait. Without closure, it'll continue to eat away at your sanity. Killian is a good example of that... not that he's crazy or anything... I mean, he wouldn't hurt anyone he cares about... yeah, okay, I'm going to go now." He walks away hitting himself in the head. Violet starts to see a pattern with Alan when he gets flustered.

"Thanks, Alan," she says as he reaches the door. He turns and winks before closing the door behind him. Turning away from the books, she sits down on the lounge chair, curling into a ball and staring into space.

CHAPTER

12

Killian opens his eyes. The room is dark, but blue light from the shelves illuminates the apothecary bottles. Nathan is asleep on his chest. Killian presses his lips to Nathan's clammy forehead. The fever has gone down. He sighs with relief. He moves Nathan carefully to rest his head upon the pillow. Tucking the blankets around him, he brushes his cheek before leaving him. Where the metal and bone meet in Killian's shoulder, there is a dull ache, a sign the weather is getting cold and wet. He tries to stretch it out but knows it won't help.

The door creaks open and swings back into place. Little Lilly stands there with tears in her eyes and bright red cheeks. "Uh-oh," Killian says quietly. "You're not sick, are you?" Lilly nods, her curls bouncing. He picks her up gently and lays her in the same bed as Nathan, giving her a spoon full of the syrup he had given Nathan earlier. "You'll feel better soon," he assures her gently, rubbing her head. Bringing out the jar, he rubs ointment on her feet and chest as well. Tucking them in snuggly, he lets them rest. Lilly snuggles up to Nathan's back.

It's still very early as he quietly makes his way back into the bunk room. Violet is on her side. Carefully he crawls into the small bed with her. Her hair is draped over her eyes and her breathing is shallow. Carefully he brushes her hair from her face. Her brow flinches. "I know you're awake," he says, tucking his hands under the pillow. Violet's eyes open. "Did you sleep at all?"

"A little bit," she says, stretching her legs over his. "How's Nathan?"

"His fever broke, but Lilly came in with a fever just a bit ago. They're resting together."

"That's good. Poor Lilly." Violet shakes her head. "What was Nathan showing you yesterday?"

"A picture of you and I when we were young. He said he found it in Jack's ship after you came back."

"I was wondering where it went. What did you say?"

"I told him the truth. When I told him I was his real father, he hugged me a lot."

"That's good. That means he's happy." Killian's grin reaches ear to ear, and Violet can't help but smile with him. She reaches out and touches her palm to his cheek. Placing his hand on top of hers, he holds it tightly.

"When the kids are feeling better, you should come with us," Killian says. Violet stares into his eyes. "As long as you stay by my side. I don't want anything to happen to you."

"Thank you," Violet says, pulling him closer, pressing her lips to his.

Killian tucks his head in the crook of her neck. "Let's stay like this forever," he says, wrapping his arm more tightly around her body. Violet agrees, holding him tightly and tracing her fingers along his back. Before he knows it, he drifts off.

Waking up to an empty bed, he quickly gets dressed. Stacy is at the bar, finishing off her liquid breakfast. Jack, Clara and Ember sit at the table. They are already finished eating and are watching Alan and Violet play chess. Clara stands up and goes into the kitchen, then comes back with a plate of food for him. "Thank you," Killian says, taking a seat next to Violet.

"Checkmate," Violet says as she moves her piece with a smirk.

"That's not checkmate!" Alan laughs, then stares at the board more intensely, his smile turning into a frown. Jack bursts into laughter and groans as his ribs protest. "You cheated! She cheated!" Alan exclaims, pointing his finger in her face.

"Someone's being a sore loser," Killian says, looking down at his food with a smile.

Violet kisses Killian on the cheek. Stacy sighs in disgust. Violet gets up from the table to check on Lilly and Nathan. He watches her disappear behind the doors of the infirmary.

"What the heck just happened?" Alan grumbles, staring at the board, scratching his head. Ember takes Violet's place and smiles at Alan. "Now you, I can beat you. Let's do this," he says as he rearranges the board to start a new game.

Stacy walks into the kitchen, looking for a snack. She slams the refrigerator door. Killian looks up at her, catching her eye. She nods in the direction she starts walking. Killian sighs, continuing to eat his breakfast. Jack stands up as he sees Stacy walk into the library. He follows her but enters through the other door. Stacy is surprised to find the old man has come instead of Killian. He very seriously approaches her, leaning against the wall picking at her fingers. "Can I help you?" Stacy asks without looking up.

Jack stands before her with his arms folded. "I know who you are. You don't belong here and you need to leave." Stacy laughs. "Go home, you wretched girl," he growls.

"You don't know me, old man," she says in exasperation. "Go back to bed."

"Development Six, Nox Company. Your father or grandfather is Jacques Nox."

Stacy's eyes open wide. "I have business here. I'll leave when I'm finished."

"What business could you have with my family?" he spits out.

"The great thing about my business is that it's none of yours," Stacy says with a sneer.

Jack jets toward her. "I'll make it my business!" Frightened, she puts her arms up and backs away. Jack grabs her wrists as he babbles angrily about her people. Stacy's back slams into the wall.

Killian rinses his plate and thanks Clara again for breakfast. She smiles kindly. Walking towards the library, he hears a cry from Stacy and bursts through the door. Killian, in his entire life, has never seen Jack lose his temper. Seeing Jack yelling angrily at Stacy has him in shock.

Crossing the room in seconds, he pulls Jack away from her. Stacy begins laughing hysterically. Wheezing, Jack breathlessly holds onto the back of a chair. He stares at her wild-eyed. "I see now, wise man. You're afraid!" Stacy laughs. "Shame on you, Jack."

"What's going on here?" Killian asks.

"This is Jack Wiseman. Wise Man. Everyone thought he was dead because he's been hidden away for so long. Tell me, did you keep it secret so that Stratos Development wouldn't kill you? Or were you protecting yourself from your new family? I'm sure if they knew your role in all of this, they would've murdered you in cold blood. Wait... how old are you now? You have to be at least 130."

"Jack?" Killian waits for answers.

"Go on, Jack, tell him. You helped raise him, right? He can't be too angry with you." Laughter bubbles from her lips once more. Jack curses himself and grumbles under his breath, avoiding eye contact. "Oh, my lovely Killian. Jack made all of this possible. He created the bio-scouts, the airships, the guns, the bombs that destroyed your cities. He even had a helping hand in the construction of the maven. Technically he killed your parents.

Isn't that right, Jackie boy?" she says, patting Jack hard on the shoulder. "He must've felt guilty. So much blood on his hands."

"You're putting Killian's life in danger," Jack growls. "He knows too much."

"Killian already knows about me. He forced it out of me. Telling him about you is just a bonus."

"Jack, you've been lying to us all this time?" Killian asks. How can this man who has helped raise him have kept this secret from him?

"Anyone who knew the truth was killed. I kept my mouth shut to protect you and everyone else. I didn't lie. I just kept some details to myself." Jack was pleading with eyes, watching Killian taking it in.

Killian shook his head in disappointment. "You will tell the others," he says. Stacy begins to protest, threatening their safety. "They have a right to know, and then we'll never speak of this again, in this shelter or elsewhere. If they are truly watching us wherever we go, I don't want them to know what we're up to." Stacy tilts her head curiously. Before either of them can respond, he walks out.

* * *

Everyone is gathered in the library. Before speaking, Killian verifies the security of the room. Stacy reassures him that no foreign devices remain. Killian makes it clear that he is giving them information that can never leave the room. If anyone were to find out they know, it would mean their life. Clara asks Ember to check on the children, and stay there until someone comes for her. Killian looks around the room at their faces. Alan, Violet and Clara sit silently, waiting for him to go on. Stacy is staring at him, shaking her head. Jack leans against the wall with his arms folded.

Killian asks Jack to inform him of everything he knows. Jack grumbles as he stands before them. Taking a deep breath, he starts at the beginning in a low voice. "I was recruited by Stratos when I was 22." When he sees the confusion on their faces he sighs. "The Stratos Developments are cities in the sky, reserved for high society. They're hidden away from view by massive simulated storms. I was recruited to create a simpler life for those on Earth, as well as the developments. We were given freedom to create things as we saw fit. After years of projects, I found out they'd been mass-producing most of them without my consent. I was invited to stand as a council member for Magister Samuel Sinai. Little did I know our first meeting would be about the recent overpopulation situation.

"I was outvoted when they decided to start a civil war. They would create a reason for people to fight each other. I refused to be involved. I left the station and the war started soon after that. They turned my projects into weapons. The bio-scouts' genetic modification samples were turned into maven. They even provided certain cities with more advanced weaponry. Safe Haven was made to protect those who couldn't protect themselves."

Jack becomes silent and takes a seat in one of the easy chairs. Clara looks at him sympathetically, shaking her head. Killian watches Stacy playing with her fingers until she looks up and their eyes lock. He nods. She shakes her head vigorously, understanding what he wants her to do. His glare sends a chill down her spine. He moves to stand, and she quickly gets to her feet. "Okay, okay." She holds her hands out, indicating he should stay seated. She takes Jack's place, standing in front of them. "I'm one of those privileged to live in Development Six." They stare at her incredulously. "My father is John Nox, currently one of the council members for Magister Sinai. He currently possesses the company that controls the bio-scouts and security for the developments. When he dies, that responsibility goes to the most accomplished of their offspring. I'm the only child in my family, so my father's inheritance comes to me."

166

"If that's true, why are you here?" Alan asks, dumbfounded.

"I hate watching the bottom dwellers killing each other for no reason."

"You could have fooled me." Alan says under his breath.

"Over time the civil war was broadcast. At first it was made available to show why people shouldn't leave the developments. It was news. Progress. People kept asking for updates. They were waiting until it was safe to leave the developments and recolonize on Earth, but people have grown content with living in the sky and prefer to keep it hidden," she says nervously as their faces turn dark. "I came here to show them that you're real people and you shouldn't be treated like this, but my father has been keeping me off screen. He wants me to return and resume my responsibilities." Stacy makes eye contact with Killian. "I have three days left before they send an extraction team." She sits down as everyone watches her silently.

"Stacy has bargained with her father," Killian adds. "She was able to make a recruitment. She's asked me to help her from the inside, to bring an end to this war." Violet glares at Stacy. "I've declined. I'm not about to leave my family. Instead, I believe we can stop it from the outside, without giving away the fact that we know about them. If we can return to that government building, we might be able to learn more about the sky cities and the other threats among us."

"That building is fed what they want you to see," Stacy says.

"If they're capable of accessing our systems, then we can access theirs. Violet, you said someone was helping you access those files?" Violet nods. "With Stacy and Jack's knowledge of the developments, we might have a chance."

"You want to hack into the Development mainframe?" Stacy says. "If they catch us, they'll have you killed before you have the chance to tell a soul."

"What else can we do?"

"Come with me. You can help me stop this from the inside. Help me sway the people against this."

"Alan would also be capable of doing so," Killian adds. Alan raises a finger trying to interrupt.

"No offense," Stacy says, "but no one would take Alan seriously." Alan sits back, obviously offended for not being included in this discussion involving him. Violet pats his hand consolingly.

"From now on, this is not to be a topic of conversation. We don't know who or what may be listening. They've been in this shelter, and they may come again. We'll leave tomorrow to see about that building." Everyone nods in agreement.

Stacy, now angry, gets up with a huff and begins preparing for the trip. Clara and Jack leave to have their own private conversation. Alan seems lost in his own thoughts. Violet catches Killian's hand as he walks past her. She looks up at him intensely. He kneels down next to her. "What does she expect you to accomplish if you left with her?" she asks.

"Yeah, recruited for what?" Alan adds.

"I don't know. She won't go into detail. Stacy says she can't do it on her own, but I have a feeling she's hiding something."

"So, you want me to do it?" Alan asks in offense.

"No, I don't think it's safe. I feel like it's a trap."

"They're sending people to collect her. Is it safe keeping her around?"

Killian shrugs. He's conflicted, and Violet can see it weighing down his shoulders. "You're thinking about going, aren't you?" she says, interrupting his thoughts.

He looks into her eyes and she sees it's true. "I don't want to leave you, but I do want this war to end. If we're able to get enough information from this place, we can create a plan. Maybe then she won't need to recruit," Killian says hopefully. Violet's stomach turns at the thought of him leaving. Trying to suppress her anxiety, she puts it out of her mind, focusing on what they can do now.

Violet goes to relieve Ember. Lilly is asleep next to Nathan, as he pulls on her curls until they're straight. He finds entertainment in letting them loose and watching them bounce back into place. "Is everything alright?" Ember asks nervously.

Violet reassures her with a gentle hug. "You don't have to worry about a thing. Tomorrow we're going to search for a building that might help us. You guys will stay here with Jack and Clara." Ember doesn't question any further. Nathan looks sorrowful. Violet hates the idea of leaving him, but it's important that if her friend is alive, he cooperate without any casualties.

The first time they met comes to mind. *It is late in the evening, but the moon and stars are bright enough to light the empty roads. Crickets are chirping. The air is warm with a light breeze. Violet is searching an empty city on foot. Her footsteps are muffled by the wildlife taking over the grounds. The road is lined with empty shops that have been picked clean of any goods. Glass windows are shattered, and pieces litter the ground, crunching under her boots as she moves into the street. Farther into town the buildings become taller. A yellow light catches her eye in one of the taller buildings. Though it is far off, she lines up against the wall and moves stealthily like a cat.*

As she comes closer, she can see the building more clearly. It is at least five stories tall, the outside covered in glass windows. The light moves up two floors and stops. Violet waits and watches for movement from across the lot, hidden in the shadows. She crouches as she crosses the lot as quickly as possible. The large glass doors are propped open with a small rock, hardly noticeable until it drops as she pulls the heavy door. It opens up to a lobby. The furniture is blanketed with dust. On the left are two elevators, on the right a large staircase. Seeing as there is no electricity (or so she thinks), she climbs the stairs to the third floor. On this floor there are many desks sectioned off by four-foot walls. Nothing has been touched in many years. The floor is carpeted, but there is a noticeable path where the dust has lifted. She silently follows the path until she comes to an open door. Light from the room flicks across the floor. She carefully peeks around the corner. The wall of screens is playing a silent video feed. One of the screens displays a view from inside the building, and she is watching herself. No one is in the room. She steps past the door and on the desk in front of her is a gray hat and aviator goggles.

Violet takes a step toward the desk to look closer. Within a heartbeat, something sweeps her feet out from under her, and she finds herself laying on the floor. Gasping for breath, pain spreads across her back. Her wrists are held over her head with one large hand as someone sits on her hips. A large, cold blade is held to her throat. It all happens so quickly that she is stunned into capture. Inches away from her face, a man with Asian features stares into her eyes. The proximity and allure causes her to blush. She is speechless and incapable of movement. He seems to stare at her in bewilderment. When she feels his fingers digging into her wrists she closes her eyes, clenching her teeth, and flexes her hands, trying to let the circulation flow once more. When he sees the pain in her face, his hand loosens. When she opens her eyes, he has a blush of his own.

Violet's thoughts are interrupted by Killian shaking her shoulder. He laughs when he sees the flush on her cheeks. "Are you okay? You were in another world." She smiles and nods, abashed. "Are you getting sick too?"

"No, I'm fine," she says, avoiding the subject. She kisses Nathan on the cheek as she leaves to let him and Lilly rest, Killian following her out. Ember and Alan are sharing music preferences as they pull out discs and records. Violet sits down next to them on the floor. Alan puts on one of his favorites and Ember wrinkles her nose. The music is a mixture of instrumental and electronic. Once the lyrics come on, she enjoys it more and smiles. Violet lays on the cold floor sprawled out, staring at the cement ceiling. The lights shine brightly in her eyes, making her see spots when she blinks. Killian watches her curiously from the easy chair. Alan stands over her and holds his hands out to her. She hesitates at first, but eventually takes his hands. He pulls Violet to her feet and spins her. Holding her waist, he leads her into a sway with the beat. He sings along to the song with a cartoonishly seductive look that can't be taken seriously. Ember begins giggling and it becomes contagious. Violet can't hold back the laughter as he serenades her.

Killian taps Alan's shoulder as he spins her again. Alan allows him to cut in as he takes Ember up into his arms and spins about the room, her giggling echoing through the hall. Killian, not much of a dancer, sways to the music while staring into her eyes. She smiles but feels ashamed for the feelings that linger from the past. Staring back into his smiling eyes, she is overwhelmed with love and guilt. It feels as if someone is squeezing her heart. She wraps her arms around his neck and hugs him tight to her as they sway.

CHAPTER

13

The morning is quiet as they pack for their trip. Stacy is dressed in a fitted cropped turtleneck that crisscrosses in the back, and skin-tight leather pants with zippers across her legs, allowing her to shorten them to many lengths. She pulls on a hooded bolero and straps her leather armor on her right shoulder, before bending over seductively to lace up her knee-high boots. Violet watches her from across the hall with contempt. She could have finished getting dressed in her room. Though Killian easily ignores her, Alan keeps fumbling as he straps on his cowl harness over a long-sleeved tee. It was a nice change from his strange worn-out printed t-shirts. Killian draws her attention. His hair is pulled into a small bun, and a few strays fall in his face, as he blows at them and draws the strings tight on his pack. Wearing a black tank-top, he shrugs into his leather jacket with the high collar, and straps on his shin guards over his patched-up military slacks. She can't help but admire their thorough process of getting ready.

Each of them are responsible for their own gear and provisions, and they work silently. Alan checks and rechecks that his med kit is fully stocked and functional. This is the first time in a long while since he will have been so far away from the shelter, and it is obvious he is uneasy. Stacy checks her weapons, clean and loaded with extra ammunition. Killian can't help but double-check to make sure Violet has everything she needs. She doesn't know whether she should be happy about his concern, or offended by his lack of confidence in her. Clara fusses over Violet like a proud mother, making sure she has her floor-length frock buttoned correctly and her holster bag strapped tight around her hip, packed with essentials. Humored by her behavior, she allows it to continue until Clara is satisfied, giving her a quick squeeze.

Since the trip will take them further than usual, they prepare for an all-nighter. Nathan is feeling better and watches his mother and father prepare to leave. Violet feels guilty for leaving him behind, but he's taking it better than she imagined, not like when she left before. Jack and Clara are there to comfort him, rubbing his arm and patting his shoulder.

They pack the gear upon the three skyriders in the cargo bay. Killian hugs Nathan firmly and asks him to take care of the family while they are gone. Nathan nods, and she is incapable of holding eye contact with him as he tears up. Killian tussles his hair and kisses him on the forehead. Violet squeezes him so tight he squeaks. "I love you, my beautiful boy. We'll be back as soon as possible. We'll check in as often as we can." Nathan nods as tears begin streaming down his cheeks. Her throat tightens as he reverts into the silent child she found in Safe Haven. Seeing her hesitation, Jack urges her on. Turning her sorrow into determination, she returns to the cargo bay where Killian waits with a sympathetic smile and extra pair of goggles for her.

Mounting the rumbling skyrider, she wraps her arms around his waist. Stacy takes the lead and Alan follows behind Killian. Leaving the cargo bay, they head towards the glowing orange tree at the center of the dark cave. They veer right and head straight for the waterfall. Lifting her hood on her frock, nothing could have prepared her for the pressure from the heavy rush of water. Violet squeezes tightly around Killian, as if the water would pull them apart. She gasps as the cold seeps through her frock.

After recovering from the shock of cold water, she is able to admire the crystal blue river raging below them, despite the brisk air whipping past. She shivers as the air makes her wet clothes even colder. The sky is gray with heavy cloud cover. Violet holds tighter to Killian, hoping to leech onto his warmth. Taking one hand from the clutch, he pats her hands wrapped tightly around his abdomen. The mountain air is sweet with pine aroma. Goats and other little critters scamper away when their vehicles rumble past. Violet is fascinated by all of the wildlife. Every time she spots a different creature, she squeals and points. Killian shakes his head, and though she can't hear his laughter over the rumbling engines, she can feel it in his chest. The most they would ever see in their little Safe Haven were birds, rabbits and squirrels, occasionally a deer or two. The pigs and chickens they raised didn't count, as they were considered food. Violet spots a pack of wolves below them and watches in awe as they move with speed and grace. Like a school of fish, one moves to the left and they all follow the same path. As they slowly fade into the distance, she checks her compass and tries to study her surroundings, storing in her mind the landmarks that would help her return if she were to ever be separated.

Stacy, still leading, slows down occasionally to check the map and make sure they're still on-course. A little over an hour in, the surroundings start to flatten. The pine trees start to thin and different trees spread across the land in different shades of orange and yellow. Passing through ghost towns during the day was something no one made a habit of, so seeing it in the light of day has Violet's jaw dropped open. Abandoned automobiles, completely rusted over, are scattered everywhere, covered in moss and ivy. The buildings have trees growing through them, and most of the paved roads have been covered in dirt and brush. Stopping near a large pond, they take a break, shaking off the jitters from the skyriders.

Killian and Stacy look over the map and argue about which path would be safest. Violet walks through tall grass until she finds the pond with lily pads spread across the water. The clouds have cleared, revealing the blue sky and a warm sun. She takes a seat, spreading the grass flat around her. She admires the chirps and squeaks from the critters thriving in the area. Her heart skips a beat and her breath catches when cold scales slither across her hand.

"It's just a garter snake," Alan says, seeing her stiffen. "It's not poisonous." It slithers out of sight and her shoulders relax. Alan scans the area before taking a seat next to her. "Pretty spot," he says, still watching his surroundings cautiously.

"You can relax," Violet says. "You know maven are around when nature stops talking."

He smiles and closes his eyes, tilting his head back, soaking up the rays of sun. "I hate leaving the shelter," he admits.

"Why did you come along?"

"Killian wanted a medic in case something bad happened," Alan sighs.

Violet pats him on the shoulder. "Well, I'm glad you came. Otherwise, it would've been an awkward silent trip." She tilts her head back. Killian is no longer standing by Stacy. There is a rustling in the grass. Killian peeks through, scaring Alan out of his skin.

Killian's laughter echoes across the water. "Time to move," he says. Violet punches Killian in the arm, shaking her head, though holding in her laugh and trying not to smile. "Ow!" He laughs again. "That's going to bruise. You shouldn't be so abusive."

"You deserved it," she says in satisfaction.

Once again, they mount the skyriders and move through the forested towns. Some areas of the town are completely flooded, and the stone buildings are stained brown from rainfall. Where there was once a need for a bridge, the water is now all dried up. The bridge is on the verge of collapsing. Another hour passes and they come across twisted spiraling metal that looks like a warped railroad. There are several more clustered together. They fly over a large wheel with little pods attached around the rim. Vegetation clings to everything, claiming its territory. They come to another city, one of the larger ones in the area. The tallest building is leaning, as its foundation has shifted. She recognizes the building and is thankful, as her butt has become numb.

Not wanting to alert anyone or anything of their presence, they hide the skyriders in a tight alley. They pull vines over the vehicles until they blend in. In case there are wanderers, they wouldn't want to lose their transportation. Each of them carry their own packs. Alan is more tense now that they are on foot, with little cover from the trees and shrubbery. His hand hovers over his weapon at all times as they move through the city, hugging the buildings' walls. Violet takes the lead now, recognizing her surroundings. The roads in this city are much wider and have more open spaces. This city was abandoned long before anyone needed to bomb it, as most of the buildings are intact, though most of the shops they pass have been ransacked. There is a loud gurgling growl and everyone turns to face the sound with weapons ready, but it is just Alan. He throws up his hands in alarm. "I'm hungry," he says, an apologetic smile crossing his face.

Violet giggles and leads them to a small cafe. Hopping through the broken window, they check the shop thoroughly before relaxing into one of the musty old couches. The afternoon light warms the dark wood walls. They eat a small meal quietly. There is art displayed on the walls with the title and price below each piece. Money hasn't been of any use for centuries; most people traded work or goods for items they wanted. Violet wipes the dust from one of the pieces, revealing a photograph. She takes a bite of her sandwich. There is a pale woman with long black hair in a thin white gown, crowned in a gold leafed wreath with lit candles. She is walking through snow with bare feet, looking around with curiosity. It is a beautiful piece, though somewhat lonely.

Alan eats quickly and stares out the open window, listening to the quiet city. Killian and Stacy whisper quietly over the map. The building is closed, but Stacy argues on whether Violet should be allowed to lead. When her voice begins to rise, Alan clasps a hand over her mouth. No one has noticed he has gotten to his feet. His lips purse and he glares at her in a threatening way.

"We should keep moving, Alan is getting antsy," Violet whispers. Killian nods, finishing off his meal. Stacy swats Alan's hand away and hastily gets to her feet. She waits near the window, tapping her foot impatiently. Violet moves past her, jumping out the window. Her long frock whips Stacy in the face, and Alan snorts as he tries to hold in his laughter. Her face turns red and she is seething as Killian and Alan pass through the window. Following behind, she angrily stalks after them. Killian, walking alongside Violet, scopes out the terrain. Violet doesn't question her path, even though it is her first time coming in the daylight. She knows the signs of an unwelcome presence, and she feels secure in walking out in the open.

Nine blocks further into the city, they come to an open lot with a five-story building made of steel and glass. The front entrance is blocked off with rubble that has fallen from the second floor, thanks to the explosion. Sticking out from the rubble is a maven's corpse, all except its caved-in skull still intact. The glass still stands, though cracks spiderweb from the ground up. Violet cringes, remembering the heat of the explosion.

Shaking off those feelings, she leads them carefully around the back. The ground dips under the building. There are two large gates. She signals them to follow. Coming up to the gate, she examines it, hoping it is not too difficult to open. This gate used to stay open. Trying not to give herself false hope, she pushes it to the back of her mind. Getting a good grip, she lifts up the corner as high as she can. There is enough room for them to crawl through. Stacy glowers before tossing her pack through the gate and crawling through. Her bare abdomen scrapes against the asphalt, and she curses as she wipes away the dirt from her scraped skin. The gate is heavy, and Violet's arms begin to shake as Killian passes through. Stacy stands there watching instead of assisting. Killian helps her hold it up on the other side, and when Alan passes through, Violet lets go. The gate drops with a loud clunk that echoes through the empty streets. Killian curses, as he is unable to hold it up on his own. Alan helps lifting with all his strength. The veins on his forehead and neck swell as he clenches his teeth. Though Killian uses his mechanical arm, he can feel all the weight in his shoulder, and it aches in his chest.

"Seriously?" Stacy and Violet say in unison. Stacy gives in, not wanting to waste more time, and helps hold it up. They are able to lift it high enough for Violet to squeeze through. They carefully let down the gate and sigh in relief as they shake out their arms. Getting back to her feet, Violet pulls out her pistol. The others follow suit. There are a few vehicles in the underground lot, but otherwise it's empty, with one light nearest the door. She is weary of the dark shadows, watching carefully for movement. Killian hisses as she strays too far from the pack. She waits for them to catch up. They follow close behind as Violet leads them to the red door.

The door is left ajar with a small rock at the foot. *Maybe he's alive*, Violet thinks hopefully as her heart begins to race. The others struggle to keep up with her pace while still clearing the building. Checking carefully around each corner, they make their way up the stairs to the third floor. Violet stops dead in her tracks. The dust-coated carpet has fresh markings. *If he's dead, this carpet would have a thick layer of dust after two years. Unless someone else is here.* There is a clear path from the stairs leading to the room. Killian taps her on the shoulder. "Are you okay?" he whispers. She realizes she is breathing heavily. She nods and moves along.

Violet follows the path down the hallway and around the next few desks, separated by four-foot walls. She turns to the right and there is a closed door with no windows. She hesitates with her hand on the handle. Her heart feels as if it will break out of her chest. Turning the handle, she pushes the door open. The screens lining the wall are dark. The long tables are empty. No sign of him. Her heart skips a beat. Walking in, she peeks around the door, making sure she isn't making the same mistake as last time. She comes back out of the room and holsters her pistol. "No one's here," she says, sounding defeated.

Killian puts away his own weapon and goes around her into the control room. Stacy follows, bumping Violet's shoulder as she passes. Tilting her head back, Violet raises her eyes to the ceiling as her hands ball into fists. Alan pats her shoulder sympathetically. Her eyes begin to prickle. He could still be alive, though they haven't checked the rest of the building yet. Violet had always come in the night, though he was always here long before she would arrive. She looks around the open floor. The light from the afternoon sun shines brightly through the glass windows.

"Violet, how do you turn these on?" Alan whispers loudly. Violet takes in a long deep breath and sighs, turning around. Stacy is sitting in one of the few black swivel chairs with her feet upon the long table, munching on the sandwich she hadn't finished during lunch. Killian is pushing buttons on a keyboard and Alan is checking around the screens, looking for an 'on' switch. She shakes her head.

As she is about to take a step, she sees movement in the corner of her eye. All too quickly she is tackled to the ground. With quick reflexes, she twists her body and kicks their hips up, flipping them onto their backs. Lifting her legs over her head, she flips herself upright so that she sits on his chest. Her legs trap their arms and her pistol is already pulled and cocked. Killian, seeing her taken down, runs to the door in a panic, ready to shoot her attacker, only to find Violet on top of them. She is panting, but a wicked grin is stretched across her face as she stares down at the man breathing heavily. He smiles back up at her after the shock of her quick movements wears off.

"I thought you were dead!" they both say in unison, breathlessly. Alan, a little slower and cautious, appears behind Killian with his weapon drawn. Violet uncocks the pistol in her hand and holsters it. Placing her hands on his chest, she moves her knees off his arms. The man frowns as he notices the subtle veins reaching around her neck and hairline. He sits up, his large hand gently taking hold of her jaw, turning it slightly in his fingerless gloved hand, lifting the hair from her neck with the other hand. With his thumb he traces the remainder of the dark veins at the back of her neck. "What happened to you?" he asks.

Violet covers her neck with her hand and her cheeks flush. "It's complicated, but it has to do with the explosion in the entrance." She stands up, holding her hands out to help him up as well. He takes her hands and, when he is upright, pulls her into a bear hug. She hugs him just as tightly, and both gasp for air before loosening their grip with a chuckle. The hug lasts longer than Killian and Alan are comfortable with. Killian shifts his weight, still aiming at the man's back. Alan clears his throat.

"Since when do you bring company with you, Kitten?" the man says. Violet shakes her head, still trying to swallow the lump in her throat.

"Kitten?" Alan scoffs under his breath.

Violet turns him to face the group, unfazed by the pet name she is so used to. Killian is still ready to shoot. She presses her hand on Killian's gun, pointing it downward, shaking her head. Alan puts his away, but looks him over skeptically, noticing he is well-kept in his attire. He wears a royal blue scarf, a black t-shirt, and black denim jeans with padded knees and a brown vest. The only items looking worn is his gray overcoat and the knitted hat on his head, its edges somewhat frayed. The worn leather straps around his shoulders hold two katanas. "This is Killian Grey," Violet says, pointing to her party in turn. "That's Alan Andrews, and in the other room is Stacy Nox." Stacy tilts her head with the mention of her name.

Killian holds his right hand out, frustrated he has to look up to him, as he is almost a foot taller. The man clasps hands and says, "Kim Yoojin." Killian's grip tightens at hearing his name. *You...gin.* Violet's words repeat in his head. *She was dreaming about him that morning. Is he the reason she wanted to come?* Yoojin rips his hand away as the metal hand starts to crush him.

"Kitten's husband," Alan adds, as he nods in Killian's direction. Violet looks to Alan, giving him a cold look.

"You got hitched, Violet?" She feels uneasy when he uses her given name. He smiles down at her, even though you can sense the sadness in his voice.

"No, I didn't," Violet says timidly. She sees the hurt on Killian's face for a second and then it is gone. "But he's the person I've been looking for all this time. I just couldn't remember him." Yoojin tilts his head curiously. Alan nudges Killian's shoulder. Killian shakes his head and Alan drops it. Stacy has a wry smile as she watches their interactions.

"What happened to Charlie?" Yoojin asks.

"Turns out Charlie wasn't who I thought he was."

"And Nathan?" Yoojin asks in concern.

"He's safe." Violet smiles. Sensing Killian's eyes burning holes into her, Violet changes the subject. "We need your help. You know these computers best." Killian nudges her side. She looks over her shoulder and Killian gives her the eye. Choosing her words carefully, she tries to explain. Their exchange doesn't go unnoticed by Yoojin. "First of all, we need any footage you may have of cyborgs, and where they may have come from."

"Cyborgs? Like this guy?" Yoojin looks Killian over.

"No, he just has a mechanical arm. I'm talking about full-on machines disguised as humans."

"I can help you look, but I haven't seen anything. Or anything I'm aware of, anyway."

"We also need locations of all of the communities or colonies still standing."

"Oh yeah?" Yoojin folds his arms, squinting down at her, scrutinizing. Violet looks up at him with pleading eyes. His light brown eyes soften as it turns to concern. "What is this for?"

Killian answers for her. "We need to inform them there's a way to fight the maven. We also want the war to end. If we can come together instead of killing each other, everyone would be better off. Don't you agree?" Yoojin nods in agreement and Killian goes back into the room. Alan stands there waiting for Yoojin and Violet to follow.

"Help me?" Violet asks again. Yoojin nods, turning her around and nudging her into the room. As they enter, Killian manages to turn the system on, but as it is new to him he doesn't know how to navigate it. Violet takes a seat in the back and watches Yoojin ask politely to take control. Killian gets up and Yoojin takes a seat, plopping his goggles and hat on the desk beside him. His hair is cut short but has a nice little flip in the front. Killian stands over him, watching everything he does, storing it for later.

Alan sits next to Violet and watches them uneasily. He leans close to her and whispers, "Isn't Kim a girl's name?"

Violet laughs. "Kim's his last name. His first name is Yoojin."

"Oh, Eugene."

"No, emphasize the Yoo. *Yoo*-jin."

"I'm just going to call him Kim." Alan folds his arms. "Why does he call you Kitten?" he whispers again, but Killian hears him and glances back with fire in his eyes. Alan straightens up, closing his mouth.

Violet feels a pang of guilt. "It's just a nickname. It doesn't mean anything," she says, though she acknowledges that it is definitely a term of endearment.

"Did you have a nickname for him?" he asks. Violet can tell Killian is listening, because he isn't giving full attention to what Yoojin is doing.

She leans in much closer and whispers as quietly as possible, "Woofie." It isn't quite quiet enough, though, and Yoojin turns slightly, a smile raising his cheeks. Alan bursts into laughter and it continues until tears stream down his cheeks. Killian glares back at him, obviously fuming at the topic of conversation. Violet turns bright red and doesn't make eye contact. *I shouldn't have told him.* She curses herself for saying anything.

Yoojin makes sure Killian understands how to use the system before handing over the keyboard. Stacy joins him in front of the screens, taking down notes in the atlas as he points out certain details. Yoojin joins Alan and Violet in the back. "This is going to take a while," he says, pointing at the screens. "How 'bout you explain how complicated things actually are."

Violet takes a deep breath and lets it out with a sigh. "Where do I start?"

"How about with how you ended up coming here to find your long lost husband," he jests.

Violet smirks. Taking her time not to leave anything out, she tells him the whole story. Describing her father's death puts a vivid image in everyone's minds, and Yoojin watches Killian's back as he speaks with Stacy. Eventually she finishes, gulping down water as her voice has gone hoarse from talking for so long. Yoojin nods, taking in what she's told him.

"So how did *you* meet Violet?" Alan interrupts the silence.

"She tried to sneak up on me and failed… miserably."

"He scared the crap out of me," Violet adds. "I thought he was going to kill me, but he ended up being a sweet guy."

"I try." He winks.

"We became close friends. He taught me how to fight, and helped me search for Killian." Yoojin smiles back at her. Looking back at Killian, he notices they are watching the feed from a large urban area. "Is that Fallen City?" he asks. No one answers. Violet and Alan throw a glance at each other. "Why are you checking Fallen City? No one can survive there. How did you even find that feed?"

"This might be where the cyborgs came from," Killian responds.

"I've never been able to access this feed."

"You're welcome," Killian responds. They spot a handful of seekers roaming the city streets, but no other signs of life. Stacy points out certain buildings on the smaller screen, so that those behind them can't see. They finish up and switch to searching for other colonies. Finding hidden colonies is like finding a needle in a haystack, and they realize quickly that it could take weeks before they find another colony, if they're hidden as thoroughly as Safe Haven was. Killian and Stacy whisper to each other in such low voices, it's impossible to understand their conversation.

"Mr. Kim." Killian gets his attention. Yoojin turns around with arms folded and leans on the desk. Violet raises an eyebrow to his formal address. "It'll take more time than we have to find the colonies. Perhaps you can show us yours."

"My home is not within range. You won't be able to find anything here." Killian looks down at Stacy. She looks up at him, then back at Yoojin for a moment, before writing down another note in the atlas and slamming it shut.

As she puts it away in her pack, Killian shuts off the system. "We should get going. It's getting late. We still need to find a safe place to sleep."

"But you didn't even find what we're looking for," Violet says.

"We can come back another time," Killian says sternly. Violet feels uneasy as Killian picks his pack up and waits for the others to follow suit. Stacy is quick to her feet. Alan, just as confused as Violet, collects himself.

"I know a safe place," Yoojin offers.

"We appreciate your help here, but we'll be fine on our own from here on out," Killian insists.

Violet shakes her head in frustration. "We'd love you to show us a safe place to sleep," she contradicts. Alan nods in agreement. He would rather not waste time searching for safety in the middle of the night. Killian exhales loudly and leaves the room, throwing his pack over his shoulder, Stacy following close behind.

Yoojin stands and holds his hand out to the door. "After you, Kitten."

Alan starts chuckling. "Woofie," he says to himself. Violet blushes and leaves with her head down, so the loose hairs from her braid hide it. They leave the building as quietly as they came, following the same path. Killian occasionally looks over his shoulder, checking on Violet.

As they come into the underground garage, she groans at the thought of lifting the gate again. The sun has already fallen below the buildings. The sky has cleared and stars are becoming visible. The crickets chirp loudly. Walking up to the gate, Killian and Stacy check for any signs of danger before they turn and wait for her. She picks up her pace to catch up with them, then squats and lifts the gate with her legs.

"Whoa, whoa, whoa!" Yoojin nudges her away as he takes her place to lower the gate. It's so heavy it drops loudly. "Jeez, you're a hulk. When did you get so strong?"

"She's a mutant. I thought she explained this already," Stacy says impatiently.

Yoojin gets into his satchel and pulls out a crowbar and a steel scissor jack. Lifting the gate with the crowbar, he shoves the jack underneath and pumps it until it's high enough for them to get out. Stacy and Violet go first, followed by Killian and Alan. The chirping crickets become silent as they crawl under, and it's suddenly too quiet. "We need to move," Alan whispers anxiously. Yoojin throws his satchel through first. Not noticing that someone had accidentally bumped the jack, he crawls under, headfirst.

Killian, Alan and Stacy are moving quickly in the direction they came. Violet stops halfway through the lot, waiting for Yoojin. He is almost through when the jack slips and the gate falls on his leg. He wails in pain. Violet is at his side in seconds. She lifts the gate and he pulls himself out just as a maven calls. Its cackling caw gives Violet goosebumps. Fear strikes everyone's faces. They suddenly see five maven charging for them from a couple blocks away. Yoojin stands up, but his leg is broken and he loses his balance.

"Violet, run!" Killian yells.

"Go, Violet," Yoojin says through gritted teeth.

"Don't be stupid! I'm not leaving you!" she says angrily, bolting for the front entrance. She can hear Alan and Killian screaming for her to come back. She skids to a stop at the entrance with the maven corpse. Grabbing the spikes, she holds it up and stomps on the arm, breaking the spikes free. "Get Yoojin!" she commands. They hesitate. Alan runs for Yoojin, who is painfully making his way across the lot.

Violet starts running back to the group. The first maven is close enough to get shots out, and shards of bone pass her as she dodges them. She picks one up, throwing it as she spins around and continues running. They are gaining on her, and if they get any closer to the group, all of them will be in danger. She skids to a stop. "Keep running!" Violet demands. Not waiting to see if they listen, she faces the maven, taking a deep breath. The maven cries out again and the sound vibrates in her ears.

Violet holds the two-foot spears in each hand and deflects the bone spikes the Maven shoots at her. Taking one of the spears, she digs the sharpest end into her inner arm and makes a sizable cut. Spreading her blood along the tips, she charges the closest one and just as it swings it's spears she ducks, sweeping its legs out from under it. She hits with such force the pain shoots up her shin and she screams out in pain. The maven starts to get up and she rams the bloodied spike into its chest. It screeches and starts to convulse. There are shots fired and she sees three mavens have passed her, heading for her group. The fifth is standing over her ready to strike. Violet rips the spike from the grounded maven's chest. Swinging it high, she hits it's arm just as it blasts out a spike. Throwing the bloodied spike in the same direction the spike was shot. The maven runs, deflecting the first spike as her second pierces through its eye, it bursts like a balloon filled with molasses.

The maven next to her screams with rage and stabs at her. She dodges it. He jabs a second time and she grabs hold, twisting her body into it. With great force, she stabs her last spear into the side of its ribcage, then rips it out and rubs the blood from her hand into its wound before taking off after the others. The group is moving as fast as they can, firing off shots.

Violet twists the spear into her arm, coating it with blood, before throwing it at the closest maven. It cries out, reaching awkwardly for the spear embedded in its back, before beginning to seize. Violet is gaining on the last maven, but it is too close to the group. The back of her tongue prickles and she feels like she will lose her lunch. Swallowing it back, she focuses on gaining speed. Killian catches a spike with his bionic arm. Just as it reaches them, Killian swings his right arm and it shatters against the maven's thick exoskeleton, metal bits flying in every direction.

Violet cries out as she leaps onto the maven and thrusts a tight fist into its back with such force that it breaks through. She feels the bones in her own hand snap and crunch as she crushes through a second layer of exoskeleton. Killian is stunned, as maven blood splatters across his face. As she rips her arm out of the collapsing maven, she screams in pain. She looks as though she has been splashed with a bucket of ink. The maven falls to the ground, convulsing. Her ears still buzz, as though the maven are still communicating. She spins around searching for more as she grips her arm, hoping to relieve her mangled hand.

Violet spots a maven standing across the lot, half its body hidden behind a thick tree. It doesn't move, but its black eyes watch them… or more specifically, watch her. Killian yells at her to follow as they start to move, but she only hears a loud buzzing in her ears and stares at the still maven. Killian wraps his left arm around her waist and pulls her away out of its sight. They run as fast as they can away from the building. Stacy pulls Yoojin's other hand over her shoulder, compelling them to move faster. Violet's ears don't stop buzzing until they've gone three more blocks.

The sun is gone, and with it their light. The crickets have started their comforting music once more. The adrenaline fades and the pain in her hand amplifies. She moans with every movement, along with Yoojin. They make it to their skyriders and quickly uncover them. Loading up the wounded first, Stacy takes Yoojin and Violet Alan, since Killian driving with one arm is unfit for passengers. Yoojin leads them out of the city. Twenty minutes later they come to a large brick tower. They find shelter for their vehicles inside a little garage nearby. The tower has watertight doors. Alan turns the hand wheel until it clicks, and he pulls the heavy door open. Stairs curve around the large tower that stands over 75 feet tall. Alan closes the door behind them, locking it tight. When they reach the top, it reveals a wide open space with barred windows every three feet.

"What is this place?" Killian asks.

"A water tower," Yoojin pants. Alan gets to work on them as soon as Yoojin is seated next to Violet. Pulling out his med kit, he gives each of them pills to stop the swelling. They gulp them down with water. He then pulls out two syringes wrapped in plastic. Killian helps Violet out of her frock, cringing as she grits her teeth and moans in pain. Alan fills the syringes with morphine and asks Stacy for assistance in administering them. She does so, taking pleasure in stabbing them with needles. The pain slowly starts to fade. Alan pulls out his scanner. Checking Yoojin first, he learns he has a stable fracture in his left tibia. He sends Stacy out to find something to use as splints. She asks Killian to come along. He looks to Violet and she nods, sending him on his way. Alan scans her hand. The X-ray shows two cracked metacarpi, two broken phalanges, and one thumb dislocated at the proximal and metacarpal. On top of that, her wrist is sprained.

Alan sews up the open gash in her arm first. He prepares her with a thick rag to bite down on, while Yoojin holds her free hand. He first repositions her thumb. It hurts at first, but once in place some of the pain lessens. She is unable to open her hand. One finger at a time, he pops the two phalanges back into place. She screams out in pain, while trying not to crush Yoojin's hand, as Alan straightens the bones. Killian comes bounding up the stairs while Stacy locks it shut again. Now at Violet's side, he takes the hand Yoojin was holding, petting it gently. Stacy comes up the stairs and drops a pile of wood pieces and PVC pipe they found. Alan sifts through them, finding a smaller piece for her fingers. He puts small rolls of gauze between the fingers before taping them to the splint, then straps another piece to her hand, keeping it and her wrist somewhat flat. When he finishes, he wraps it thickly with gauze all the way to her elbow. Moving back to Yoojin, he uses the longer pieces of PVC pipe to splint his leg.

"Hey, Violet," Alan gets her attention. She's becoming drowsy, but looks at him with lazy eyes. "Where did you learn to move like that? I've never seen anything like it."

"This guy," she replies, as she jabs Yoojin with her elbow with a giggle.

Yoojin smiles at her fondly. "You've improved far beyond what I have taught you."

"That's cuz…" she replies woozily. "Cuz I'm, uh, a mutant." She snuggles up to Killian's pack.

"A badass mutant," Alan adds. Violet waves the finger on her good hand at Alan approvingly.

The morphine has taken hold, and Violet and Yoojin fall asleep next to each other. Killian doesn't take his eyes from her as he eats a meal of protein bars and water. Seeing her chest rise and fall rhythmically, he relaxes a bit. The night is cold; but being surrounded by windows, they don't risk lighting a fire and bringing attention to themselves. Stacy helps Killian remove his armor and leather jacket. The right sleeve is shredded. Alan pulls out a screwdriver and starts removing what is left of Killian's bionic arm.

After their quiet meal they all huddle together for warmth, pondering what to do next.

CHAPTER

14

Yoojin wakes up, his leg throbbing. The morning light illuminates the tower. Everyone still sleeps. Next to him, Violet's brows are knitted together. He carefully props himself up on one elbow. He wants to smooth out her frown, but doesn't want to wake her. After some time, Violet opens her eyes and looks up at Yoojin. He quickly looks away. Violet smiles, knowing he had been watching her, though he would never admit it. She tries to lift herself up and gasps, forgetting her hand is still healing. "You okay? Do you need help?" Yoojin whispers.

"I'm okay, thank you." Putting her weight on the other hand, she sits up.

"You should keep that elevated." Violet looks around for something that might be used as a sling, and Yoojin pulls his cobalt blue scarf from his neck. He points a finger at her and curls it towards him. She scoots as close as possible. Lifting her arm gently, he slides the soft fabric under her arm and folds it over. Violet lifts her hair with her free hand so he can tie it up at the back of her neck. His fingers brush her back when he finishes.

"Thank you. I would hug you, but I might hurt myself, so this will have to do." Violet rests her head on his shoulder. He wraps his hand around her waist, hugging her in return. Lifting her head, she turns to look for her pack. Killian is watching her. He doesn't have to say anything; she can tell he's upset. At first she feels guilty, until Stacy moves. She's still asleep, but her arm is wrapped around his middle, and her face is pressed into his shoulder. Her relationship with Yoojin had always been innocent, but with Killian and Stacy it was a different story. Killian has no right to be angry with her.

She gets to her feet in frustration. Stomping down the stairs, Killian yells after her, "Where are you going by yourself?"

"Nature calls!" she shouts over her shoulder, as good an excuse as any.

"Go with her, Stacy." Killian shakes her off of his shoulder.

"No, I'm sleeping," she groans.

"I'll go," Alan grumbles as he pulls his arms into his jacket with a big yawn. "Come on, might as well take both of the cripples," he says, lending a shoulder to Yoojin on his way. Violet, currently having only one good arm, struggles with the hand wheel but eventually gets it moving. As Yoojin and Alan make it to the bottom, Violet has the door open. Feeling like a caged animal, she hurries out the door, taking deep breaths. The air is thick with fog. Noticing the chill in the air, she shivers, regretting leaving her frock behind. "Don't go too far!" Alan yells after Violet, watching her disappear into the mist.

Killian lays back down and stares up at the ceiling. Stacy snuggles up closer. Shoving her off, she groans in protest. Forgetting his metal arm is gone, he goes to lean on it, only to tip over, falling on his side. Stacy watches him sympathetically. He uses his left hand to get to his feet. Taking hold of one of the bars at the window, he presses his forehead against the cold iron as he stares out over the murky woods.

"You know," Stacy says, folding her legs under her, "even with the information we have, you could never make it through Fallen City without someone on the inside helping you."

"I know."

"And it would probably take years to find all of the colonies and convince them to stop fighting each other. And if Yoojin is who I think he is, you could all be in a lot of danger."

"You think he'd try to hurt Violet?"

"Maybe not him, but his family would never allow his camaraderie with her. His family could destroy everything."

"If you're right..."

"If I'm right, then the best way to help them would be to come with me. Ensure that the Kims will never find your family. My father has complete control over their knowledge. You and I will be taking over the company, which means we'd have that control."

"You don't understand what you're asking me to do."

"You're right. I don't know what it feels like to leave your long-lost love and newfound child behind. I'll probably never really understand, but you have to look at it this way. You'd be making it so much better for them and all of humanity."

Killian spots Violet kicking at bushes and small rocks. Even when she's angry and frustrated at him, he has an overwhelming love for her. Stacy gets to her feet and comes to stand behind him. "If I left with you," he asks, "what would be the plan when we got there?"

"For starters, we'd set you up with a new arm. A better one than that piece of tin you put together. We'd get cleaned up, presentable. You'd help me take over the company. We'd start winning over those with open hearts. If we can convince the people that the bottom dwellers are real, valuable people, they might see things differently." She leans in and whispers quietly, "We'd be able to communicate with everyone below us. We could stop the war." Stepping back, she adds, "We could also watch over your family from there."

Killian nods. "She'll hate me for leaving."

"If she really loves you, she'll let you do what you need to, to keep your family alive and safe." She grabs hold of the iron bars and looks down on Violet. Killian nods again, knowing what he must do, and how much it is going to tear his family apart.

Downstairs, Alan calls for Violet. She looks over her shoulder and up at the tower. Stacy disappears into the shadows and all she can see is Killian looking down on her. Anxiety is written across his face. It feels as though a snake is constricting around her heart. She shivers as the cold morning dew soaks into her skin. Trying to stay out of their sight for some privacy, she goes a bit deeper into the woods. Finding a convenient spot, she drops trou' and squats. She hears the crack of a stick. Turning her head, she sees nothing but thick mist and hears nothing out of the ordinary. Finishing up quickly, she pulls up her pants, but before she can button herself there is a sharp pain in her shoulder. Her nose and mouth are covered simultaneously. With a gasp she inhales, and the world starts to spin. She is dragged away, unable to fight her attacker. She tries to yell out when he removes the cloth, but her muscles become heavy and can only groan in protest.

After a while, her attacker grows tired and drops her on a soft patch of grass. Her heart is racing, her head is becoming clearer, but she is unable to move any muscles. Just breathing is a chore in itself. The man sighs. "Maybe I shouldn't have used that drug until we got further away. You're quite heavy," he laughs, out of breath. He is sitting beside her, but she is unable to see him, as her head is turned away from him. He brushes her cheek as he breathes heavily. "It didn't take me long to find you. Thank you for making it easy to separate you from them." He turns her head so that she is looking up at the ash gray sky, revealing Charlie looming over her. He climbs on top of her, making it harder to breath. He leans forward so all she can see is him. His eyes have circles under them, and he rubs at his shoulder as he speaks to her. His unkempt red hair highlights the madness in his eyes.

"You're probably curious as to why you're incapable of moving. I injected you with a paralytic. It'll wear off in about an hour. I came across it while trying to save my own life. You know, he shot me in the shoulder and left me for dead?" He clicks his tongue. "Killian is quite the trooper, isn't he? I've tried to kill him, what, three times now? It just doesn't take." He wipes the sweat from his brow. All Violet can do is listen and watch as he pulls his fingers through his damp hair.

"Why him?" he asks, and for a moment he seems truly befuddled, as he looks out around him. "Why could you never let go of him? I loved you more than he ever did. How could you just look past me and always go to him? I would've done anything for you." His expression becomes sour as he looks down at her. "Answer me!" he screams as he wraps his hands around her throat and squeezes. His eyes clear and he chuckles. "I forgot, you're paralyzed... sorry." He releases her throat, allowing her to breath once again. He bends down, kissing the marks on her neck. "Honestly, I wish he would just die, but every time I try, he gets away from me. I desperately want to hurt him. I want to see the pain and fear in his eyes." He shakes his head.

"Unfortunately, the only way I can truly hurt him is through you," he says as he unbuttons his jacket. Panic starts to set in now. "I can take away the only thing he cares about." He sits up to pull his coat off. Leaning forward again, he smiles down at her. He flips open a pocketknife. With his free hand he caresses her face and neck. He moves out of her view. Seeing only gray sky, she feels his hands groping and pulling at the loose top she is wearing. He rips her shirt down the middle and kisses her chest. Tears start to swell up and spill down the sides of her face. He sighs. "Such a perfect body. A few scars but still perfect." He comes into view again. "I wish there was another way to hurt him. I won't enjoy this, Violet, I really won't. Such a waste…" Charlie presses his lips to hers, parting them with his tongue. She tries to scream, but a weak moan and more tears are the only things she is capable of. He is breathing heavily when he pulls back to watch her eyes, as the blade is shoved into her side and he slowly removes it. A moan of agony escapes her, and Charlie strokes her face. She feels it a second time as it punctures her lung. It is becoming harder to breathe now, as she chokes on the blood filling her lung.

She sees the darkness closing in on her peripheral vision when Charlie is thrown off her. Her head is knocked to the side, along with Charlie. "I should have killed you when I had the chance!" Killian roars. He sits on Charlie's chest, holding his arms down with his legs, and with his sole hand he snatches the blade. "You'll never be able hurt anyone ever again," he says to Charlie in his ear. Violet can't look away as Killian slowly pierces the blade into Charlie's eye socket. Charlie screams and kicks his legs. His hands, pinned to the ground, turn to claws as he tries to break free. Killian bares his teeth like a rabid dog as he moves on to the next eye. It gushes with a clear liquid and then blood. So many tears are filling her eyes, and she welcomes the blurred vision, so that she doesn't have to see the grotesque scene.

"Killian!" Alan yells as Killian begins stabbing the blade further past his sockets. Charlie has already stopped screaming. Stacy is trying to pull Killian off Charlie without success. "Stacy, keep the pressure on," he yells as he presses a cloth to Violet's side. She is wheezing with each breath. Alan tackles Killian to the ground, hitting him in the chest. "What is wrong with you?!" he yells, disgusted. He doesn't bother checking Charlie and focuses on Violet.

"He was killing her!" Killian yells with a broken voice.

"Why didn't you call out for help, instead of letting Violet bleed out while you torture a man to death?!"

Killian looks at her then, seeing the black tears filling her eyes as she stares at him. "She's alive?" Killian crawls to her, wiping the tears with his bloodied sleeve. "I'm sorry," he whispers to her. Alan shoves him out of the way as he picks her up into his arms. She can feel the pain with every step he takes. Her broken hand bumps against his chest with every stride. The way he is holding her makes it harder to catch a breath, and she can feel herself losing consciousness.

Yoojin is waiting at the door of the water tower where they had left him. "What happened?" he asks anxiously. Alan doesn't answer, but climbs the stairs as if she were as light as a feather. Laying her down, he scans her quickly. Seeing her lung has collapsed, he grabs his largest syringe. Carefully, he removes the excess blood. He puts a mask over her mouth and nose, and presses a button to begin a machine breathing for her. She is able to breathe but is still unable to even blink. Alan closes up her wounds, confirming that there is no other internal damage. Killian is at her side, holding her hand helplessly. Stacy is slowly following Yoojin up the stairs, making sure he doesn't fall.

After a long silence, Alan speaks directly at Yoojin as he comes to her side. "She'll be alright. We're lucky she has a mutation. She heals much faster than any of us. All the scars you see here—" He points out the pink scars from the maven attacks. "These are all from last week." Yoojin nods. He doesn't say anything when he sees Killian looking at him like he will bite his head off. "Watch over her while I go wash my hands," Alan says, patting Yoojin's shoulder with his cleaner hand. "You… come with me." He points at Killian.

"I'm not leaving her," Killian hisses.

"I said get up!" Alan grabs Killian by his collar and drags him away from Violet until he follows on his own.

"Blast it Alan, what do you want? She needs me in there!" he says as he follows Alan to the nearby creek.

"What the hell was that? I didn't even recognize you. You looked out of your mind, sick, psychotic!"

"That man has hurt my family all this time. How am I supposed to react when I see him stabbing the love of my life?!"

"Kill him quickly and take care of her! That's what I would expect! Instead, you left the love of your life on the ground bleeding, desperate for breath, forcing her to watch your twisted revenge." Killian hides his face in his hands, knowing Alan is right. "Do me a favor, Killian. Get your head on straight, before you lose everything… again." Washing his bloodied hands in the creek, Alan dries them on a fresh cloth and tosses it at Killian's head. "And clean yourself up," he says in disgust. "His blood is all over you." He leaves Killian to his thoughts.

CHAPTER
15

Stacy is helping Alan pack up when Killian returns. Violet is sitting up and able to move once again. Her chest is wrapped with thick gauze, protecting her wounds and covering her chest. Yoojin helps Violet into her frock, darkened from maven blood. With her splinted hand, she is unable to fit it through the sleeve, so he wraps it over her shoulder and slings it. Violet cannot look Killian in the eyes as he comes up the stairs. Killian, seeing her reaction, collects his pack and makes his way back down the stairs.

"Kitten, I don't know what happened out there, but you could come with me. You keep getting hurt with them. You'd be safe with me. You and Nathan would be safe."

Violet looks down, pondering her options. Looking up at Alan, he keeps his mouth shut, but she can see he's still angry with Killian. Stacy glares in their direction. "I can't do that," she rasps.

Yoojin looks down at her free hand. Taking hold of it, he brings it to his lips and looks her in the eye. "You know where I'll be. If you need anything, come find me," Yoojin says sincerely. "Though it might be a couple weeks before this foot heals." Violet nods with a smile that doesn't reach her eyes.

Alan comes to her side now, lifting her up in his arms as she gasps in pain. Stacy comes to aid Yoojin, but he hops along on his own. Meeting Killian at the garage, Yoojin approaches him. "Since we're moving out, I'd appreciate it if you could bring me to my ride," Yoojin says.

"Happy to," Killian responds in a low voice.

Heading back into the city, they avoid the area where they were attacked, Yoojin leading them instead to a storage facility. Unlocking the padlock with a key from his pocket, he slides the red painted door open. Alan's eyes sparkle and his jaw drops. He dismounts from the skyrider. Inside is a vehicle somewhat the shape of an egg. Its large windshield is tinted blue. Yoojin hobbles to the side of the vehicle. He pulls a latch and the windshield swings open. It is large enough to seat two, one in the front and a backseat passenger. Stacy and Killian make eye contact and look away.

"What is it?!" Alan marvels.

"A hover-pod." Yoojin smiles, patting the pod like a loyal dog.

"It's so… I've never seen anything like it." Alan walks toward it like it might bite him if he comes too close. Holding his hands out to touch it, he murmurs, "So pretty."

"Would you like to sit in it?"

"Shyeah!" Alan climbs in and caresses the white leather seats.

Killian hops off the skyrider and approaches Yoojin. "Thank you for helping us find what we needed." He holds out his left hand and they shake.

Yoojin turns to Stacy and says, "Nice meeting you." She salutes him and stuffs her hands in her pockets. Yoojin turns to Alan. "Thank you for the meds and splint. If you ever need the favor returned…"

"This is enough. We're good." He waves a hand as he gently touches the buttons and switches. Yoojin laughs. Turning to Violet, he turns serious.

"Come with us?" Violet says weakly.

"Naw." He glances at Killian. "I need to get home." Violet tries to climb off the rider, but he stops her. "You need to rest. Thanks for not leaving me for dead, Kitten," he says softly. She leans her body towards him and he catches her against his chest. Wrapping her arm around his waist, he does the same, resting his head atop hers. She gasps when his hug tightens and he releases her, apologizing again and again. She starts to laugh but regrets it instantly.

Alan comes over reluctantly to help Yoojin into his hover-pod, Killian standing beside Violet as Yoojin starts it up. Watching Yoojin leave is dismal for Violet. She looks at Killian but can only see the murderous rage from before. No longer is the sweet boy from the docks here with her. In his stead is a terrifying man, intoxicated by hatred. Killian can see the fear in her eyes when she looks away. His heart is breaking into pieces.

Getting back on the road, they make their way back home. Avoiding major cities, the trip takes a bit longer. With the meds Alan gave Violet for breakfast, she becomes drowsy. They have to stop frequently, as she keeps going limp and almost falls off the back several times. Alan puts Violet in front of him and she falls asleep in his arms, making it just as difficult to drive steadily. They make do, however, and arrive early in the evening.

Alan helps Violet off. "Go on in. I'll get your gear."

"Thanks. Sorry I made it hard for you and used all of your gauze." Violet pats him on the back. Alan shakes his head with a smirk.

Walking through the door, she's greeted by Nathan slamming into her legs, hugging them tight. Violet loses her balance, catching herself on the wall. "I missed you," he says, burying his face in her belly.

"I missed you too, love," she says, hugging him with one hand

"What happened to your arm?" Nathan looks up at her with concern.

"I accidentally broke it. Clumsy me," she says brightly.

"Does it hurt?"

"A little. Uncle Alan fixed it up really well. I need to rest. Come sit with me." Nathan nods, hugging her again.

Killian comes through the doors and Nathan rushes to him. "Whoa, hey buddy," Killian says, dropping his bag and swooping him up with one arm, a large smile gracing his face. "Did you take care of everyone for me while I was gone?" Nathan nods vigorously. "That's my boy." He kisses him on the forehead before setting him down.

"Where did your arm go?" Nathan asks while groping his shoulder.

"I broke it. I can always make a new one." Killian winks. Nathan smiles and runs to catch up with his mother, holding onto her hand.

"Well, aren't you two peas in a pod," Jack chuckles.

"Together we still have two working arms," Killian says. Violet carefully sits on the couch, ignoring their conversation. Nathan cuddles up to her for a little while.

Lilly and Ember start setting the table for a meal as the others get cleaned up. Fresh clothes are already laid out for them on each of their bunks. Violet presumes Clara had something to do with it. The men are given nice dress shirts, vests and slacks. No one questions it except for Stacy, who barges into the bunk room still wrapped in a towel, holding a powder blue dress out, touching it as little as possible. "What is this? Why is it in my room?" She stops in her tracks when she walks in on Killian and Alan.

"Just get dressed, Stacy. It'll be nice," Killian demands as he buttons his blue brocade vest with one hand. Alan helps him with his matching cravat tie before doing his own. Looking over his shoulder, Stacy is still staring in the doorway. "Stacy, go." She shakes her head, backing out of the room.

Violet is changing in Jack and Clara's room. Slipping into the burgundy velvet dress is easy enough, but fixing her hair is another thing. She keeps it in its long loose braid and manages to wrap it into a bun at the nape of her neck. She is able to hold it in place with her freshly splinted hand while pinning it in place with the other. When she's satisfied, she joins the others in the dining room. Ember, Lilly and Nathan are also dressed in proper garb as they wait patiently at the table covered in white linen. Jack's cheeks are rosy, and she can tell he's gotten into the stash at the bar. Alan and Killian come out together as Violet takes a seat. The children giggle and poke fun at the frills and lace they aren't used to wearing. Killian and Alan flush when seeing Violet in the low-cut velvet gown. Suddenly she feels more self-conscious.

Clara comes out of the kitchen holding a large pot roast. The aroma wafts through the halls. Everyone is seated, waiting anxiously to eat, but they wait impatiently for Stacy to come out. Finally, she emerges, her silver wavy locks draped over one shoulder and tied with a ribbon. She is wearing a blue silk dress with lace overlay. The dress is unlike any she has ever worn, even in the Stratos Development. It is so frilly and dainty that she can't help but love it, smiling bashfully. Alan turns his head and explodes into laughter. Her smile quickly turns sour as she stares him down. Red spreads across her face and down her neck to her chest as she balls her fists. The laughter is contagious but they try so hard not to, biting their lips and coughing to disguise their chuckles.

Clara quickly stands with excitement. "You look lovely, my dear," she says as she leads her to the table and sits her down next to Lilly. They both shift uncomfortably, knowing they don't like one another.

"It looks good on you, Stacy," Killian adds.

Stacy smiles at him, holding the deep red flush in her cheeks. "Thank you," she responds.

Finally Alan settles himself, wiping the tears from his eyes. "I'm sorry, Nox. I just haven't ever seen you in anything other than the color black, and in a dress no less." He sighs. "You do look beautiful, though. It's a pleasure to be in a room with so many lovely ladies." He looks around the room. Lilly and Ember giggle.

"Such a charmer," Clara laughs. "Now that Stacy's here, shall we?" She gestures to the food on the table.

It's the first civil dinner since joining together. The conversation is light. Even Stacy participates, careful not to offend anyone. They feast on the pot roast with carrots and celery, and fresh baked bread. Wine is passed around the table, putting everyone in high spirits. Even the children are able to partake, though it is watered down for them. They finish off with a bread pudding. By the end of their feast, everyone is giggling and rosy-cheeked. Stacy pulls out an old camera from the library. She takes a photo of the group sitting about the table joyously. Alan takes over the camera, taking photos of everyone.

Jack puts on some music and holds his hand out to Clara, asking her to dance. "Such a gentleman, how could I say no?" Clara laughs. Taking his hand, they begin spinning around the room in a waltz.

"May I?" Killian asks Violet in the same manner as Jack.

"I'm sorry. I'm just not up for it."

"She still needs to rest," Alan scolds. "She heals fast, but not *that* fast." Killian settles in beside her on the couch to keep her company.

After numerous photos, Alan sets the camera down. "M'lady?" he says to Stacy in a deep voice.

Stacy looks up at him, contemplating, then sighs and says, "Sure, why not?" Soon everyone is on the floor dancing. With uneven numbers, Violet urges Killian to participate. As they switch partners, Stacy grabs Killian. Killian keeps an eye on Violet all the while.

"I think I'll retire to the bunks after this song," Stacy says, drawing Killian's attention back to her.

He looks at her curiously. "You seem to be enjoying yourself. Are you not?"

"I am." She smiles up at him and holds him closer as they move to the rhythm. "It's just… tomorrow we're leaving, unless you've changed your mind."

He looks at her seriously now. "I haven't changed my mind," he says solemnly.

She nods, keeping a serious expression. "Since we don't know when we'll return, you should take this time to be with your family."

"That's thoughtful of you."

"Well, I may be selfish, but I'm not heartless… sort of." She scrunches her face and Killian laughs. With that the song ends. She kisses him on the cheek before taking her leave. She thanks Clara for dinner and the dress on her way out. Clara smiles brightly at Stacy's warm attitude.

Before long, the children start to yawn, Jack and Clara along with them. Alan offers to put the children to bed but Killian declines. Jack and Clara retire after tucking in the girls. Killian helps Nathan get comfortable. "Thank you for taking care of everyone while I was gone," he says.

"You're welcome." Nathan smiles.

"I want you to know that I have to leave tomorrow. I don't know for how long. I need you to continue watching over them for me, okay?"

"Where are you going?" Nathan asks in concern.

"I'm going to end this war for you and your mama. So we can all live together safely." Nathan is quiet for a long while, thinking of what to say, tears filling his eyes. "Don't cry, little man. I'll be back before you know it. I just need to make the world a better place for all of you here." Nathan nods with a quivering lip. Killian kisses his forehead and hugs him tight. "Can you be brave and take care of them for me?" His throat tightens and he tries to swallow the swelling knot.

"I will," he says with a shaking voice.

"Don't take this job too seriously, though. I still want you to play and have fun too."

"Yes sir." Killian kisses him again as he gets to his feet. "Thank you for being my dad."

"It's my pleasure," Killian chokes out. "Get some rest, little man," he whispers.

Killian leaves the bunk and takes a deep breath, wiping away the tears that are welling up in his eyes. Putting his hands in his pockets, he comes back to Alan and Violet. Alan, seeing the look in his eyes, cuts their conversation short and bids her goodnight, kissing the top of her hand as he bows out. Looking back at Violet, she is watching Killian cautiously.

Killian sits down with her once more. Being so close to him, she is unable to hide the tears forming in her eyes. He stares down at her, speechless. "You're leaving, aren't you?" she says, unable to look into his eyes.

He bites his lip as tears fall down his cheeks, mimicking her own. "Yes."

"You're going to break Nathan's heart."

"I'm doing this for him. For both of you." Violet nods. "I'm sorry," he says in a hushed voice. "I love you." She turns to face him. "I promise—"

"Don't promise me anything," she says, cutting him off. "Promises mean nothing if you keep breaking them." She stares into her hands.

"Look at me." Killian pulls her chin to face him.

Violet closes her eyes tight. "Please don't touch me," she says as fresh tears fall.

Killian drops his hand. "You're scared of me," he says solemnly.

Violet is silent for a moment. "I've never seen you like that. It came so easily to you."

"When it comes to you, it *is* easy. I would kill again if it means keeping you safe. You said you could forgive my mistakes if I forgive yours."

"It seems that's something we both struggle with, though," Violet responds.

"Perhaps it's better that I'm leaving," he responds bitterly. "We'll both have the time we need to get over our pasts." Violet is speechless. The ache and the fear battling in her heart keeps her silent. Disgusted with himself and angry at what he's done to their relationship, he stands up to leave but hesitates. Kneeling down, he waits until she looks into his eyes. "I love you and I love our child. I'll never let my emotions change me like that again. One day I hope you'll forgive me. Just, please don't give up on me, on us. I love you more than anything in this world." A tear streams down Violet's face as she finally sees the boy she fell in love with again. He quickly takes his leave. She reaches out to him, but hesitates. When her nerves have calmed, she crawls into bed with Nathan. He clings to her in his sleep and she takes comfort in him.

* * *

The lights in the bunk room brighten as they alert Violet of a new day. Morning has come too soon. Pulling herself away from the still sleeping Nathan, she gets dressed. She attempts taking a deep breath, which is a mistake as she doubles over in pain. Taking some painkillers from the infirmary, she puts on a smile as she starts the day. Clara helps her with breakfast. Though Violet pretends to be cheery, Clara can tell something is off. Taking care not to make things worse, she keeps quiet. Nathan comes out with a melancholy attitude. He clings to his mother's leg as she works in the kitchen. When Killian rises, Nathan joins him at the table he is setting.

Stacy emerges, looking as though she hadn't slept much. Violet avoids making eye contact, but Stacy catches her on her way to the bunks. She pulls an envelope out of her pocket and hands it to her. Looking at Stacy, she's puzzled. "These are for you. Take it." Taking hold of Violet's wrist, she shoves the yellow envelope into her hand and walks away. Opening the envelope, she finds printouts of the photos from last night. Her throat tightens when she sees the photo of Killian and Nathan dancing together. She stayed up until all hours of the evening to develop these memories.

Stacy watches her from beside Killian at the table. Violet looks at her and smiles, which is thanks enough to Stacy. She bows her head, looking over to Killian. "Don't pack anything. Keep this in a safe place," she says in a low voice, sliding over a picture of Violet and Nathan embracing.

He smiles and hides the photo in a hidden pocket in his high-top boots. "Thank you. When's it happening?"

"I don't know, I haven't had word." Killian nods.

Clara brings out breakfast and everyone joins for their last meal together, though few of them know it at the time. Putting on a strong veil of happiness, everyone enjoys the meal with little small talk.

After breakfast things continue as usual. "Let's play hide and seek," Lilly begs Nathan, tugging on his sleeve, though he seems uninterested, looking back at the father he has only known for several days. Killian urges him to go, giving him a tight squeeze and a kiss on the forehead. Reluctantly he follows Lilly and Ember into the atrium.

Alan jokes around with Jack as they enjoy the music playing. Stacy watches them with almost a look of amusement. "Careful,"

Killian whispers to her. "You don't want them thinking you enjoy their company."

"As annoying as he is, I *am* going to miss him. Just a little bit."

"Turning soft?" Stacy elbows Killian in the side. Looking over his shoulder, he sees Violet glance at him and head towards the cargo bay. Killian follows her. She sits down at the edge, taking her shoes off to dip her toes in the water. He sits down beside her, doing the same.

"Be careful," Violet says. "Don't trust anyone."

"Alright," Killian says. Violet closes her eyes, focusing on her breaths. There is a rustling sound behind them. He looks back but doesn't see anyone. He hears it again and nudges her. He stands, putting his wet feet back into his boots, then quietly moves towards the area where he heard the sound. Another sound draws his attention back to the open cave. Violet is alert, listening carefully now. The hiss and grumbling of a ship is nearby. "Violet, go inside and get Stacy." She does as she is told, moving quickly through the swinging doors, leaving a path of wet footprints.

The sound of the ship breaking through the wall of falling water echoes through the cave. It slowly comes into view. The large ship hovers at the edge of the platform as the doors slide open. Two armored men run out, taking aim at Killian. He throws his hand up, gritting his teeth. He hears the sound behind him again. Glancing back, he sees a small figure through the cracks of the wood crate, which has his heart pounding out of his chest. Two more armored suits come out, flanking the others.

"Stacy!" Violet yells. "I think they're here." Stacy runs out towards the cargo bay.

Lilly comes out of the atrium, yelling, "Nathan! Come out, come out, wherever you are!"

Panic begins to rise in Violet as she runs through the shelter, checking every room as quickly as possible. Hearing her calling for

Nathan, the others begin searching. "No, no, no!" she says to herself as she heads towards the doors of the cargo bay.

Peeking through the window, she sees Killian and Stacy with their hands up. One of the suits walks behind Stacy, leading her into the ship. Nathan is cowering in a ball behind the crates as one tips over, crashing behind him. The suits are alerted and start to move towards him. Violet bursts through the doors with her hands up, moving towards the suits. Shoving Stacy onto the ship, another suit restrains her. All four suits converge on Violet, as two more leave the ship to restrain Killian as he comes to help her.

The suits are yelling commands for her to hit the ground with her hands behind her head. Killian is struggling to free himself. He yells for them to leave her as they drag him onto the ship. Violet obeys their commands, dropping to her knees as they surround her. Stacy is yelling at them to leave her. Everyone yelling at once causes chaos, and Violet hears nothing but buzzing in her ears. She looks at Killian. Shaking her head, she wants him to calm down and let it happen. They use zip ties on her wrists, pulling them so tight it bites at her skin. The splint guards the other wrist.

Killian doesn't listen to her silent request and breaks free, snatching the weapon from a suit's holster. One shot hits the suit in front of Violet, and sparks fly from his chest as he falls to the ground. All weapons are suddenly on Killian. Stacy again commands them to stand down, but they do not hear her shouting. Things start to slow down as Violet sees one of the suits about to fire on Killian. She snaps free from the thick zip ties and throws the aim off just as the shot goes off.

"Mommy!" Nathan screams. Like a ripple effect, the others follow suit. Violet reacts before the shots are fired, knocking the aim off Killian again. Several bullets ricochet off the ship in all directions, as they hit their own suits and bounce off the metal framing in the bay. The three men go down. Looking back at Killian, he is white as snow, as the two men on the ship restrain him from taking his weapon. Stacy is on the ground, holding her hands to her head, as she stares pale-faced past Violet.

Following her gaze, Violet turns to see Jack falling to his knees. He pulls Nathan into his arms. Killian is in shock, staring wide-eyed as the doors shut in front of him and the ship leaves their wounded behind. Jack cries out. Violet weakly falls to her knees in front of him. Blood soaks his clothing as Violet takes her child into her arms.

"Nathan?" She touches his cheek. His eyes are closed and the color in his face fades. "Nathan?" Violet croons as she pets his soft cheeks and brushes the hair from his face. "I'm here, sweet boy." Violet's throat tightens and she can feel herself falling to pieces. "Come on, baby, please don't leave me," she says as she rocks him in her arms. Nathan begins to lose his warmth with the loss of blood. "Nathan!" Violet cries, shaking him as if he might wake. Alan touches her shoulders. "Don't touch me!" Her scream echoes through the cave. "I'm so sorry, my baby. I shouldn't have left you. I should've stayed with you. I should've stayed. I am so sorry." She cries into his chest. "I love you so much. I am so sorry," she says again and again, between kisses on his pale lips and cheeks.

Alan pulls Nathan from her grasp as Clara and Jack hold her back. Her throat tears as she screams. It echoes several times throughout the cave. Tearing her eyes from the pool of blood on the cold cement, she buries her face as she cries out in pain. There is no physical pain, only the agony. *I killed him.*

CHAPTER
16

Shots fired near his head have his ears ringing. He feels a tight grasp around his arm, yanking him back. No longer does he have the strength or the will to fight back as he watches his only son bleed out in Jack's arms. Killian is thrown into the car and cuffed to the seat. The doors slam shut and he can no longer see his family. His mouth is dry and tears spill down his cheeks as he stares into space. All he can see is his boy in Jack's arms. He lingers on the thought. Perhaps he could have prevented it. He saw the look in Violet's eyes telling him to stay put, but he didn't listen. He has always acted before thinking of the consequences.

Stacy watches him from the other side of the car, tears of her own streaming down her pale face. Her silver hair is in disarray from the tussle with the suits. Killian stares at the floor. His eyes don't hold any light. Stacy glares down at the two men in suits that have caused him so much pain. Some of them have taken off their helmets, breaking protocol to wipe the sweat from their brow. When they see the wicked smile on Stacy's face, they quickly return their helmets, cursing themselves, knowing punishment will follow their arrival.

The ride is long and quiet. Returning home is something Stacy never thought she would have to endure. Peeking out the windows, she can see the fallen city growing larger in the distance. The storm clouds swarm angrily about the towering skyscrapers. Lightning brightens what has been darkened by the thick cloud mass. The crashing thunder shakes them. As they come into the city, the winds rock the vehicle. The buildings are mostly just bare bones. The glass windows have shattered away, and what once had occupied them has been stripped away with the fierce winds. Nothing grows in this city, and the ground is covered in copper-toned dirt amongst the rubble. The wind roars against the car, sending debris into the sides of the vehicle. The lightning strikes it several times.

Alarms go off in the cockpit as the wind thrashes them about. The pilot flips a red cover, revealing a keypad. They enter the code and the wind calms. It becomes quiet once more and the lightning strikes the empty buildings once again. Heading straight for the tallest building, the suits arm themselves and watch Killian carefully, as they hold onto the straps on the ceiling in front of the doors. This building is so tall that it is partially hidden by clouds. Stacy watches what little light was left outside turn to pitch black. They enter a small port in the building. Mechanical arms take hold, jostling the car. They are pulled in deeper.

Eventually the ship comes to a stop, slamming Stacy's back against the hard seat. Killian is hardly fazed by the jarring movements. The rizzing sound of escaping air and clanking of mechanisms at work sound off until the doors slide open once more. They are greeted by two more armed people. The grated floors are lit by a white light underneath, the only light illuminating the corridor.

"Move out," one of the suits commands. Two more remove Killian's restraints. Stacy stays close to him as they step out of the car. The air is warm and heavy, with the scent of burnt rubber and metal. Suits surround them as they accompany them down the corridor.

Finally they stop in a room highlighted in blue. "Please remove all clothing and enter your designated chamber," a woman asks in a calm voice. Two chamber doors open, with a symbol for each sex. Stacy is separated from Killian as they are stripped of all clothing and shoved into a chamber. The door shuts and everyone is showered in a blue liquid that sends a bristling sensation across their entire body, and is then rinsed off. The pressure from the jets prick the skin. Brisk air flows through the chamber, leaving them dry.

The doors open and at the center of the room, a table has risen from the ground with a matching uniform for each of them. "Please get dressed and wait for further instruction," the same woman says. The gray uniform is tight fitting and covers them from neck to toe. Someone dresses Killian as he stares off into oblivion. The sleeve hangs from his right shoulder, so they tie it off in a knot.

The now empty table sinks back into the ground. A circle of light activates. "Please stand inside the circle and keep all limbs within the line. Thank you." The four suits help Killian and Stacy into the circle. Railing rises around them and the floor begins to rise. There is a hole in the ceiling with a blinding white light. As they ascend through the building, they gain speed. They feel something detach from the floor, and you can feel the weight of gravity as they accelerate further. The walls of the elevator change from gray cement walls to an unusual metal. Stacy watches Killian with concern; he looks as if his life has been sucked out of him. His head hangs low with his shoulders hunched. She reaches out and touches his arm. It is as if he is numb to everything around him.

Within 25 minutes the weight of gravity is lifted. The elevator slows its speed and comes to a stop. The doors open. The corridor is labeled 'Level 03 Department of Health and Scientific

Exploration.' A scruffy man in his mid-thirties is waiting in a long white coat and gray trousers. He is lean with strong cheekbones, and greets them with a large grin. Pushing past their guards, he takes Killian's hand in both of his hands and shakes it vigorously. "It's a pleasure to meet you, Mr. Grey," he says. "I've been watching your work for quite some time. Welcome, welcome." Killian pays no mind to the man grasping his hand. "My name is Doctor Oric, but please call me Zane." He places Killian's hand in the crook of his elbow. "Please, come with me and we'll get you all cleaned up." He leads him out of the elevator.

Stacy begins to follow but the guards hold her back. "Dr. Oric," she calls, "we're not to be separated. He's been through a traumatic experience!"

"Don't you worry, Ms. Nox. I'll present him to you in perfect condition." He waves her away without taking his eyes from his new specimen.

"No, I need to stay with him!" she argues, but the doors close in front of her and she is whisked away to her own destination.

Dr. Oric leads Killian down the brightly lit hallway into his laboratory. The room is very large and circular in shape. The windows to the right reveal an open sky. Looking out over the earth below, all that can be seen are miles of dark clouds being lit by lightning, keeping them hidden from below. "When they told me you were joining us, I got to work on something special for you. I worked thirty-eight hours straight coming up with the design."

He taps a panel and it lights up with blue keys hovering over it. He enters a code and a hovering table comes out of the wall to the center of the room. From the ceiling, several mechanical arms descend. He leads Killian to the middle of the room, removes the gray suit and tosses it aside. A woman comes into the room dressed in a white skintight suit. Her thick black hair is slicked back into a tight bun, her dark brown skin contrasting with her white clothing. She picks up the article of clothing and disposes of it.

"Ah, Ella," Oric says. "He'll need your company during this procedure. Make him as comfortable as possible." He smiles at Killian as he helps him onto the table.

"Of course," she says as she takes the doctor's place. She takes Killian's hand. "Please lie down," she says sweetly. He does as he is told. Gently she brushes her fingers through his hair with her free hand. Resting her palm against his temple, she places her thumb below his eye and her index above his brow. "He is experiencing mental anguish. Do I have permission to treat him?"

"Permission granted."

"Administering treatment." She turns his head so that he is looking her in the eyes. She smiles down at him and holds his wrist with her index and middle finger over the largest vein, his pupils dilating. "I am sorry for your loss," she says. Killian tries to comprehend his situation to no avail.

"Let's start the procedure, Ella."

"Administering anesthesia," she says while still smiling into Killian's eyes. It quickly takes effect, though he is unsure of when or where it is coming from. They are keeping him awake for the procedure, but he no longer feels the woman touching his hand and face. The mechanical arms move gracefully as they whirr with each movement. He feels the pressure as they drill the new plates into his shoulder. Dr. Oric orchestrates it behind his screen.

"Ella, I thought you administered anesthesia?"

"Yes, doctor."

"Then why is he in pain?"

"He is not in physical pain, doctor," she says, still staring into Killian's eyes.

"Is he mentally unstable?"

"Currently his mental stability is fluctuating, due to the chemical imbalance we are inflicting. He is also coming out of shock."

"Let's keep him for a couple of days. Please inform Chairman Nox of his extended stay."

Ella stares past Killian for a moment. "Message has been delivered."

"Thank you, Ella."

"You are welcome, doctor."

Dr. Oric sits down in his chair, twirling the pen in his hand as he watches the operation. Over the next hour, the arm begins to come together. Killian falls captive to his exhaustion during the procedure. When it is finished, skin-toned plates cover the vital parts of the arm and he almost looks whole again. Letting him rest, they move the patient to a room in which he can recover.

The doctor inspects the new arm with satisfaction. "I need to check on our guinea pigs. Stay with him, Ella. Make sure he stays comfortable."

"Of course, doctor." She lays next to Killian and brushes her fingers through his hair as she watches over him. As he settles into a dreamless sleep, she imitates sleep as she holds his wrist, keeping track of his vitals.

* * *

Stacy sits on the oval shaped bed in her whitewashed room, waiting, anxiously biting at her nails. Everything in this room has a curved edge. At the other end of the room is a hidden door which quietly slides open. Stacy glances over and sighs with a roll of her eyes. A young woman enters the room wearing a short white tunic, with a cutout in the shape of a triangle revealing a lot of her chest. Though she has a small chest, Stacy is disgusted by the very little clothing she is given. Her hair is ghostly white, bobbed to her chin, her bangs cut in a perfect line. Her face is thin and sharp. "Oh,

Eustachia!" she squeals. The girl clings to her, wrapping her arms around her neck. "I have missed you so much," she says in a candy-coated voice. "Did you miss me?"

"Nope—"

The girl cuts her off. "I have not known what to do with myself since you have been gone. Look at you, what a mess! Let us get you cleaned up. Won't Mr. and Mrs. Nox be excited to see you home..." She continues talking as she walks to the corner of the room in which the floor is embedded with white smooth stones. Pressing a button on the wall starts a waterfall from the ceiling. The woman pulls Stacy's clothing off and begins unraveling the disheveled braids. Stacy ignores her assigned companion as she prunes and polishes every inch of her body. Her rambling becomes intolerable.

"Please shut up, Kat!"

"Am I talking too much? I am sorry. We are still best friends, right?"

"You're a freaking gynoid."

"Ha ha! You are too funny!"

"Kat, not another word, not even a confirmation, or I'll disable you."

She nods in agreement with a glistening smile. Taking deep breaths, Stacy tries to calm herself, knowing she cannot do anything to the intolerable thing yanking at her hair. After a couple of hours she has finally finished. Stacy is now sporting her family color, wearing a white floor-length gown made of a very light fabric, with a gold-plated collar curving around her breast and up about her neck. Her silver hair is parted in three sections, the middle pulled tightly and formed into a bun, with the sides hanging loose around her face. The parts in her hair resemble the three white triangles tattooed under her eye, which match the gold cuff around her wrist, the gold triangle being the family emblem.

With a satisfied smile, Kat takes Stacy's hand and drags her out of her room to meet her parents in the dining room. Her mother Dinah stands from the table and goes to greet Stacy, kissing her on the cheek. She is wearing a gown similar to Stacy's, with a gold angular tiara that rests on her forehead. "I'm so happy you're home," she says. "You look beautiful." Stacy tries to smile for her mother's sake. John stands and waits for them to sit before greeting her. He is tall, with dark hair and white streaks on either side. He wears a white suit with a gold tie clip in the same shape of Dinah's tiara. They take their places on either side of the table, with John at the head.

"Your little escapade with that man at the shelter has been very difficult to keep quiet," he says. "Keeping out our family's involvement with Grey's recruitment is imperative. There'll be many adjustments needed. I'll announce his recruitment next week, and you'll pretend you've never met him." He twitches a finger in the air and Kat brings out the first course of the meal. He is served first, and Stacy takes note of the smile he gives Kat in passing.

"Why can't you say I recruited him after seeing his impressive skills amongst the bottom dwellers?"

"You've only just recovered from a severe illness that has kept you confined to the Department of Health. It's my job, Eustachia, to protect this family and everything we've built," John says in frustration.

"Please don't call me that."

"I *will* call you by your given name. Now that you've returned, I want you to start repairing your reputation. Don't use ridiculous nicknames, and make a public apology for your absence. Explain that your health has improved and you'll be returning to your duties. The people need to see that you can be trusted with the safety and security of Development 6."

"What illness did I supposedly have?" Stacy sighs.

"That's a personal matter that concerns no one. You won't need to discuss details about your absence."

"What about Killian?"

"You'll be separated until he's been introduced into society. We don't want anyone to get the wrong idea. Besides, he's not mentally capable of being released into the public yet."

"How long will that take?!"

"Doctor Oric will decide, and you are not to interfere. If I hear word you've gone against me again, I'll have him cast out from the nearest airlock. Am I understood?"

"Undeniably." Stacy glares him down, though he has not looked her in the eye since she entered the room.

* * *

Killian opens his eyes to the beauty with dark brown skin laying next to him. Her eyes open slowly and she smiles. He sits up, feeling uneasy, realizing he is not wearing any clothing and that only a thin blanket covers him. She still holds his wrist as she sits up with him.

Doctor Oric promptly enters the room. His disheveled brown hair and unkempt facial hair, accompanied by his hyperactive personality, gives off a hint of insanity. "Good morning, Killian Grey," he says. "Do you mind if I call you Killian? I feel as though we'll be good friends. I'm Dr. Oric, but you can call me Zane. Of course, I told you this already...." He taps his chin, looking up at the ceiling. Throwing his hands up in the air, he says, "You're recovering nicely. How do you feel?" He sits down in a swivel chair and slides up next to the bedside. Picking up the new arm he attached the evening before, he begins inspecting it.

"Fine," Killian rasps.

"Good, good," Zane smiles as he stares into Killian's eyes.

Killian begins to feel uncomfortable under his unwavering gaze. "Where's Stacy?"

"Stacy? Stacy... Stacy..." He strokes his beard as he tries to recall.

"Eustachia Nox," Ella chimes in. Killian glances at Ella.

"Oh, *Stacy*," Zane laughs. He presses his hand on the white wall and it lights up. "*Stacy* is making her public announcement of good health."

On a video screen, he sees her behind a podium with her hair pulled up in a professional manner. Her attire is clean, white and simple, with a gold collar in the shape of the family emblem. She smiles brightly as she speaks, thanking the audience for being patient while she worked through her sickness. She apologizes for not being available to fulfill her duty as the firstborn of the Nox family. She promises to be more present from now on in all future events. The audience claps and calls out with questions. Stacy steps to the side of the podium and bows low before walking off the stage. Music starts and the video transitions to current events. A shot of Killian comes on the screen, an image of him smiling with the background blurred out. The man announces Killian Grey as a new recruitment for the first time in a hundred years.

Zane flips the screen off at the snap of his fingers. "Wait, turn it back on!" Killian demands, getting to his feet to touch the wall.

"You asked about Eustachia. Now it's time for some tests. You can watch the program on your own time," Zane says indifferently as he gets to his feet.

Killian is quick to his feet, and with his new limb he clasps his mechanical hand around Zane's throat and shoves him into the wall. "Take me to her."

"E-Ella?" Zane barely chokes out.

"Yes, doctor." Ella stands beside Killian and takes his left hand. A calm washes over him and he feels his body grow weak. He loses his balance and takes a couple steps back, releasing Zane.

Zane rubs at his neck and clears his throat. "Well, we need to run a few tests before you can be introduced into society. Make sure you haven't contracted something contagious, and a psych evaluation. Don't want you running off to kill the precious *nobles*... or me." Zane laughs. Ella helps Killian into the robe, tying it off in the back, then leads him out of the room. Entering the main operating room in which the surgery was performed, he notices the strange unnatural design. There are no hard edges; even the windowsills are soft and rounded. The walls, ceiling and floor are all polished and bland in color. A very sterile room. They continue through a hallway, with many glass doors leading to rooms that have drains at the center. Many other patients are being studied as they stare off into nothingness. All of them are equipped with the same robe and glasses that wrap around their head, made of a metal of sorts. There is a narrow opening in which the eyes can see through. They sit in reclined chairs in which their ankles and wrists have been restrained. Beneath their robe, wires and tubes have been attached, connecting them to the back wall.

Killian is brought into his own small room. Ella leads him to the chair and he weakly lops down into it. Ella equips him with the glasses, adjusting them to fit perfectly around the shape of his head. "What is this?" He clumsily stops her hands, knocking the glasses askew.

"Everyone entering society must go through a psychological test." Ella smiles. He lets her adjust the glasses. She and the Doctor stand behind the glass door as it seals. Killian nervously waits for something to happen. Zane smiles as he activates the glasses. The narrow opening turns dark, cutting off all light, leaving him in darkness.

"Please don't take any of what you see personally. It's just part of the test," Zane says over a speaker. Killian sighs, knowing he won't enjoy whatever happens next. His head lulls back, feeling drunk from Ella's touch.

First comes the sound of the ocean. The image comes after, and a wave of nostalgia flows over him. He looks down and finds the apricot-colored sand. Looking around him, he takes in the multicolored sky to the right, and to the left is a star-speckled sky. Then comes the scent of the salty air and he laughs. "Safe Haven?" he asks as he bends down to take a handful of sand, though in reality he is sitting very still. Somehow he feels each granule of sand as it slips through his fingers. The sand falling from his hand transforms into water, changing the scene to the waterfall.

"Very nice," Dr. Oric says, touching the glass board in his hands, revealing Killian's brain activity. He shares it with Ella and she smiles. He scrolls up on the board, changing the scene in Killian's mind several times, and different people appear in front of him in different scenarios. Zane takes note of the changes. Ella takes over for Zane when he tires of the same results. He sits in the corner of the room, impatiently tapping his foot and scratching the scruff on his neck. He begins pacing and stretching his arms out, twisting his back. "I'm going to check on other patients. You can take it from here, Ella. Inform me if anything changes."

Ella continues with the scheduled scenarios, in which Killian encounters different types of people and situations, and he has to choose to move on or help them, as if it is a game. Within hours, Killian forgets that it is simulated, and carries on as if it is real to him. Ella then connects the tubes and wires from the back wall to his body, giving him nutrition and testing his blood. When children are involved, Killian feels obligated to protect them, though when it comes to those who would get in the way of his goal, he does what is necessary to survive. The testing continues throughout the night.

* * *

A couple days have passed. Dr. Oric comes back to check on his newest specimen. Killian has tubes and wires connecting him to the wall, like the other patients. He sighs before taking the board from Ella. Sliding his finger across the screen, he does not seem impressed. "These results are fairly stable. Start the program. Let's get this done already." Ella nods and joins Killian at the center of the room, strapping his wrists and ankles to the chair before returning to the panel.

The scenarios become much more intense, including Violet, Nathan and the rest of his family. The results become more intriguing, and Zane watches with amusement. Killian's breathing becomes erratic. Zane taps Ella's shoulder. "When this round of scenarios end, go ahead and upload this, and finish him off if I haven't returned."

He flicks a drive into the air. She catches it with a smooth swipe. "Yes, doctor." Ella smiles up at him.

* * *

Forty-eight hours later, Ella opens the door to the lobby. Dr. Oric is drinking a hot cup of coffee, his hair wet and slicked back, beard neatly trimmed. He is checking the stats on his board when he looks up fondly. Ella is wearing her grey dress, which is proper for a droid companion of his status. The gown is sleeveless and floor-length, in a sheer fabric. Strips of a thicker fabric cover the most private of parts, leaving very little else to the imagination. Killian comes in after her. His hair is cut short around the ears and longer at the bangs, styled in a sleek fashion. His face is clean shaven, and he is dressed in a gray suit, with silver shoulder guards and slanted buttons from the shoulder to his abdomen. His dark eyes are bleak as he follows Ella to stand before Dr. Oric.

"Well, well, well," the doctor says. "Don't you clean up nicely."

"As do you, Zane," Killian says with a wry smile.

Zane slaps his knee in amusement. "It looks like you qualified under our color. I'm honored to welcome you to our family." Dr. Oric removes his white coat, revealing a gray suit of his own with a different style. Closing the distance between them, he pats Killian on the back. "Before we throw you to the wolves, I should prepare you with what to expect. Everyone in Development 6 has been informed of your recruitment, and has been given a brief history of your unfortunate past. They know what happened to your family, so they'll probably bring up Nathan and Violet. Try to be understanding; they're concerned for you. Know that you don't have to answer any questions you're not comfortable with." Killian nods, frowning down at the floor. "Are you ready?"

"As ready as I'll ever be," Killian responds with a sigh.

Zane holds his hand out, gesturing to the exit. Ella takes the lead. Entering the hallway, there are several elevators. Ella presses a button against the wall and one of the large steel doors slides open, then closes behind them. As the elevator rises, the glass walls allow Killian to look over the facility that he will be considering home from now on. After several layers of cement walls, the view opens up for a moment to a cluttered, enclosed city. There are no windows to allow natural light; it is forever dark, lit only by electricity. Neon lights and advertisements light up the streets, filled with people.

As they continue to rise several more floors, the view of the neon city is disrupted by more cement and metal flooring. When it opens up once more, Killian is nearly blinded by the bright sunlight. Without the obstruction of the tall city buildings, you can see the curve of the station, as fields of crops stretch as far as the eye can see. People are seen working the fields with hand tools. An older woman watches the elevator rise as she stretches her aching back.

Rising a bit further, they finally come to a stop. Before Killian can grasp the scenery, the doors open and he is bombarded by hundreds of people cheering. Many drones hover about, with their cameras greeting him. Zane and Ella part the sea of people to allow Killian to pass. Many of the people call out to him.

"I'm so sorry for your loss!"

"We're happy to have you here!"

"May I have your autograph?"

"What made you decide to leave your family and join us here in station 6?"

"Are you still mourning the loss of your son?"

Killian attempts to ignore their pressing questions. With help, they are able to enter the nearest building. As they pass through the glass doors, the noise subsides. The people have been shut out behind them. Greeted by a young man in a sharp white tunic, they are led through the large open lobby. Many plants bring color to the plain room. "This way, please," he says, leading them down a flight of stairs and down a long narrow hallway. Climbing another flight of stairs, the man holds the door open as they pass through.

A woman wearing the same white tunic, with a headset and glass board, quietly greets them as they walk backstage, from where Stacy once stood giving her speech. "Just in time," the woman says. "I want to introduce you in five minutes. All you have to do is smile and wave at the audience. Stand at the podium beside Magister Sinai. He may ask you some questions." The woman positions Killian to the side of the stage and waits for the cue. The magister is gesturing with his hands enthusiastically as he speaks. He is dressed in a black suit that is fitted perfectly to hide his rounded gut. His daughter stands a few feet back and to his left, tall and elegant with her dark brown hair slicked back into a clean, long ponytail. Eustachia and John Nox stand to the magister's right, against a purple curtain backdrop, as he speaks. John stands tall in his white suit with gold buttons in their signature triangles. Silver streaks on either side of his head, just above his ears, highlight his darker features.

"Now, I know it's unusual to recruit one from below the skies, but we wanted to make an exception for this intelligent man. Losing his parents at a young age, he was found and raised by one of our very own. He's a clever engineer and experienced in the medical field, as well as advanced weapons. He's been through so much more than we could've ever imagined. Discovering him was by accident, as one of the seekers had crossed his path. With the most recent loss, we found it important to help and support this man. Let me introduce our newest, Killian Grey."

The woman standing behind Killian gently shoves him, and he hesitates before walking onto the stage. He waves to the audience as they cheer, and with a handsome grin he shakes hands with Magister Sinai and then his daughter, ignoring the Nox's entirely. He joins the magister at the podium and the audience calms.

"Thank you for taking me in to join your society," Killian says. "I'm eternally grateful for the hospitality and support I've received since my arrival." He turns to nod at the magister's daughter. Stacy stands there, watching him in shock.

"Of course. We're so pleased to have you with us. I see you've been assigned a position at the Department of Health and Science Exploration."

"Yes, it's very exciting."

"Wonderful! Now, Killian, I know you've been through a lot, but I'm sure everyone wants to know, how are you handling the loss of your son?"

"Honestly, I don't know how I'm even standing on my own two feet right now. When Nathan died in that cave, I couldn't help but feel anger towards myself for not being a better parent. For not keeping an eye on the children as they played." His eyes glaze over. Stacy looks down at the floor at the mention of Nathan, guilt strangling her heart.

"You've only been a parent for a couple of weeks, from what I understand. You can hardly be to blame. Was it not Violet who caused the accident?"

"It's true. She knew I was about to leave to collect supplies. She was supposed to watch the children."

"Is that why you chose to leave her behind?"

"Yes, after she hid the child from me from the beginning, trying to erase her memory of me. Not taking her responsibility as a mother seriously, I could no longer stay with her. You can hardly expect me to stay with someone who doesn't respect young lives." Stacy's jaw dropped as she stared at him, dumbfounded.

"And her mutation. Can you tell us about it?"

"She's sick. It's irreversible. Perhaps that sickness has changed her, making it impossible to function like a normal human being. If I had only seen it sooner, I might have prevented Nathan's death." A single tear streams down his cheek as he stares at the podium in front of him.

"I'm sorry to hear it. From what you've told us, it seems you've saved her life at least three times. You'd think she'd show more gratitude."

Killian clenched his teeth, keeping an eye on the podium. The tension in the room became palpable before Killian spoke again. "Though my past is painful, I'd like to move on from it, and build a new life for myself here. I'll do my best to help in my profession for the community."

"I'm glad you can stay so optimistic, Killian. We hope you can move on from the loss of your old family and embrace the new. Don't you all agree?" The audience cheers. "We'll help you overcome this tragedy," the magister says while squeezing Killian's shoulder with sincerity. Killian smiles weakly and nods. "Let's give Killian a rest for now. I'm sure you all will see more of him in the future."

Killian bows his head and the magister's daughter escorts him from the stage with a gentle smile. As they all leave the stage, Stacy follows close behind them. She shoves herself between Killian and the young lady. They stumble off-balance from the abrupt interception. "My apologies, I tripped," she says hollowly, though she makes eye contact with Killian as he catches her elbow. He helps steady her with a soft smile about his face. "Killian, would you mind if I had a word?"

"Mr. Grey," the woman corrects her.

"Thank you, Danit. Mr. Grey?"

"Ms. Nox, now is not the time to badger him with questions." Danit looks at Killian with concern.

"I'm sure he can speak for himself, *Ms. Sinai*," she says with a hint of animosity.

"Thank you, Ms. Sinai," Killian says in a soft voice. "I'm sorry, Ms. Nox, I've answered as many questions as I can, and I'm feeling quite drained. Perhaps we could speak another time."

"No, Killian," Stacy complains, but her father sharply grasps her arm, yanking her back.

"My apologies, Mr. Grey," John says as he pulls his daughter to stand behind him. Killian bows his head in thanks before he and Danit continue on their path.

The magister comes to John and shakes his hand before following after his daughter. John gives his daughter a look that would make anyone shudder, before storming off in another direction.

"What the hell is going on?" Stacy says to herself, pulling a communicator out of her bag as she watches Killian stroll out of sight. Activating the device, she waits for someone to answer on the other end. Looking up and down the hall, she makes sure she is alone.

Before she becomes too impatient, Clara comes onto the screen. "Stacy!" she exclaims. "Where's Killian? Are you both safe?"

"Yes, we're safe. We don't have a lot of time, though. Where's Violet?"

"Stacy, Violet isn't doing well. I don't know if it's a good idea to speak with her anytime soon."

"Fine, then get Alan."

"He's with Violet. I don't have their current location," Clara says hesitantly.

"Well, I need to speak to someone that knows Killian well enough."

"What is this about?"

"Something's off with Killian. We got separated for a little over a week, and now he's acting strange, like he doesn't know me. Just get someone, please."

A pause. "Yes, I'm here."

"Jack." Stacy sighs.

CHAPTER

17

The lazy air is thick with fog. With each deep breath, the smell of pine soothes Violet's soul. Opening her glazed eyes, she looks down. The heavy rocks are piled into a mound. Snow comes early, higher in the mountains. The ground is dusted with powdered ice. She is kneeling next to the last rock she placed on the grave. Her cerulean blue frock gathers on the ground, soaking up whatever ice melts beneath her. Darkness circles her eyes. Her hand balls into a fist as she brings it down onto one of the large stones and it cracks in half. Alan huffs out a breath.

"I'm so sorry," she cries. "I should've been there for you from the beginning. I should've always been by your side instead of searching for him." The rushing water from the nearby waterfall muffles the chirps calling in the distance. She looks up at the trees, looking for the creatures making the sound. She sees no signs of the birds, and the emptiness inside overwhelms her.

"I don't know what to do with myself now." She sits down with her back leaning against the rocks. "I'm worthless." She closes her eyes, taking deep breaths. The cold air makes her lungs ache.

"You're not worthless, Violet." Alan says with a shovel in hand. Violet breaks into a sob as she covers her face with clenched fists and pulls her knees to her chest. He drops the shovel and sits in the wet snow next to her, wrapping his arms around her tight to keep her from falling apart.

"I pushed Killian away and my baby. My baby!" She wails into his chest. Alan's face crumples as he tries to hold it together for the both of them.

"Killian knows you love him. He won't give up on you that easily." He says in a cracked whisper.

"Does he even know?" She chokes out.

"Stacy said she would stay in contact. We'll make sure he knows."

Violet stays in his arms sobbing while he pets her head and rubs her shoulder. Over time her breathing slows and she calms. Her expression becomes darker as she pulls away from Alan and gets to her feet. "Do you think they'll be successful?" she asks.

"I hope so."

"Did you see how they were restraining both of them? As if they couldn't be trusted," she says as she turns to face him.

"Yeah, I did." Alan gets to his feet, and they begin walking back down the mountain, side by side.

Violet sorts her thoughts for a while before speaking again, then before heading towards the opening below the falls she turns to face him. "I don't think we can rely on Stacy and whatever she had planned."

"What are you suggesting?" Alan watches her.

She kicks a rock on the ground with her lips pressed into a line. "I don't know yet."

"Whatever you're thinking, it can wait. Take some time to heal and make a solid plan. Talk to us before you decide anything. Now's not the time to be making any rash decisions."

Violet nods with a permanent frown on her face. They turn to head under the falls, making their way through the rocky terrain to a small opening to the side, which allows them to pass through without getting completely soaked. Violet slips on one of the slick rocks and Alan catches her by the arm, giving her stability. They walk along the inner wall of the cave until they reach the cargo bay.

"I'm gonna get something to eat," Alan says. "Do you want anything?" Violet shakes her head as she follows him into the hall. She stops at the infirmary door. Looking through the glass porthole, she watches the EEG, it is steady as always. No changes whatsoever.

Violet pushes the door open and lets it swing closed behind her. Taking a seat on the stool next to the bed, she looks at Nathan's pale face. Feeding and breathing tubes are taped at his nose. She strokes his warm soft cheek as he rests. Nathan has been stabilized for a few days now, so they finally felt they had the time to bury the dead that had begun to stink in the cargo bay.

She brushes Nathan's hair away from his forehead gently. "I'm sorry, my sweet baby," she croons. "I'm so sorry this happened to you." She waits, hoping for a response. "I want you to know that I love you so much. I want you to wake up so I can show you how much I love you. I want to feel your hugs and kisses and hear your adorable voice. I know you can't right now, and that's okay. I can give you all the hugs and kisses instead." She bends over to kiss him on his forehead and cheeks, as tears spill out of her eyes.

Violet takes his hand in hers and tries to warm them, as they are slightly chilled. "I might have to leave sometime soon, but if you want me to stay here with you instead, I will. Just say the word and I won't go anywhere." Violet smiles at him, but her smile falls again when there is no response. "If I do leave, I'll keep the radio close so I can talk to you and sing to you. And if you wake up, Jack will let me know and I'll come running. I'll come straight home to you."

The door swings open and Lilly pops her head in. "Hi, sweetie," Violet says as she wipes her nose and tears on her sleeves. "Did you come to tell him a story?"

"Mm-hmm," Lilly says with a meek smile. Violet opens her arms out in invitation and scoops her up onto her lap. Lilly gets comfortable, leaning her head back against Violet's shoulder. Violet pets Lilly's hair back and kisses the top of her head, hugging her tight. Lilly starts talking to Nathan as she always has, as if he were responding to her.

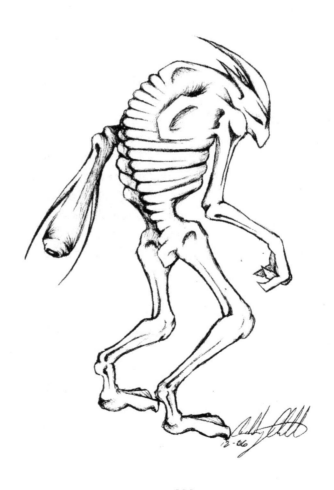

CPSIA information can be obtained
at www.ICGtesting.com
Printed in the USA
BVHW040958190122
626619BV00011B/360/J